THE KILLING JAR

THE KILLING JAR
Ann Brandvig & Rick Becker

Grey Cells Press
www.greycellpress.co.uk

Paperback ISBN 978-1-909374-22-5

ePub ISBN 978-1-909374-23-2

Cover design by Ken Dawson.
http://www.ccovers.co.uk/

Typesetting by handebooks.co.uk

Published in the USA and UK

Grey Cells Press
An Imprint of Holland House Books

Holland House
47 Greenham Road
Newbury
Berkshire
RG14 7HY
United Kingdom

www.hhousebooks.com
www.greycellspress.co.uk

To

Aaron, Amanda, Jerrell, and Isaac

Acknowledgments

We wish to thank those who read so many versions of the book: our first critics, Barbara Greenfield, Celeste O'Dell and Patricia Stevens; then Marilyn Beard Buchanan, Cissy Hepburn, and Larry and Gayle Sievers; Marlene Lee who never forgot us; and Peter Gelfan for his insight and the phrase "like crazed weasels." Most especially we want to thank Grey Cells Press and our editor, Robert Peett, for his patience and unwavering confidence in our writing.

Fatigue tugged Theda Kovac toward sleep. Her thoughts, untethered from her body, rushed here and fidgeted there. She twisted onto her side. 5.19 a.m. flashed red from the clock radio. She flicked on the lamp and watched a funnel-shaped glow rise like steam. After tenting the sheet over her bony knees, she grabbed her book, *Passionate Tomorrows.*

> *One by one Kyle unfastened Lucinda's buttons. Faint*
> *with desire, she felt a melting deep in her stomach.*

Damned prissy heroines always melting deep in their stomachs or burning high on their thighs. Say it, say crotch, say what you mean. Substituting exact anatomical terms, Theda read until Kyle's lust burst forth like a surging tsunami. She slapped the book on her nightstand and clicked off the lamp. This wasn't good sex, just lousy metaphor.

Voices bickered outside, and she waited for a defining sound—more talk or a car door slamming. When it didn't come, she stepped to her window, hitched back the curtains, and stared into the space between her hydrangeas. Goosebumps rose and tingled along her arms. Without exception, she slept with the window open. This morning the marine air flowing into Portland smelled like fresh-cut grass. Theda latched the window and climbed back into bed. Muzzy predawn light cut a V through the curtain. She rolled onto her back and watched headlights swell across the ceiling. A memory razored through her—that car flashing out of the night to run her down.

Don't be silly, that was a week ago. Every night since she'd drifted right off, so why not tonight? Something inside her clicked. Not so brave are we?

An emphatic birr, like an appliance gone crazy, yanked her back from sleep. Theda snatched her kimono from the chair and struggled with an armhole. In the kitchen, her old fridge hummed then grumbled into silence. She released her breath in a great whoosh. Now she'd sleep. But the trilling continued, and she turned, trying to track the sound.

Night still muffled the living room, piling into corners and mixing with shadows. Yes, the noise came from there, but something else was wrong. The picture window, where were the streetlights? Behind dotted Swiss curtains, the window looked mottled as if smeared by mud. She crept closer and gripped the curtains. Splotches on the glass blistered into bees, hundreds of crawling bees. She wrenched the curtain rod loose, trapping herself in a filmy net. Clumps of bees, frantic to escape, rose and darted back toward the light. Her toe snagged the curtain, and she tripped. One fiery stinger then another pierced her neck.

The bedroom. Her EpiPen was in the bedroom.

Theda crouched and waited for the drone to become one sound like water or wind. She willed herself, *move slow. Bees sense panic.* After untangling her foot, she flung the curtain over the bees. A wing tickled her lip. She almost slapped it away but couldn't risk another sting. Already her heart hammered, working against her, pumping venom.

Step, pause, breathe became a rhythm to calm the bees, to calm herself. She stumbled down the hall, past the bathroom to her bedroom, slammed the door, and stuffed her kimono into the crack at the bottom. Dizziness came over her in hot, bitter waves. *Breathe, keep breathing.* She heaved the top drawer of her dresser open. Her vision whirled with browns and reds as she flung nightgowns and shook out slips. Probing corners of the drawer, her fingers hunted the EpiPen.

It was gone.

Her scalp tickled, and she raked a bee from her hair. It fell next to a pink negligee and crawled in a stunned, drunken circle. She stumbled across the room taking in air a pinch at a time. Afraid to shut her eyes, she flung herself on the bed.

Don't pass out.

She struggled for breath like a swimmer kicking to rise up and break free of water. Two voices collided in her head. The loudest and most distinct commanded, *fight*. The other voice whispered, *It's been a grand life.* She rolled across the bed, knocked the receiver off the phone, and punched 9-1-1. The operator's words sounded far away, and in a dreamlike undertow, the voices in her head unraveled. More surprised than afraid, she followed the softer one.

A bee settled on her wrist, its thorax pulsing like a tiny heart.

Georgia Lamb

Georgia Lamb's one concession to female plumage was earrings: tickly feathers, cascading beads, hoops the size of tin can lids. She unhooked a knot of dangling silver, palmed it, and elbowed her way through smokers clustered outside the bar.

"Excuse me, lost jewelry, woman on the hunt." An amused part of her watched while she zigged and zagged around the truth. At least as a PI she'd found a job that honored her gift for mendacity.

She buffed the window with her shirtsleeve. If tonight's target, Jimmy Nesbitt, glanced outside she'd be fragmented by the bar's painted name, *Blues Heat*. She dug the phone from her pocket and aimed it through the top bulge of the letter B.

Click—Jimmy nibbling a tiny blond's neck. Click—the blond nibbling Jimmy.

Georgia eased back into the horde of smokers and sucked in blue clouds. Ninety-seven days without a puff, but standing in this drift of nicotine was like making out with an old boyfriend. It roused dangerous urges that had no place to go.

She scrolled through the pics. After most wives scanned photos of cheating husbands, they'd bellow for a divorce lawyer. Yesterday the woman had repeated her husband's name, "Jimmy," in a slippery whisper, her eyes and mouth softening, becoming almost stupid. Georgia's mother had melted in the same batshit way while describing each *male du jour*. Extra proof was needed to refute Jimmy's crappy excuses: names, places, credit card statements. Then, when she pointed to Jimmy's hand in photo five snaking up the woman's skirt, wifey couldn't fall for his nonsense. "Hey, just helping her wriggle out of a painful wedgie."

New development. A curvy brunette had replaced the petite blond. Jimmy stared reverently at cleavage and spillage. Three more shots and Georgia buried the phone in her pocket.

A young guy smiled at her. "Finally figured you out." Blond curls burst from beneath his baseball cap. "Shanghai tunnels. You're checking bars for secret passages. Doing a documentary, right?"

"How'd you guess?"

"I'm psychic."

"What you are is a big-ass liar. I like that in a man."

He swept away the cap. His hatband left a circular indentation, the only suggestion of order in his brambled hair. "Buy you a beer?"

"Sorry, I'm on the clock."

She sidestepped him and, arm in arm with a surprised couple, slipped into the bar. Her phone vibrated and she checked the number: Stockard Swanay. She'd return the call later. Seventeen years ago, Stockard had been her social worker and at times fell back into that role.

Georgia squinted into the bar's twilight. No Jimmy, no blond, not even the perky brunette. She prowled through a maze of tables and stopped at the edge of the dance floor. An overload of hormones wafted off the sweaty bodies. She spotted the blond a few feet away, sitting alone.

"Hey."

The woman's head snapped around.

Georgia grinned big. She knew her appearance fooled people—hair bunched into a ponytail that hinted of Irish country red, a summer sprinkle of freckles, but most deceptive, her one dimple acquired at age seven when she fell out of a tree. The dimple, so she'd been told, made her smile quirky, borderline sociable. Georgia pulled out a chair. "Mind if I join you? The creep stood me up." Shit, she even sounded sincere to herself.

"Sure, have at it."

The woman was late-twenties, maybe five years younger than Georgia, pretty but washed out. Georgia introduced herself, offering up both first and last name. Fingers crossed. The blond reciprocated with Lynn Presley. If Georgia needed to corroborate Jimmy's roving hands, now she had a name to track. The waitress stopped on her rounds; a gray stain creased the white apron where her midriff had rubbed against the bar. Georgia ordered beer, Lynn another double Scotch neat.

Georgia coughed. "Excuse me, not my business, but earlier, weren't you with a guy? Cute couple I thought." Georgia smiled but imagined the universal puke sign, finger down throat.

"That's when the bastard was loyal. Tell me, what do you look for in a guy?"

"I'll bite. Brains, humor's good, too. But here's the deal breaker, minimal back hair."

Lynn flashed a quick grin and turned to the band. Georgia admired the lead guitarist's chunky single-string solo; any other night she'd lean back and study his fret work. The tune ended and dancers scattered, a few stuffing dollars into the band's tip jar.

"See over there?" Lynn flicked her head toward the bar. "That's Jimmy. I come out of the can, and he's talking up Suzie Silicone like I'm too whipped to notice. I've seen her in here before, she's one of those."

Georgia wasn't in a soul-baring mood, but at this table the woman with one dimple had yowled at the moon while morphing into "one of those."

"And big surprise," Lynn said, "they exchanged phone numbers. How do I know? I reached in his pocket and pulled out this paper with, sure enough, a phone number." Lynn crinkled the scrap and dropped it next to her drink. "Here's to loyalty." She tossed back her Scotch.

Georgia's work here was done. She'd report to Jimmy's wife: Hey, guess what? Jimmy-Boy's a shitheel. One last question.

"Did he drive you here?"

"Couldn't bother." Lynn listed to the left as if tugged by a current.

Georgia understood drunks, how Valentine-gooey switched to junkyard-vicious. "Let's call you a cab."

"Mm, maybe."

A man's hand gripped Lynn's shoulder. Bristly hairs sprouted from the knuckles. Georgia lifted her lip to show off pointy canines. "You must be Jimmy."

He grunted.

"This is my new friend, Georgia," Lynn said.

Second grunt.

Georgia managed not to roll her eyes. "Hey, how'd that Mensa application work out?"

He turned to Lynn. "What'd she say?"

Jimmy wasn't exactly staggering under the weight of his IQ. Maybe she'd finish early and have time to enjoy the band.

He half twirled a chair, straddled it, and smiled slow as if Lynn's presence couldn't be absorbed all at once. Lynn let out a meet-me-by-my-locker giggle, and Georgia scratched other plans for the evening.

"Baby, let me explain," Jimmy said. "Tammy, that's who I was talking to, anyway, Tammy's brother is an old friend. I asked her for his number."

Lynn gave Georgia a boys-will-be-boys shrug.

Georgia smoothed out the paper Lynn had balled up. "If I call this number, who will pick up? I'm taking bets here. Tammy? Her long-lost brother? Amelia Earhart?"

"Bitch." The flesh under Jimmy's jaw quivered.

"Remember what we talked about?" Georgia asked Lynn. "Look at those knuckles."

His eyes scraped across Georgia. "Lynn, honey, I've apologized over and over. It was a shove, not a punch."

Georgia had meant hairy knuckles. She lifted her glass and examined the foamy tidemarks of beer. "You got one thing right, Jimmy, I'm a bitch. Here's the deal, I'm talking to Lynn first, then she'll decide."

"Talk about what?"

"Girl stuff. Well, Lynn, like I said earlier, my periods are never regular, sometimes I go through a box. Now let's talk real she-woman cramps…" When she said, "stirrups," Jimmy guzzled his beer and stomped off. He wore new cowboy boots and had a flat butt.

"Let me put you in a cab," Georgia said. "Go home, sleep it off, then decide about him."

Lynn nodded. Georgia dialed for the cab, snagged Lynn's elbow, and led her through swinging doors at the back of the bar. Georgia blinked at the bright kitchen lights as if she'd stepped out of a theater into daylight. The tang of dishwater mixed with a beefy whiff of stew.

A man in a chef's toque that slouched over an eyebrow blocked their way. "Out! Out of here now, or I toss you."

"Don't men in white hats," Georgia asked, "take an oath to save animals and protect helpless women?"

"You helpless?"

They scrambled past him and escaped through the back door into an alley. Lynn bent over, one hand braced on her knee, the other against a brick wall. Voices squabbled on the street. A car key wedged between her knuckles, Georgia peered around the corner and watched Jimmy talking to a man she didn't recognize. A cab pulled to the curb.

"Let me look." Lynn stepped from shadow. "Hey, Jimmy, come on, there's a bar down the street."

"No, you don't." Georgia hooked a finger in Lynn's belt loop and reeled her toward the cab. When all else fails, try truth. While herding Lynn into the back seat, she explained that Jimmy's wife had hired her, that Jimmy was a loser, a plain waste of time. She snapped the seatbelt, slipped the driver a twenty, and slammed the door. Sparks of pain burst from the base of her ponytail.

"Bitch."

Jimmy's voice came from behind her. He yanked a second time, and she tumbled into him, elbows flailing for a target. She shoved off the curb, letting momentum catch him in the chest. A huff and they both fell back, her full weight on him. He released her ponytail and she popped to her feet.

Run. But sprinting from the playground bully was like sticking out her tongue, *can't catch me.* She strolled away— school bell rung, recess over. At the first street, she took a left. When she reached the corner, a bus wheezed and stopped. Blue-white lights lit its interior like a traveling village. The door of the bus sighed open, and a skinny woman with a toddler shelved on her hip stepped to the sidewalk. Georgia veered around them and checked back down the street. No Jimmy. She flipped her phone open and hit redial.

After two rings Stockard picked up. "Yes?"

"A promise, I'll drop by tomorrow and grab that box."

"No, no, forget it."

The tremor in Stockard's voice stopped her. "What's wrong?"

"It's Theda. Her brother called, she's dead. Paramedics found her in the bedroom. Stung by bees early this morning. Only forty-one and she's gone."

"God, I'm sorry."

"We'll talk tomorrow."

Georgia had first met Theda Kovac outside City Hall protesting sewage spills. The tiny woman's sign, *We All Live Downstream,* had bobbed through the crowd. Threats of jail, even a Portland downpour, hadn't stopped her. Georgia pictured Theda chanting, her hair pasted to her round face in tight, red squiggles.

Georgia started to cross the street then stopped. Bees in the bedroom? That couldn't be right.

*

Georgia hustled through Waterfront Park toward the boat basin. Gilbert Kovac's bookshop must be hidden in that maze of high-end condos.

This morning Stockard had phoned. "Can you meet with Theda's brother? He has suspicions about her death."

Suspicions? With so many efficient weapons out there—guns to shoot, poisons to drink—bees should be about a hundred and forty-third on a killer's list. "Did he explain?"

"Not really. He called the police idiots."

Most PIs would laugh him out of the room, but this was Theda's brother. "Okay, I owe you," Georgia said. "And Theda."

Besides, her calendar was empty. Once she quieted the brother's imagination, she'd call Roshanda at Jiffy Temporary Services. Her job reviews stank—*Ms Lamb has a foul mouth and poor telephone etiquette; Ms Lamb claims to be allergic to skirts*—but she'd tracked Roshanda's deadbeat husband, and now Jiffy kept her in Top Ramen between PI gigs.

After Stockard hung up, Georgia searched through an online list of exterminators, calling each one and explaining the circumstances of Theda's death. "Sure," number three told her, "bees swarm into chimneys, build hives, and when the honey gets too heavy, splat, it all falls into the fireplace."

At the Justice Center in downtown Portland she walked through the lobby to the reception desk with her head down—a homicide detective might come in handy later, but for now she'd avoid Dave Thayer. They'd dated a whole three times when she worked as a paralegal, but he'd uttered the grim word "relationship." That left just two possibilities: she'd like him or she wouldn't. Bad news either way. The desk sergeant called an Officer James from the squad room. Yes, Theda's death was accidental. James handed her a copy of his report. His parting words, "Good luck. Kovac's all yours."

Georgia scanned the basin at Waterfront Park, turning in a slow circle. Fishermen ranged along the bank of the Willamette.

The one man in the park, curled in sleep on a bench, couldn't be Gilbert Kovac: his mustard-colored sports jacket was grimed black from the collar down the spine, and shaggy salt-and-pepper hair poked out in clumps. A Bible pillowed his head.

Down the hill, Georgia settled on a bench closer to the river. Years ago she and her mother would've picked the sleeping man for their game, *Find the Daddy*. They'd choose a stranger, the quirkier the better, tag him with a biography, then explain how he'd vanished from their lives. Georgia's favorite escape was the Foreign Legion.

In fourth grade, she'd learned the CliffsNotes version of sex, how tab A fits into slot B. Then Sheila Tomlin, a woman-of-the-world fifth grader, informed her, "If you don't know who your father is, you're a bastard." Georgia told her mom and *Find the Daddy* stopped. After that, she'd study herself in the full-length mirror on the bathroom door, dividing her features between mother and stranger. From her auburn hair to the color of her nipples, she was one shade darker than her mother, and though they wore the same shoe size, her second toe was longer than her mother's big toe. She'd scrutinize her body, believing that if she eliminated shared features she could, abracadabra, lift a transparency to match her father. After she hit puberty, she avoided mirrors.

A teenage boy, eyes raccooned black, dashed by. His iPod gave off muffled anger like insects trapped in a jar. A girl with surprised fuchsia hair hugged him. Thirty seconds later a man in a double-breasted suit too long for his torso stopped at the lip of the grassy bowl. He had a round face and blue eyes, but that ended the family resemblance. Theda had dressed equal parts Gypsy and hippie; this guy might've stepped from the pages of an Edwardian GQ. On his right sleeve he wore a black arm band, the kind she'd seen in old movies. Why had people stopped wearing them? But for her the big question was, what did it say about him? Was he formal and restrained or did he wear grief like a badge of honor? He dawdled down the path looking left and right, but never at her. To identify herself she should've worn a big-ass gardenia.

Five feet away he paused and dipped his head. She could see each tidy comb line in his brown hair. "Ms Lamb?"

"Yes, Georgia, Georgia Lamb. I knew Theda. She was a magnificent firecracker." Georgia patted a spot on the bench, but he walked past her to sit on her left, and placed an attaché case between them.

He drew a business card from his vest pocket and handed it to her: *J. Gilbert Kovac. Rare books. First editions. No search too difficult.* "Sorry I'm late. I had to phone Stockard, so much to do. She's helping me decide how Theda should be laid out."

What a God-awful phrase. It made Theda sound like a buffet.

"And I didn't know you were you," he said. "Besides, you're so, so—"

"Young?"

"Exactly, young."

"Over ten years legal but they still card me."

"Stockard insisted that you're competent." He straightened the pleat of his trousers and crossed his legs, exposing a sock garter. "I've been running here and there, planning the memorial, and have to rely on the recommendation of friends."

"You understand," she said, "if this isn't an accident—"

"Yes, yes. Is a case of this nature beyond your capability?"

"That's your call," Georgia said. "What makes you think it was murder?"

Gilbert described a welter of underwear and nightgowns humped around Theda's dresser. "She had to be searching for her EpiPen, nothing else makes sense. People dismissed her as scatty, but she'd been stung before and knew the consequences. After one incident, she showed me the needle and demonstrated how she'd plunged it right through her clothes into muscle."

"What did the police say?"

He looked puzzled, as if eons had passed and he could no longer remember. "Please repeat that? I have a hearing problem."

"The police, what do they think?"

"Police," he said as if tasting something rancid. "They called Theda's—they called it an accident."

"Besides the EpiPen, was anything else out of place?"

"No. Well, one tiny thing, but it's insignificant."

"Tell me anyway."

"A locked window in her bedroom. Fresh air, she said, made for the best sleeping. She always left it open, always."

He fingered the black band then looked up at her. His face was lopsided; one eyebrow was higher than the other. No, that wasn't it. Holy shit, his left ear was fake, a prosthesis attached to the stem of his glasses. Now she understood why he'd sat on her left.

"I know Theda was an environmentalist," Georgia said. "Did she have enemies?"

"My sister enjoyed battling corporations, that's why she formed the Abraxas Foundation. 'Stirring things up' she called it."

"And lately, what has she stirred up?"

"Do you know Sauvie Island?"

"Birds and pumpkin patches and nude beaches, right?"

He winced at the word *nude.* "Imagine an island the size of Manhattan twenty minutes from downtown Portland. No supermarkets. No gas stations. A sanctuary. That's where we grew up. Our Uncle Billy and a cousin, Jonathan, still live there. Northwest Metals wants to enlarge their landfill and offered to buy Billy's farm. Theda was determined to stop them." He touched his glasses as if bringing her into focus. The nudge aligned both ears.

A boat horn echoed under the Hawthorne Bridge. "Let's walk." Georgia waited for him to stand then shifted to his right so he could concentrate on details. "Stockard mentioned a gathering at Theda's house."

"Yes, Billy's so-called peace conference. He invited all those involved but neglected to tell her. At seventy-two, he suffers from episodic clarity."

A jogger wearing spandex tight as sausage casings cut in front of them. Georgia gripped Gilbert's elbow. His thank-you smile never reached his eyes.

"I need to search your sister's house," she said.

He reached under his glasses, delicately, and rubbed his eye. "Today's inconvenient, I'm watching Uncle Billy. Tomorrow's soon enough, don't you think?"

She relied on his defective hearing and muttered, "Hell no."

"Theda also had a penchant for vulgarities."

"That's how we first bonded."

"You'll have to put up with my uncle's intrusions, but if you insist, I'll meet you there in, say, an hour."

"Perfect."

Gilbert nodded a curt dismissal and turned away. When his strides lengthened, he cupped his ear.

The sleeping man had left his Bible on the bench.

*

"So we're going camping?" A gray-haired, long-faced fellow stepped from the shadows and peered into the trunk of Georgia's car.

"Not today," she said. "Getting gear, a camera and such."

"Camera? You a realtor? Is Gilbert selling Theda's house? I'm Billy."

"Nope, not a realtor. Georgia here."

Hunched over his cane, he limped up the walkway then made a halting turn. "Your voice, husky, I like that, reminds me of my first wife, the chanteuse. Now she had zest… too bad she zested after others. You sing?"

"Only in the shower."

Whistling a tune that sounded vaguely familiar, Billy

retreated up the steps and through the front door.

The absurdity of this case matched Theda Kovac's house. On a block of buttoned-down Cape Cods, the red pillars and tiled pagoda roof stood out like a clown at a black-tie party. Gilbert stepped onto the porch. His radiant smile surprised her.

"I see you've met my uncle. Everything's set. Theda's assistant will pick him up later."

Georgia fingered the shattered doorjamb.

"The nine-one-one people did that," he said. "I've hired a carpenter."

He ushered her through the door, and she dodged a giant Japanese lantern that hung in the entry. No Billy, but deeper inside she recognized television voices arguing.

"Do we shake hands, sign a contract?" Gilbert asked.

"Let me look around first." Georgia offered him a half dozen business cards. "If anyone comes up with something, have them call me."

Full of stuff all crowded together, the front room stretched the entire width of the house. A massive slate fireplace dominated the back wall. Built-in shelving displayed tchotchkes and collectibles side by side in no discernible order—cloisonné snuff boxes, hand-blown glass paperweights, Tibetan temple bells, and two Mayan corn gods. A carved zebra mask stared from the wall, and wooden giraffes faced one another in silhouette.

Gilbert stroked the fin of a carved fish. "Amazing, isn't it? Theda called this assortment Santa Fe Ming."

"Did she deal antiques?"

"Things caught her fancy, that's all. I'm certain the police saw this and wrote her off as a crazy hoarder. Just assumed she'd misplaced her EpiPen."

"Was anything in here out of place?"

"That curtain was down."

The noon sun flashed off an abstract statuette. Georgia squatted to examine it and discovered a nude, contorted yet supple with one arm outstretched, freeing herself from the restraint of bronze.

"I never understood why she kept that," Gilbert said.

Georgia crossed the room to examine the dotted Swiss curtain bunched on the floor, but she stopped at the fireplace. "The bees came down the chimney, right?"

He nodded. "I haven't touched anything. The exterminators said the damper was open, but that can't be. The chimney was cleaned in May, we use the same chimney sweep, and he always shuts the damper."

"Do you have his number? I need to call him."

Gilbert thumbed through his wallet and extended a business card. After nodding a thank you, she unzipped her knapsack and arranged a jumble of tools on the hearth. Hunkered down, she swiped inside the fireplace. No dust, no soot; the exterminators must've vacuumed. Cool air funneling down the chimney meant the damper was still open. A brass pull chain dangled from the slate face, and she gave it a tug. Stuck.

"What'cha doing?" Billy leaned on a cane, his yellow cardigan dipping almost to his knees. Glasses enlarged his eyes, and he seemed to float above her.

"Jeez, where'd you come from?"

"Judge Judy's on commercial." Billy popped something into his mouth. "I love Theda's olives. Gilbert has pits. Not him, his olives. For twins, those two were day and night."

"Did you know we were twins?" Gilbert asked Georgia.

She shook her head. Hell, she hadn't known Theda had a brother.

"When they were toddlers they invented their own language," Billy said. "Moulee, their common name was Moulee. If you called them Theda or Gilbert, they'd ignore you."

The beam of Georgia's penlight traced the corners of the firebox until she found the damper lever. Bracing herself, she yanked. No give. Damn, she'd have to crawl inside. Georgia snugged a black watch cap onto her head and tied a blue bandanna over her nose.

"She makes a good bandit. Gilbert, invite her to our party." Billy flashed a pleased grin, a half loop just like Stan Laurel.

"Party?" she asked.

"Our birthday party. We're all Virgos, the three of us, me, Gilbert, and Theda. But don't you believe it, I'm a Leo at heart." Billy growled and laughed as if he'd made a grand joke.

"Stop interrupting," Gilbert said. "Let her work."

She spread newspapers and shoved off with her heels, sliding into the firebox. Both hands gripped the lever and she wrenched it. The husk of a dead bee tumbled onto her shirt, but the damper remained open.

"Gilbert, I need that screwdriver." She extended her gloved hand. A handle thumped her palm.

"There you go." Billy's voice.

With the screwdriver blade wedged between the gate and the frame Georgia twisted until the damper clanged shut. A cloud of beeswax spilled onto her, and she rolled out sputtering, snatching off her cap and shaking off bee parts. Sorted into piles the meager scraps of yellow flakes and black bits didn't point to murder. "Okay, you two, did anything odd happen at that peace conference? A noise, something to hide the clang of the damper?"

Two blank stares.

She kept her gaze on Gilbert. Had he heard the question? "Did anything odd happen?"

"You mean that ruckus in the kitchen between Theda and her ex?" Billy asked.

"Theda's ex was here?"

"Yep. Theda and Gilbert have one thing in common, they're both lousy at judging people."

"What do you mean?" Gilbert asked. "I never liked Ted."

"Not him, Daniel Quist. Don't deny it, you make snap judgments, and then you're too stubborn to admit it."

"Hold up, you two. Gilbert, who knew Theda was allergic to

bees?"

"I'm not sure."

"Everyone knew," Billy said. "And they knew where she kept those needles, 'cause you told them."

Gilbert put a finger to his temple. "My God, he's right. I almost forgot. In the backyard, hornets buzzed us the way they do in August. I mentioned Theda's EpiPens and someone asked 'What's an EpiPen?'"

"Who?"

Both men shook their heads.

"Theda told them everything," Billy said. "Even where she kept 'em."

"She was that specific?"

"Yes, no, I think so," Gilbert said. "Everyone traipsed in and out, getting food, using the bathroom. Anyone could've taken it."

Billy stood, thumped his cane, and hobbled back to Judge Judy. Georgia followed.

"Don't encourage him," Gilbert said. "When he's like this, you'll only get gibberish."

Georgia dug a pen and legal pad from her knapsack and handed both to Gilbert. "I need a guest list from that meeting and names of any visitors after that."

"Last week Theda had a cold. No one dared visit her when she was sick. People, she'd say, sapped her healing energy."

Billy had stretched out in a behemoth La-Z-Boy, and she stepped between him and the TV. Another commercial, now a meow-meow cat food jingle, droned behind her. Billy's eyes were shut, but Georgia caught flickering movement beneath the lids.

"Who's Daniel Quist?"

His eyes opened a slit.

"You're not sleeping, might as well tell me."

Billy sat up by degrees as if cranked into place by a winch.

"My neighbor."

"Not enough."

"A neighbor who owns the farm next to me."

"How did Gilbert misjudge him?"

"I, he, um Gilbert… It's no use." Billy's gaze passed through her, lost. "I've known Daniel since he was a baby, and I can recite hundreds of things about him, but what I said a minute ago, nope, vanished. Everyone says my memory's gone. The problem's too many memories, jam-packed, like that closet on the radio show, 'Fibber Magee and Molly.' Trouble is, when I open that door, I never know what'll tumble out. My feet are cold, poor circulation."

Georgia scrounged an afghan from a loveseat and covered him. The ridges and knobs of his body seemed barely more than rumpled bedding she could straighten with the snap of a sheet.

"My two younger brothers are gone," Billy said. "Bad tickers. Figured I'd be next, not Theda. People dying wears me out."

Gilbert stood in the doorway. "Georgia's not interested in family."

Wrong. Murder was often family business.

Billy's wheezing settled into a snore.

"Come on," she said, "Let me see that list."

Gilbert followed her to the front room and handed it over.

"So far," Georgia said, "nothing indicates—"

"The roof. Stockard promised you'd be thorough. The killer had to climb the roof. At the very least I'd expect you to examine the roof." He gestured to the door. "While you were quizzing Billy, I set out a ladder. It's in the side yard by Theda's bedroom window."

She transferred tools to her fanny pack. Humor the guy then check in with Roshanda.

Georgia descended the wide porch steps and circled the house until she found the ladder. Behind blue pom-poms of hydrangea, she spotted what should be Theda's window. Locked. In a bed of plumped-up dahlias, dirt oozed around her sandals onto her toes, and she examined the ground near three smashed marigolds. No footprints, but a murderer could easily brush them away. Shielding her eyes from the sun with a hand, she stepped back to study the steep, comical roof.

She dragged the ladder to the base of a maple; its branches arched over the eave. Up one rung, then two more, she spotted a triangle of bark ripped away at the tree's first crotch, then scrambled higher, stretched, and hopped to the roof. A breeze lifted her shirt and an old exhilaration swept over her, the delight of teetering against the wind. She'd loved climbing trees. On the playground she'd swing highest, calculating which leg pump would flip her upside down. This beat the hell out of the law office where she'd worked as a paralegal, caged in a cubicle, trapped under fluorescent lights, their blue buzz like the beginning of a migraine.

The slope of the pagoda roof steepened, and Georgia crab-walked over humpy ceramic tiles to the safety of the ridge. Across the street a woman watering her roses stopped and watched a brown Ford Taurus pull to the curb. Two quick toots. The front door slammed and Gilbert appeared from under the porch, a hand at his uncle's elbow. Billy whistled the same ditty all the way down the walk. When he reached the "fa-la-la-la" refrain, she almost joined in singing "deck the halls with boughs of holly."

Gilbert thanked the driver, and in a voice, friendly and efficient, she answered, "No trouble. Billy's a joy."

Before he ducked into the passenger seat, Billy spied Georgia. "Now you're a bird. If you had wings you'd look like Jonathan when he jumped off the barn. Come to my party. I stole one of your cards."

The car disappeared around the corner, and the neighbor went back to her roses. Georgia crept along the ridge, gripped the rough brick, and stared into the chimney. Coarse striations of gray and black streaked flue tiles cracked by years of heat.

Her penlight flashed on a brown swatch of fabric snagged by the broken clay. The fibers were beyond her fingertips. She retrieved pliers from her fanny pack and tried again, pushing harder. Her feet slipped, but her arm, swallowed by the chimney, stopped a slalom off the roof. The pliers clattered onto the hearth.

Deep cleansing breaths cleared the fear and adrenaline. Her rump perched on the peak, she leaned against the brick and fumbled in the fanny pack, pulling out a length of twelve-gauge wire. A hook bent at one end, she bobbed the wire, twisting until it snared the cloth and she could ease it up. Burlap. She crawled across the roof. Soot blotched the ends of the roofing tiles down to the lip of the eave. Pinched between sharp flanges where sections of gutter joined, she found yellow strands from a nylon rope and more threads of burlap.

Georgia drew a mental line from the chimney, to the smears, to the hedge at the side of the house. So, someone could have hoisted a bee hive onto the roof, maybe in a burlap bag; someone fit and agile, climbing the maple just as she had done, then creeping silently to the ridge. Stuffed into the chimney like a cork, the bag would've trapped the bees. Had the killer hidden in the shrubbery and waited for Theda's frantic search before a sharp yank of the rope removed the bag and the evidence?

Back in the house she called Gilbert's name. No answer. Here was her chance to snoop down and dirty. She tiptoed into Theda's bedroom, and a childish thrill trembled through her, the same rush she'd felt when her mom took her to late-night parties. The guests all seemed so smart and witty, but after an evening of drinks, their voices slurred and they morphed into pod people. Medicine cabinets and bedrooms hid the best secrets—who wore dentures, dyed their hair, smoked pot, who cheated, who found out and filed for divorce. She knew her mom's friends better than her mom.

When she opened Theda's bedroom door, it snagged a red kimono, and she wrenched it loose. A glossy romance novel, *Passionate Tomorrows*, was splayed face down on the nightstand.

She stepped over piles of underwear and opened the top drawer of Theda's dresser. Empty. Eyes closed, she imagined the scene. Theda discovers the swarm in the living room and tries to escape. The bathroom's closer, but panicked she rushes past, comes in slamming the door, and tears the top drawer apart looking for an EpiPen. Overcome by the venom, she dies after calling 9-1-1.

Stealing the EpiPen was risky; its absence would be noticed. Georgia slid out the second drawer. Summer nightgowns, Theda would open this almost every day. The same for the t-shirts and shorts in the third drawer. The bottom drawer smelled of camphor. Here the balance was right: enough out of place so Theda might not find it, but close enough to be explained away. Georgia unfolded a bulky sweater, and a mothball rolled across the floor. She reached in, sweeping the corners, until her fingers curled around a plastic tube.

"That's it."

Georgia hadn't heard Gilbert enter the room. When he reached for the EpiPen, she gently deflected his arm, and he jerked back as if she had slapped him. She rummaged a paper bag from her pack and dropped it in. "Evidence."

He nodded and then pinched at his palm.

"What's the matter?"

"I picked up a splinter from the ladder."

"Hold on a sec." She opened her fanny pack and handed him tweezers. "Now, this land deal with Northwest Metals, we talking big money?"

"Millions, but more important than money, Theda wanted to change land use laws. 'Setting a precedent,' that was her catchphrase. Her ex, Ted Brody, represents Northwest Metals."

"Hmm, the odd couple. Okay. Her will, who inherits what?"

"A small bequest to Billy, but I'm the main beneficiary."

"And who's your heir?"

"Theda, now just Billy."

Gilbert was at his hand again.

"For a minute, let's assume both you and Theda were targets. Would the order of your deaths affect the inheritance?"

"You mean if I'd died first?"

She nodded.

"If I died first, her estate went to the Audubon Society—in other words, the beneficiary would've been birds." He winced, rubbed his palm on his trousers, and held up a gray sliver with the tweezers.

Georgia smiled at his prize. "I'll snap a few pictures then I'm out of here."

First she shot the dresser with clothes jumbled around, then the rest of the house: hallway, second bedroom, bathroom, living room, and back yard. She left her camera on the porch and crossed the street. Theda's neighbor, the one she'd seen from the roof, still tended her roses.

Georgia cleared her throat three times before the woman acknowledged her. Eyebrows, plucked thin as a spider's leg, emphasized her false eyelashes, but she had good bones. Ten years ago she must've been a looker; another five might pass before she realized it was no longer true.

"Excuse me," Georgia said, "I need to ask a few questions."

"When I'm through watering, I can—"

"I'm investigating Ms Kovac's death."

The woman released the lever on the nozzle, and water dripped to a stop. "Sorry, officer, I thought it was an accident."

"Can't discuss an ongoing case. And you are?"

The woman air-patted fussy, stiff hair. "Iris, Iris Blossom."

"A perfect name to match your beautiful yard." A battalion of rose bushes, planted a meticulous eighteen inches apart, conquered a square of bark dust. Georgia christened it *the kitty litter look.* "Did you know Ms Kovac?"

"Only to say hi. We, well, she wasn't my type."

"And what type was she?"

"Eccentric, an aging bohemian, you know, a hippy type. She

had strong beliefs."

What, weak beliefs are better?

"A month after she moved in, she had her pagoda roof tiled red. That's all anyone notices anymore."

"Do you work in your garden every day?"

"Roses require extra care. Black spot, you know." Her nose wrinkled. "So I monitor their water intake. Ms Kovac suggested I xeriscape, but that's so Arizona." Theda's suggestion earned another nose wrinkling. "After all, there's a reason Portland is called The City of Roses."

"Have you noticed any strangers around her house?"

"The morning she died I was sound asleep."

"And before that?"

"I remember a woman, at first I thought she must be one of those hippie-dippy characters who drifted in and out of there."

"Why?"

"She had a handbag that looked more like a serape, but the rest of her didn't fit."

"Please explain."

"Her dress was tailored, expensive. And she had big blond hair."

"Was it coiffed, like yours?"

"Hers was bleached. I'm a natural blond."

Sure, and Georgia was Alfred E. Neuman's love child. "Anything else?"

"I didn't see her face. She stood on the porch talking to Ms Kovac. I did notice that her arms were lobster red. Sunburn."

"How long did they talk?"

"More like argue, I couldn't make out any words, but they both waved their arms around like they were angry. It must've been at least five minutes, but I couldn't make out their words, and I'm not sure if they went inside."

Georgia thanked the woman, and both stepped from shade into hot, motionless air. When she kicked a mushy apple out of their path, a hornet zipped past her face.

"If I think of anything else," the woman said. "How do I contact you?"

Oops. "After I run things through forensics, if the tests are positive, I'll be back."

"So very, very sad, but as Mr. Blossom says, one must look for the silver lining. And now with her gone, they might rethink that roof."

A tradeoff, Theda's death for a humdrum roof. Blossom yammered on and Georgia concentrated on the powder in the creases of the woman's neck.

She found Gilbert sitting on Theda's bed with his face buried in the red kimono. Seventeen years ago, after her mother died, Georgia had opened a box labeled Salvation Army and rescued a black negligee with tattered lace. Each night she'd smooth it over her pillow and inhale perfume, whiskey, and tobacco fumes from those thin brown cigarettes her mother had smoked. Before she toppled into sleep, she'd hear silver bracelets jangling and feel her mother enfold her.

Billy Kovac

"Aren't you frisky?" Marci Heath sat on Billy's couch and patted the cushion next to her.

Billy escaped across the room to the green chair, his first wife's favorite, not his. The tufted velvet reminded him of a casket lining.

"Now don't be shy," Marci said.

He liked his women with a little padding. Marci Heath barely had enough flesh to cover all her bones.

She giggled. "Just because there's snow on the roof doesn't mean there's no fire in the furnace. Your last years should be carefree, fun. Wouldn't you be happier in town, a smaller place, no stairs, no upkeep? You could sell your land for a hefty sum."

"That's not what Jonathan told me to do."

"I've spoken with your nephew, and he agrees with me."

Billy almost blurted out, "Liar," but there might be a spark of truth in what she said. Billy had always worried that Jonathan might turn into his father, and since Theda's death, his nephew had become prickly, even snapped at him. The thought felt like betrayal, and Billy snared a tender memory—a little blond boy sleeping on his couch, the bridge of his nose red where his glasses had pinched.

"I brought brochures." Marci lifted her gaping beige purse. "Let's look at them together, doesn't that sound fun?"

"I want water," Billy said, "with ice."

After Marci disappeared through the kitchen's swinging door, he limped to the couch and scavenged through her purse. In the side pocket he found a cell phone—tiny, pink, and sparkly: a little girl's toy—and pamphlets with Senior Meadows scrolled across the top. He tucked her phone into his pocket and shoved the brochures behind a cushion.

She returned with his water, and he gulped it down.

"Now, let's look at those pamphlets." She plucked out another of the damn things and sat on the arm of his chair.

"I have to go to the bathroom." At this age nobody questioned his bladder. He stood, angled toward the bathroom, and walked fast, even though his hip grated in its socket when he shifted weight from his right foot to the left. He slammed the bathroom door, sat on the toilet lid, and wrestled the pink phone from his pocket. A business card drifted to the floor. He squinted at the detective's name and punched in the numbers.

One ring. Two rings. With each ring, he counted a pockmark his cane had left on the linoleum. Six. Seven. Eight.

"Hello?"

"I'm trapped in my bathroom."

"Billy? Is that you?"

"Yes, it's me, Billy. The skinny woman's after me."

"And you're in the bathroom? Is the door locked?"

"Can't remember. My hip hurt and she—"

"If you don't feel safe, lock the door now, but don't hang up."

When he pushed off the toilet, a seam of pain crackled down his leg. He fumbled at the latch with sweaty fingers.

"Billy, please open up." Marci's voice came at him all sugary. "Pretty, pretty please." The doorknob jiggled. "Naughty boy, my phone's gone, did you take it?"

He unlocked the window, hiked up the glass, and tossed the phone. "Your phone's outside."

While he leaned against the wall, his thoughts straggled off one by one. Unsure how much time had slipped past, he shook his head. A minute? Might be an hour. His legs ached. Had he fallen asleep standing there like a horse? All he knew was that menace lurked on the other side of the door. His confusion ballooned and while holding his hand to the light, he examined his knuckles and the thin gnarl of bone.

Tinker Toys. At this age we're all built like Tinker Toys.

4

The door opened, revealing an oblong slice of Billy's face. His watery brown eye studied her.

"That witch gone?"

"Vanished into thin air."

Billy slumped against Georgia and they toddled into the living room. She helped him into a rocking chair and caught the scent of a piney aftershave he hadn't worn earlier; maybe he slapped it on while trapped in the bathroom.

"You okay?" she asked. "Can I get you anything?"

"She's gone?"

"No one here but us. What happened?"

"I don't frighten easy, but she scared the bejesus out of me."

"What happened?"

"Wasn't words as much as intense." When he leaned forward, his bony head looked too big for his shoulders.

"What did she do?"

"Scared me, scared me bad. Tried to flirt, all cuddly and smiles. The woman has too many teeth for her mouth."

"I'll call Gilbert."

"He'll think I'm being—" Billy's voice fumbled away.

"Being what?"

"Old."

"When I was up on Theda's roof, you said I looked like Jonathan before he jumped off the barn. Tell me about that."

"Jonathan is Gilbert's cousin. He must've been five or six when he made wings out of twigs and Christmas paper then jumped. Wanted to fly away. Lucky he didn't break his neck."

Georgia imagined a boy flapping paper wings, trying to escape. And then the fall.

"My mom was in her forties when she had Jonathan's father. Everybody fussed, said it was a miracle. But the big celebration came when he died."

"Why's that?"

"Ask me something else."

"Tell me more about Jonathan."

"Can't." Billy mimed locking his lips with a key.

"Will you tell me some other time?"

"When Jonathan says it's safe."

Safe? "Earlier you said Daniel Quist owned the farm next door."

Billy's lips were shiny with saliva, and he wiped his mouth with back of his hand. "Yesterday I saw Daniel out on the road fraternizing with the suits from Northwest Metals."

"You said Gilbert doesn't like Daniel. Why not?"

Billy used his foot like a brake to stop the rocker. "He thought Daniel did it on purpose."

"Did what?"

"Tried to run Theda down with his car."

"Good God, when was this?"

"At the fundraiser."

Why hadn't Gilbert mentioned this? "Please, tell me what happened, it's important."

"There was music in the Grange Hall, dancing, and drinking. Theda was in the parking lot when I saw Daniel's car race out of the dark. His brother, Luke, shoved Theda clear and the bumper clipped him instead. Gilbert made a fuss and called the sheriff, said Daniel tried to run Theda down 'cause he doesn't like tree-huggers."

"And what do you think?"

"Drunken stupidity, just drunken stupidity. Now he's stuck on the farm."

"And this Daniel's not a tree-hugger?"

"Don't know who believes what, don't much care."

Georgia heard a car approach the house.

"She's come back," Billy said, his eyes growing large.

Georgia peeked between the curtains. "It's not Heath." She opened the door and stepped onto the long porch.

A woman, her arms loaded with groceries, slammed the car door shut with her hip. "I'm Margaret, Billy's housekeeper, who are you?"

"A new friend, Georgia Lamb."

Margaret, barely five feet tall, had a charming little monkey face. Georgia helped carry groceries into the house then detailed Billy's escape. Margaret described his agitation after an earlier visit from Heath.

Before Georgia left she borrowed an empty gas can.

*

Gravel crunched underfoot as Georgia tramped down the long driveway. The gas can swung at her side, and she hummed "Sportin' Life Blues" in time with her steps. The day had begun cool but now had the makings of a scorcher, and she wiped her forehead with her sleeve. A lone red-tailed hawk in search of prey spiraled upward on thermals; at the top of the climb the bird slipped to the side and sank before rising again. When she finished here she'd hunt up her own dinner.

A white clapboard house at least a century old, the Quist place came without frills. The drapes were clamped shut against the heat. A doorbell chimed inside, but no one answered. Somewhere a tractor droned.

"Anyone home?"

Just the cluck of chickens.

Behind the house a high-peaked red barn sheltered rows of farm machinery. To one side, the long, low pole building filled with tools looked like a shop. Under an open shed roof, bags of fertilizer were stacked eight high. She turned a corner and, ugh, a new smell smacked her, cows or pigs she guessed. A dust devil churned above the cornfield. Time to go a-tractor huntin'.

Within seconds Georgia was lost between corn rows, the stalks rustling above her head. An engine grew louder, and she followed the sound, stepping into the open where a mammoth green John Deere tractor, its tires taller than her, towed a wide metal rake. Ready for another pass down the length of the field, it turned away. She dodged around it, but a cloud of powdery topsoil engulfed her and swirled into her eyes and nose. Stumbling across furrows she tripped, then scrambled upright and waved the beast to a stop.

The driver throttled back, and the tractor wheezed to a muted grumble. "You trying to get killed?"

Cool air from the open cab washed over Georgia, and Willie Nelson's voice dribbled out of the CD player. She wiped grit away with one hand and held up the gas can with the other.

"Try this." He tossed a water bottle.

"Thanks." She threw in a curtsey. "Spare any gasoline for a lady in distress?"

She had to admit curly brown hair and shocking blue eyes made for one good-looking guy. The day-old beard and plaid shirt with sleeves rolled over his biceps gave him a macho working-guy charm.

He held his cap out to block the sun and scanned the cloudless sky. "Guess I can use a break. Come on back to the barn and we'll tap the tank."

A groan and the tractor went quiet.

"Why in the hell doesn't this island have a gas station?"

"Our secret plan. How else can we meet new pretty girls? Don't want inbreeding."

When he swung a leg out and caught the first rung of a short ladder, the left cuff of his Levis rode up and snagged an electronic tracking bracelet fastened to his ankle. Stuck on the farm Billy had said. This had to be the drunken speedster, Daniel, under house arrest. Never mind bees dumped down a chimney, with that thing strapped on, he couldn't have left the farm. God, if she could just eliminate the next suspect this easily.

"Now that's some fashion statement. Puts you in the same league as Lindsay Lohan and Charlie Sheen. Should I be afraid?"

He unhooked the cuff from the bracelet and shook his pant leg down. "Anybody can do stupid things. This one's mine and, nah, I'm not dangerous. Come on." He started back the way she'd come.

"I've screwed up a few times myself, maybe not that bad, or maybe I never got caught."

He didn't respond, and Georgia regrouped. "Lived here your whole life?"

"Not yet." With the hint of a smile he watched her from under the bill of his cap.

Again the snap and pop of attraction hit her. Way too young. My god, he still had that new car smell. She held out her hand. "I'm Georgia Lamb."

"Daniel Quist."

"Family farm?"

"Yep." He breathed deeply and seemed to grow. "We weren't the earliest, not like the Bybees or Reeders or Gillihans, but we showed up not long after."

"And I thought those road names were picked out of a hat. Let me guess, you have a wall of family pictures in those old-fashioned frames."

"Not one wall, two." He brushed aside cornstalks and let her pass.

"I can't imagine a real family, never had one."

"Maybe you're better off without all that push and pull. Family isn't scientific like breeding Herefords. Two people have a fling after a dance and then, shazaam, family."

"My parents shazaamed once then split. My life would've been easier if I'd at least met them both." She hadn't meant to give up this information. With most men, she delighted in being dishonest, tossing out a false name to match a false biography.

But lying to him made her uneasy. Go figure. Oh well, sharing family scars—*you show me yours, I'll show you mine*—was a good tactic

"Less family might be better," he said. "Sometimes they're like chickens."

"Huh? Farm metaphors don't come easy to me. Please explain."

"Not important."

They stepped into the open, the barn ahead of them.

"Quist? Quist?" she said. "Sounds familiar. A news story, something about brothers."

"I bet." Daniel headed toward the twin red tanks standing next to the barn. "See, that's what I mean. My brother, he acts like everything's all right between us."

She let his silence grow awkward. Isolation, alienation from family, and a little flirting—she'd need the whole damned arsenal. "And it isn't?"

"I hurt him, that's all."

"Why?"

"Don't know."

"Bet you've thought it through a hundred times. Trust me, if you say it out loud, it won't sound so bad."

"First I almost ran them down, then they found me passed out drunk in the back seat of the car." Daniel unscrewed the top of the gas can and opened the spigot on the tank. "I heard Mom say, 'We both knew someday Daniel would—' How can she say that? Think that I'd—"

A low-slung black Honda threw up a curtain of dust as it turned down the driveway.

He closed the spigot.

The Honda stopped fifteen feet away and a near replica of Daniel stepped out, this one taller and, if possible, better looking. What'd they put in the water? This must be Theda's savior, Luke. The awkward attempt at a moustache set him apart from Daniel. That and the gray plastic neck brace.

"Mom's working late today, loads of new students to register." Luke gave Georgia a once over, and his smile curled into a smirk. "Well, Danny Boy, looks like you trapped another one."

Daniel uncoiled from his crouch. Though an inch shorter than Luke, he was broader and bulkier. He screwed the cap on the can and handed it to Georgia.

"That your car back in the trees?" Luke asked. "Figured you for a birder."

She nodded. "My car, but no birder. Just a tourist who thinks that a gas pump every quarter mile should be guaranteed by the Constitution." She turned back to Daniel. "What's the damage?"

"Nothing. You have enough to get off the Island, but keep a little in the can in case you need to prime the thing. About a mile south towards town there's a gas station in Linnton."

"Thanks." She looked around, trying to loiter. The two brothers stared at her and waited. She finally gave them a wave and began an amble toward the car.

"You make a decision yet?" Luke asked his brother.

"Not yet." Daniel's voice had gone flat.

"C'mon, I need to know by the end of the week. This damned place belongs to you, so you decide. If it were my land—"

"I said, not yet."

"Don't you care?"

They leaned toward each other, and Georgia pictured kid goats huffing and pawing the ground. She headed back toward them. "Hey, no pissing contest until I'm out of range."

Daniel's finger jabbed air. "Watch it, little brother, next time I'm drunk, you'll be the target." He stomped back into the corn.

Luke reached for the gas can, and she didn't object.

"What just happened?" she asked.

"Apologies for my big brother. The farm life, lack of human contact."

"He only grunted once and never scratched in an inappropriate place, scout's honor. In fact he was helpful, even lurched toward charm. He told me how he's going through a hard time, the accident and all."

"Accident, my ass." Luke started up the driveway.

PI Lesson *38: once they start to rant, just stoke the fire. "That's what your big brother called it, an accident."

"No, he was stupid drunk. When he barreled down on us, I saw his eyes, wild, animal fury—all blackout drunk, yelling about goddamn tree-huggers. If I hadn't, well, jumped in front of her, he would've killed Theda. I saved his butt."

"He said he passed out in the car's back seat."

Luke shrugged. "I go off to college, they're going to keep the farm. I come back and the family's gone nuts, my brother and sister want to sell the place; they even convinced Mom it's for the best."

"What's your stake here?"

"This island is holy, and I'm fighting to save it."

"Geez, that's deep." Shit. Had he caught her sarcasm? Nope, he beamed right back at her.

"Who am I if I betray my ideals?"

Except for a freighter churning down the Columbia River, a hush closed around them.

"How bad were you hurt?"

"Enough to end my football career. Cracked vertebra."

"And Daniel, how's he doing?"

"I'll give him one thing, he hasn't had a drink. Of course that tracking bracelet can detect alcohol in his sweat. And the Antabuse."

"Antabuse doesn't cut the craving, it tears out your guts."

"You know about Antabuse?"

"A relative of mine tried it for three seconds."

He stopped at the mailbox. A green pickup with a great blue heron painted on the door streaked past and honked. He waved. A young woman, her bobbed black hair wild in the breeze, waved back.

Georgia continued up the road swinging the half-full gas can even more than she'd swung the empty one. So Billy was right, Northwest Metals was pressuring Daniel to sell, but what was the deadline Luke mentioned? His return to college? Something else? And why had Daniel passed out in the back seat and not the front? Was someone else driving? Lies could be as revealing as the truth, and she'd just heard a big, fat one: Luke said he'd seen the "wild, animal fury" in Daniel's eyes.

In the dark?

*

Sagging gray clouds weighted the sky, and the swollen mass seemed within reach. Georgia tapped out a cadence on the porch railing, a series of triplets. If Gilbert didn't return her call in ten minutes, she'd drive to his house.

Was he trying to mislead her? His sister is almost run down by a drunk and he fails to mention it. Was he protecting Daniel Quist? From what? That made no sense. Had grief overwhelmed him? She understood how loss changes you. After her mother's death, when the universe whirled out of control, she'd stiffen at each closed door, expecting it to fly open and whack her face. To get through the pain she'd given herself over to habit—*I'm an early riser, now shift down into third gear, from the bed take twenty steps into the bathroom and pee*. Maybe Theda's death had exhausted him and punched holes in his memory.

Inside the apartment she heard a bleep then Gilbert's voice. She made a ten-second dash, but too late, he'd hung up. She hit replay: "Gilbert Kovac here, I'm exhausted, I'll call back tomorrow. And don't trust anything Billy tells you."

She opened windows to purge stale air and folded back a shoji screen in the corner of the living room. Here was her office. Someday she'd rent an upstairs room with a bathroom and a view of the street, but she kept that aspiration to herself, the same way she'd hidden her girlhood dream of becoming a prima ballerina. That hope had been shattered when her instructor, Vasciliof, snarled in his thick Russian accent, "Lousy, you have lousy turnout. Strive to become the swan, not to remain the penguin that you are."

Short file cabinets supported an unfinished closet door that served as a desk. Georgia dumped her knapsack and rolled up a blue plastic IKEA chair. Her laptop blinked into action, and she snagged a key ring from her bag, thumbed to the flash drive, and slid it into a USB port—backup, backup, backup.

A quick search for Sauvie Island didn't give much, just the usual travelogue schmaltz—mazes in cornfields and hayrides for kids. Local newspaper websites focused on specifics: Northwest Metals, landfills, Theda's protests. And headlines lured Georgia into other Island stories: "Chinook Indian Village Excavated," "Zoning Change Hearing Postponed Pending Traffic Study," "Prohibition Era Moonshine Found in Root Cellar." After a flurry of printing, she'd built a satisfying pile of information. A few more keystrokes opened Google Earth, and she zoomed to the confluence of the Willamette and Columbia Rivers. Shaped like a primordial bird, Sauvie Island stretched northwest from Portland toward the Pacific Ocean. Northwest Metals owned the eastern tip of the Island, and wedged between the landfill and the Quist place, Billy's farm was the key. Without it, no deal.

She shoved aside a camcorder and opened a pack of 3 x 5 cards. Across the top of the first she scribbled *blond on porch?* That woman might have been the last person to see Theda alive. Georgia hesitated then on a second card wrote *follow the cash.* And on a third, one word, *Bees.* Pinned to a cork board the three became the nucleus of her investigation.

She wrestled a metal box from the file cabinet, removed a shoulder holster, and laid it on the desk. A scuffed line, three notches from the new hole she'd made, indicated that the last owner must've been big, probably a man. She buckled the worn leather strap, and it molded across her shoulder snug as an old purse strap. When she slipped out the Glock, the odor of gun oil filled the room. The last time she'd used it was on a firing range with Thayer, their third and last date. She remembered the way he studied her as she aimed. Maybe that's why she hit a bull's-eye. Until she went to bed, the gun remained on her desk. A kind of reintroduction.

*

This was not the hippie hovel Georgia had expected. She stared up at a two-story wooden building, gray with black trim, circa 1895, Portland's version of a New York brownstone. Plaques marked each office, and she walked the hall until she found the name of Theda's environmental group, Abraxas Foundation, stamped on brass. Behind this door was the woman who had terrorized Billy. Georgia imagined kicking it down, but she needed an armload of papers, so play nice. No cage rattling yet.

The door opened into a silent white room, an ante room with a magazine stand between two chairs. Sunlight sparked off the metal edges of framed Audubon prints, and a collection of primitive masks stared back at her. Opposite that wall, a gallery of black-and-white photographs pictured Theda schmoozing with city politicos. Two doors, both ajar, bracketed the far wall. One door revealed file cabinets, from the other Georgia caught a murmur. Relying on the Persian carpet to quiet her steps, she stood between the doors and eavesdropped.

"Give me a minute." Must be Heath's voice. "I think someone's in the office. Hello? Who's there?"

Silence.

"No one." Same voice, same pause, a phone call. Tap, tap, tap. Pen against the desk? Toe on the wood floor? Impatience for sure. "Yes, of course, call back later."

Georgia scooted to the front door and slammed it with a satisfying wallop then called out, "Anyone home?"

"In here, in here."

From Billy's description she expected a buck-toothed shrew, but Heath's smile was sunny as her yellow dress. She resembled a door-to-door evangelist, complete with a freshly scrubbed we-will-save-you glow. Something was going on in this woman's life. The rush of money? Love? Pregnancy? Power?

Heath stood and leaned across the desk. They shook hands.

"Hello, I'm Georgia Lamb. We almost met yesterday when you picked up Billy."

"Marci Heath, Theda Kovac's assistant. Please, take a seat."

Georgia mimicked the saccharine smile and dropped a business card on the desk next to a china cup brimming with hot chocolate and itty-bitty marshmallows. When no beverages were offered, Georgia understood she'd be rushed out the door. She wriggled her rump deeper into the plushy leather chair. "Mr. Kovac hired me to look into—"

"He's not dependable." In a nervous gesture Heath centered her nameplate. Georgia assumed that Marci with an "i" had not taken long to commandeer the big office. "You know he suffers from dementia."

"What? Gilbert is—"

"No, no, sorry, I thought you meant Billy."

Heath had rushed ahead and stepped, oops, splat in the middle of a steaming pile.

Georgia forced wide-eyed naiveté. "Why would Billy hire a PI?"

"Billy, Billy, Billy." Heath crooned his name like an endearment. "Yesterday I heard so many wild imaginings, I wouldn't have been surprised if the cavalry showed up." She laughed one of those please-join-me laughs.

Georgia obliged.

"Let's start again," Heath said.

"I'd like that. Mr. Kovac hired me to look into his sister's death."

"I can't believe he'd have questions."

"New developments must be pursued."

Marci Heath reread the card, turning it over in her hand.

"For a starter," Georgia said, "fill me in on your relationship with Theda."

"I still can't believe she's gone. Each morning I expect her to burst through that door. Did you ever meet her?" Heath didn't wait for an answer. "She was quite poetic about her mission, a woman of principle who wanted to bring light into a dark world—her words. I'm still confused, why does poor Gilbert need a private investigator?"

"I'll be examining the financials," Georgia said. "Numbers tell stories. The annual reports and anything related to the fight on Sauvie Island, I need it all."

"Would you like some promotional material?"

Georgia leashed in her inner Rottweiler. "Thanks, but that's hardly sufficient."

Heath left the room, her high heels clicking on the hardwood. She obviously preferred Manolo Blahniks to Mary Janes. Sashaying like a pro on four-inch stilts took practice. She came back and dumped glossy pamphlets on the desk. "I'd like to help," she said, "but that information is strictly—"

Georgia pushed the phone across the desk. "Let's call Mr. Kovac, he's listed as a trustee, he can authorize it." She waited for Heath's grin to sag.

"Gilbert's such a dear, this morning he called to reassure me, said I shouldn't worry about my position here."

So that was it. Confident of Gilbert's support, Heath could stonewall. Were they working together? Did he have a crush on Miss Buttons and Bows? Blackmail? Was she privy to Gilbert's secrets?

"I wouldn't depend on information from Gilbert," Heath said. "A week ago he wanted—" She covered her mouth. "I've said too much."

Georgia got it: Heath wanted her to beg. What the hell.

"Now you've made me curious. Come on, spit it out, a week ago, he wanted what?"

"It's, it's something I overheard. No one else knows. A conversation between him and Theda."

Again Georgia smiled. Being nice was exhausting. "You might as well tell me, I'm not leaving until you do."

"Oh, all right." A toothy grin replaced the clenched lips. "Guess I don't have a choice, but it's hush–hush. Gilbert burst into the office and demanded money from Theda, a loan to prop up his bookstore. Theda refused. She told him to imagine the forests that would be saved if more bookstores closed. And he said if books were animals facing extinction, she wouldn't hesitate. I tried not to listen, but it's a tiny office."

"I understand. Now please, I need those papers."

"I want to oblige, but it's a logistical problem, lawyers." Heath fidgeted with a pearl ring, her only bit of jewelry. "And the Sauvie Island papers might take longer."

"Well, then, I look forward to many chummy afternoons here with you."

"Everything's a mess. Theda did things without telling me, chaos, just chaos, and now I don't know where anything is. I was her gofer, a lowly secretary, nothing more. She called me her assistant, a mere kindness on her part."

Heath should've waited for an answer when she asked if Georgia had known Theda. Anyone who met Theda knew she hated euphemisms. If Theda called Heath her assistant, that's what she was.

Kindness my ass.

*

Damn, what happened to it?

Georgia rummaged through her knapsack, tugging out a manila folder full of printouts, two pens and a pencil, a couple of notebooks, and stacked them neatly beside a Slurpee-sized café mocha. There it is. She popped open a bag of corn chips. The Heath woman might play snotty with the Abraxas paperwork, but at least Georgia could enjoy a late breakfast.

Across the red brick amphitheater of Pioneer Courthouse Square, posters above a makeshift stage proclaimed "Senior Citizen's Hawaiian Prom." A trio knocked out a rendition of "Tiny Bubbles," and blue-haired women in muumuus two-stepped with old guys in floral shirts. In fifty years, no, make that forty, would she be out there tango-strutting or shopping for matching parrot shirts?

The fluorescent lights in the county records room had hummed like her nerves, and she rubbed her temples to chase away a headache before thumbing through the folder. According to Motor Vehicle records red-haired, green-eyed Theodosia J. Kovac drove a Toyota Prius and had only two tickets, no DUI's or high speed chases. After the interview with Heath this dose of banality soothed her.

Wings flashed as a pigeon landed on the brick terrace. Georgia broke corn chips in her palm and flicked crumbs in a semicircle at her feet. More pigeons cooed and pecked; a flutter and the entire colony descended. She scattered the last scraps above them like a benediction. On the next tier a tweedy man dipped into a bag of popcorn. The flock would be saved.

County records surprised her. Theda owned twenty-two pieces of property either alone or jointly with The Abraxas Foundation, much of it prime commercial real estate in downtown Portland. A registered Democrat, she had voted in every election. On paper Theda Kovac might have been a mild-mannered Presbyterian who worried most about her dahlias. But with all this property for collateral she could have floated Gilbert a loan. So why not?

A high-pitched giggle snapped Georgia's concentration. Pierced and brazen, teasing one another, a gang of street kids sprawled along the wall at the south end of the Square. Georgia locked eyes with a blond wraith. Flustered by her exposed innocence, the girl, maybe fifteen, toyed with a hoop earring and glanced away. Georgia knew that perplexity. At least Stockard made sure she'd always had a home, not a cot in a shelter or the backseat of some john's Chevy. A MAX light-rail train slowed to a stop, and the crowd detoured around the kids, avoiding them in the rush to get back to the suburbs.

A new Theda emerged from the police files. Maybe Presbyterian, definitely not mild-mannered. Last year, chained to a heritage oak tree, she'd stopped a developer from bulldozing an old house. Arrested for disorderly conduct, she'd been given probation.

Georgia ticked off names from Gilbert's guest list. Daniel Quist was on record as sole owner of his family farm. Gilbert's cousin, Jonathan Kovac, had created his own real estate fiefdom on Sauvie Island—a half dozen large pieces of acreage. And court filings confirmed Theda's ex, Ted Brody, as the agent for Northwest Metal.

An older man, maybe in his mid-thirties, approached the blond girl. He held out a small object as if offering bread crusts to a skittish sparrow. Georgia silently coached, *trust your instincts, not him.* The girl snatched the man's gift and scooted over, a sign for him to sit beside her.

Georgia ran her finger down the list again. For motive she always considered the magic triad: love, revenge, money. Ted Brody, the real estate broker for Northwest Metals and Theda's ex, was an interesting money link. A call to his office elicited the business version of bite my butt. "Mr. Brody is out and couldn't possibly squeeze in another appointment for at least a week."

At the bottom of this murder, she smelled money and lots of it.

She turned back to the Square. The blond girl was gone, and so was the man.

*

Georgia tossed the tote bag crammed with documents onto the back seat of her Corolla. Abraxas was a nonprofit, and she could pull annual reports off the web, but she wanted to root around in internal documents. Maybe Stockard could supply more background, and anyway she needed to pick up that damned box.

She resisted the urge to peel out. Instead she jacked up the CD player, Brownie McGhee. At least one thing felt right, today's sky—moving clouds, piercing light, a sky full of possibilities. Georgia craved things going on up there, eerie pewter tints, crimson sunsets, clouds stretched thin as a stage scrim, anything but monochromatic blue.

Five car-lengths back from Twenty-First the stoplight switched to yellow then red. Georgia punched the gas and slipped through the intersection. Boxed in by the congestion, a Portland cop gave her the evil eye. A quick left on Thurman, and she stopped in the driveway of a Spanish stucco, slid down in the seat, and checked to see if the cop had followed. Curtains parted in the window and a wizened, gray-haired woman stared back. Georgia smiled at the stranger and bumped both palms against her forehead in a "stupid me" gesture. She checked left then right, still no cop, and backed into the street. She'd been playing these driving games for too many years.

One night when Georgia was fourteen, her mom chauffeured them home from a party. After the car coughed and stalled on railroad tracks, her mother's head lolled against the steering wheel. Engulfed by whiskey fumes, Georgia heaved her mother back against the seat. No train threatened, but she slapped her mother's face hard. The next morning she'd found a driving instructor. Kip, his honest-to-God name, was printed on his driver's license. He was nineteen. She'd spotted him in his parents' driveway. She lied, told him she was sixteen, said her parents belonged to a cult that banned women from driving.

He said, "No shit."

Her "Would you teach me?" came from a silky, secret place.

The saddest part of the whole thing was that she'd been crazier about Kip than any man since and still remembered the chafe of his whiskers. She convinced him that her one dimple was a gypsy sign for telling the future and that fate had united them. Together they waxed his bronze Dodge Charger in meticulous circles, the chamois soft as moss on her palm.

"You take to driving like a fish takes to water," he told her, and he was right. With windows rolled down and hair whipping and stinging across her eyes, she discovered love. Then some snitch—she'd always blamed one of the Harper girls—told Kip her real age. His memory still gave her an ache, all that passion, short and intense like church camp religion.

A month later Georgia took the keys from her drunk mother, opened the passenger door and said, "I'll get us home." To avoid police, she drove lights-out on side streets. The plan worked, but her mother began staying later at parties, drinking until she passed out. Eager men helped Georgia spill her into the car. She'd park in the garage, and if she couldn't rouse her mother, she'd leave her there to sleep it off. Her mom never asked how she'd learned to drive.

Georgia spotted a parking space in front of Stockard's house smack in the middle of Northwest Portland, a miracle on any day of the week. She'd angled in next to the curb when her phone rang. Gilbert. About time he returned her call.

"Ms. Lamb, I've been in an accident."

Concern slid past the anger that clogged her throat. "Are you okay?"

"The doctor said I have a minor head injury."

"What happened?"

"A dog. A week ago I would've thought someone had let in a stray. But if the killer knew about Theda and bees, they probably know about me and dogs. I was alone in the store shelving books. This wild dog attacked. The wheels on my cart slipped, and, and, anyway I'm lucky I wasn't killed."

"Where are you?"

"Legacy Hospital, emergency."

"I'm on my way."

Georgia made a tight U-turn, bumper kissed a silver BMW, and drove full-pedal through yellow lights to the hospital. She found Gilbert with a doctor in a curtained cubicle. A bump, already purpling, rose from his forehead.

The doctor told Gilbert, "No concussion, but avoid excitement."

While they waited for his prescription, she quizzed him about the attack. "Any idea how the dog got in the store?"

"None. I didn't see any customers and thought I was alone. That's why I was so frightened and he was, he was—"

"Did he snap or growl at you?"

Gilbert stood and leaned against the wall. "Please, please, no more dog questions."

Georgia eased him into a chair and let him catch his breath. "Last night I waited for you to—"

"I apologize for not calling back," he said, "I was exhausted."

"But you talked to Marci Heath?"

Except for the false ear, his face flushed. "We have a special relationship. Marci confides in me, and she's worried about her job. I needed to reassure her."

Yep, a crush on Heath. "Did you tell her I found Billy in his bathroom?"

"You've got Marci all wrong. Someone like you wouldn't understand. Marci, she's shy like me."

*

Gilbert Kovac's creampuff Victorian was painted in at least four trim colors. Georgia had expected something austere. While she coasted to the curb, she told him, "Let me call animal control before you leave."

"Please don't. I've called before, and, and it wasn't pleasant."

"You need to explain." This time she wouldn't let him distract her.

His eyes narrowed in a shrewd expression Georgia hadn't expected.

"I'm useless if you hold back," she said. "I need the truth."

"The last time—" He cleared his throat. "The last time I called animal control, they said I...the man said I was 'hysterical.' Now and then I might overreact, Theda thought so, but she wasn't always right."

"And this overreacting, is there a reason?"

"Dogs, I don't like dogs."

"Is that how you lost your ear?"

"Stockard said you're perceptive, most people don't notice."

Holy crap Batman, did he really believe that? "Tell me about the dog."

"I arrived at the shop early, about half past—"

"No, the first dog."

His shoulders stiffened. "I can't remember the dog's name. Isn't that odd? I can picture it, a mongrel, but the name's gone. It looked a lot like the dog in my bookstore. Do you think that's important?"

"Go on about the first attack."

"I'll tell you what I can, but the memory's jumbled up with my nightmares." He picked at his thumbnail, followed Georgia's gaze, and then placed one hand over the other.

Was Gilbert being evasive or was he just nervous? "How old were you?"

"Fourteen, I'd just started high school. After the accident we left the island. Theda loved it there and blamed me for the move. I've never missed it. Everything was too, too physical. Who's bravest, biggest, toughest. I don't value those qualities. Theda said that I changed after that." His hands relaxed.

Georgia pictured those long, elegant fingers gliding over piano keys or curved around the neck of a violin. "You play an instrument, don't you?"

"Cello. Did Theda tell you?"

"No, a guess. Sorry, go ahead."

"A group of us, just kids, were tossing a ball. That part's still vivid. I've never been comfortable around animals and after the dog nipped at our legs, I was nervous but knew if I said anything, the others would tease me. Then the dog's growl changed, changed enough so we quit playing." The memory popped beads of perspiration on his forehead. "When the dog lunged, I curled up. Later, Theda said I looked like a sow bug touched with a stick. I must have been in shock because I don't remember pain, only blood, warm and spilling from my chewed-off ear into my mouth. She saved me, beat the dog with a rake, all the time screaming at me, 'Are you dead? Are you dead?' And now she's dead from an insect bite. A puny buzz of life. Two pricks on her neck. Let's talk in my house, I'll make tea."

"Why didn't you tell me about Daniel Quist?"

"Daniel Quist?"

"About him almost running down Theda."

"How'd you find out?"

"Doesn't matter. Why didn't you tell me earlier?"

He was at his thumbnail again. "Pride, and I suppose guilt, yes guilt. That was the last argument Theda and I ever had. At the time, I made a big deal out of it. But Theda convinced me I was unreasonable. We've known the Quists for years, Daniel was drunk. I didn't want to admit I was wrong." Gilbert fumbled with his keys. "The bookstore has always been my sanctuary, now I'm nervous about going inside my own house. Please, let me fix you some tea."

"I need to get to your bookstore now, face off with that dog. Did you lock up the store when you left?"

"I think so, I meant to, yes, I'm almost sure I did." He unhooked a key from the ring and gave it to her.

"The dog could be important," she said. "I need to get there before someone let's it out."

On the drive to the bookstore, she stopped to buy rope, heavy gloves, pepper spray, and a baseball bat. As she pulled out of the parking lot, she flipped down her visor. Sunlight had burned off the clouds from that wonderful, complicated sky.

5

Gilbert Kovac

A green box without markings was centered on Gilbert's porch. He nudged it with his toe. When it toppled, he snatched it up, sensing soft thumps inside. He eased the flaps back. The box tumbled from his hands, bouncing on each porch step, dumping ragged rubber lips and tattered ears, pieces torn from Halloween masks, across the walkway.

His phone buzzed—Uncle Billy. *Not now!* But when his finger stretched to cut off the call, he accidentally hit *Talk*.

"Why'd you stuff me into that hussy's car?"

"Billy, is that you?" Gilbert wasn't sure if the agitation came from Billy's voice or a bad connection. "Are you referring to Marci Heath?"

"How many hussies do you know?"

Gilbert stared at bulbous, green lips that had fallen onto bark chips. When he turned to the front door, he stepped on another mouth, this one with fangs painted red to imitate dripping blood. "I don't know any hussies, and Marci, she's been quite helpful since—"

"She wants to put me in a home and take my farm. How's that for helpful?"

"I don't understand— Listen, I really have to go."

"I'm not finished. The woman buttered me up, laughed at everything I said."

"Billy, the next time you have an appointment, I won't send Heath."

"What about Georgia, that PI lady?"

"She's busy. Billy, I really must—"

"Listen here, you think I'm imagining things, but that Marci's doing it to you, too. I'm not surprised that you're blind to the ways of women like her."

Gilbert grabbed at a different topic. "What about the birthday party? When is it?"

"Don't worry about that. Even if I have one, you're off my list."

"Theda and I always—"

"You hate parties. Did you forget that?"

Billy was right. Meeting new people was like struggling with a foreign language. What to ask? How to answer? And when the conversation peters out, which of course it does, how to fill the void?

"Well, I phoned you, so there's hope. But for now, you're crossed off. A big fat X. Let me sort things. I need to talk with Jonathan and sort things."

"Billy." Gilbert heard a tremor in his own voice. "Billy, please don't be angry, not now."

"You can come next year, chances are by then I'll forget. That's a promise; I'm so sure, I'll invite you right now. Gilbert, please come to my birthday party next year." Billy hung up.

Gilbert scrambled to stuff everything back into the box. After unlocking his front door, he placed the box on the entry table and pressed his hand against his false ear. Under the silicone, deep down in the ear canal, it itched. He shut his eyes, but still pictured the twisted rubber bits and remembered heated arguments with Theda. She'd always blamed herself for the accident, and he'd used that guilt. When they fought, when he feared frustration might split his skull, he'd rip off his glasses and gesture, his pink silicone ear bobbing on the stem like a giant wad of bubble gum.

6

Georgia Lamb

Pepper spray in her left hand, baseball bat in her right, Georgia tapped the door. With a kick it swung wide. Wood thwacked the wall, and glass rattled in the frame. Then silence. Square off in the open.

The scrape of her shoes mixed with another sound she didn't recognize. She slithered along the wall toward the rear of the store. Leaning forward, she checked down the next aisle. A cart had been knocked over, books jumbled across the floor, and one bookshelf akimbo leaned on another. A long paper banner sagged above the mess. Georgia made out a few words, "Clearance Sale..." The wreckage supported Gilbert's story: he'd been stocking books when a dog attacked. But then what happened? Had the dog knocked him over? Or had the cart wheeled away and thrown him off balance? She whistled and listened.

Her phone rang. She tucked the bat under her arm and reached for her cell but heard a clicking and turned toward it. A shape stirred at the edge of her vision. Another ring. Let it go to voice mail. The baseball bat shifted against her armpit, and she raised it above her shoulder, ready to strike. More clicks, and then she saw it.

The image whanged at her like an elbow cracked on a doorframe. A dog the size of a German shepherd, its tan fur wiry like a terrier's, skulked toward her. It stopped ten feet away, a string of spittle swaying from its mouth. Nostrils quivered, testing her scent. Then, one leg extended, it plunked down and began licking itself. The pose reminded Georgia of a tricycle tipped on its side.

"Bitch to bitch, what are you doing here?"

With minimal curiosity, the dog's ears perked before returning to basic ablutions.

"Oops, pardon my gender faux pas, but now that I've had a more intimate peek, bitch to butch, what are you doing here?" She patted her thigh. "Come on, you old pooch."

Where was the snarling Cujo? Or were there other possibilities? A cruel practical joke? Maybe. Could Gilbert have lured the dog into his bookstore and staged the whole thing, even the lump on his head? Sure. But why? To divert suspicion? From what? Georgia believed that the simplest explanations worked best—this hound had just strolled in for a visit and Gilbert panicked.

The dog, large and pudgy, waddled over. He sniffed her shoe, approved the scent then inspected her knees. His grizzled, tan fur was short except for the mane framing his face. This six-inch frizz, half-blond and half-black, reminded her of grow-out on a bad dye job. His date-soft eyes gave her a pang, and when she reached out, the dog swiped her wrist with his tongue. She examined his collar and found no license or ID.

"You're lucky," Georgia said, "I've been through the system, and I wouldn't do that to you. What I need here is a flop-eared pup, not an old codger. Face it, your adoptability quotient is a three out of ten."

The ridge, where eyebrows should've been, quirked.

"Hey you, listen up, it's time for the talk. The truth, what seduced you to come in here? Promises of a new chew toy? Huh? Huh? If someone dangles a sirloin tip in front of your nose, what then? Easy, that's what they'll call you. I've been around that block, and it's not pretty. Come on, you."

She pursed her lips and with a kissy-smack summoned the dog. Side by side they strolled up the aisle. At the front door he stretched to lick the floor. Georgia squatted and watched him slurp up a squiggle of raw hamburger.

To hell with simple.

*

The familiar plink-plink of Stockard's doorbell reminded Georgia of the phone call she'd left unanswered at the bookstore. When she checked her phone, she saw Gilbert's name and hit call back. Across the street children flipped a Frisbee. Gilbert didn't answer. On the second try he picked up. Out of breath, he sputtered assurances that he was okay before launching into a story about a green box and grisly rubber scraps tumbling down his porch steps.

"Try to calm down," she said. "I'll be there in an hour."

She pressed the doorbell again. Nothing. Stockard must be out back.

Georgia followed a narrow path between rows of hollyhocks. Stockard was weeding elbow-deep through the yellow button heads of santolina. In sunlight her white, frizzy hair was as transparent as a dandelion puff. Blush orange tomatoes spilled over their cages, and pole beans twined through bamboo teepees. Water dribbling from a hose spidered out to squash and cucumbers.

Stockard braced her back and stood. Plastic cherries stapled to the band of her straw hat jiggled like red antennae, and she called across the yard. "How's Gilbert?"

"A lump on his forehead, no concussion. But that's not all." Georgia told her about the green box.

Stockard motioned toward the mimosa tree. "Let's sit in the shade. I made lemonade, a powdery concoction, but wonderfully deceptive, lacking only the pulp, I do miss the pulp."

Between Adirondack chairs painted canary yellow, a matching table held a plate of macaroons—Georgia's favorite—and a pitcher. Stockard poured two glasses.

"God, I miss Theda." Although the brim of her hat shaded her face, Georgia noticed the puffy eyes. Stockard stuffed a hankie back into the ridiculous pocket sewn onto her coveralls.

The fabric's red roosters looked familiar. "I never told you how Theda changed your life. When you became my client, I worried that my growing attachment was unprofessional, that you were a substitute for the child I never had. She told me, 'Nonsense, the relationship is good for both of you.' And she was right. Now, what happened? Did a dog wander into Gilbert's shop?"

"Not wander, it was enticed. I found hamburger inside the front door. At the vet's I had the dog scanned for an ID chip, but no luck."

"Where's the dog now?"

"My place. An ad on Craig's List might turn up an owner. If not I'll canvass the neighborhood, maybe find a witness to the dog drop. My big question is, does Gilbert have enemies?"

"None that I know of."

"Family feuds?"

"Squabbles with his uncle. He doesn't have much to do with his cousin, Jonathan."

"Tell me about Gilbert's hearing problem."

"Hearing problem? He doesn't have a hearing problem."

"When we first met, he asked me to speak up, said he has trouble hearing."

Stockard placed her hat on the table and leaned back. "Let me explain, Theda was the darling in that family, and Gilbert dissolved into the wallpaper. But while he recovered from the dog attack, their mother doted on him. When the attention waned, and of course it did, Gilbert claimed he'd gone deaf."

"Psychosomatic, you think?"

"That was the diagnosis. They moved off the island, and his hearing returned."

"Did Theda ever tell you how Gilbert lost his ear?"

"I asked once, and she blurted that it was her fault, she should've stopped the dog sooner. I could tell the subject was painful."

Georgia watched a dragonfly rise like a tiny helicopter from a holly bush. According to Gilbert, Theda was his savior.

"Something's funky here. He misconstrues facts and forgets important details. So I have to ask myself, what's the problem? Why is he stonewalling?"

"Remember his sister just died."

"Sure, but on the other hand he's nearly bankrupt and after the will is probated—"

"Stop right there." Stockard's eyebrows gathered into a white V. "You can't think Gilbert would kill Theda."

A car honked and they both turned to the noise.

"Before you go off on me, listen, I can't exclude him. Everyone is suspect."

"Even me?"

Georgia smiled.

"Fine, but name a motive."

"The bookstore's going under. Signs advertising a clearance sale are already posted."

"Eventually Theda would've helped. And if he's behind this, which I'll never believe, why hire you?"

"Could be he's delusional, or more cunning than we realize. Hire the inexperienced girl detective and divert suspicion. This dog incident was frightening, but not dangerous. He becomes a victim and avoids suspicion. When I question him, he's evasive."

"You seem to have it in for poor Gilbert."

"Granted, we didn't hit it off."

"Let's try more what-ifs," Stockard said. "Say Gilbert is the next target in some vendetta. That fits, and someone who knows about his canine phobia lures the dog into the shop, hoping the scare would result in an accident. Here's a stretch, one of Theda's acolytes plans to torment him until he confesses to Theda's murder. Or why not corporate bad guys, horrible minions of a capitalist pirate with evil intent? Any of these scenarios are just as likely as your suspicions."

They stared one another down until Georgia shrugged.

"I hate sitting around," Stockard said. "How can I help?

Unlike you, I enjoy rummaging through musty records."

Georgia detailed what she'd found so far then handed Stockard the guest list Gilbert had given her. "I can use more background on these names. Gambling debts, culinary quirks, do they keep their toenails trimmed, anything. You name it, I need it."

"Money, do you think that's the motive?"

"It keeps popping up, and for now seems the best possibility. Since I'm here, why don't I grab the box you've been bugging me about?"

"Sure you want to mess with that? Now that you're busy with—"

"Next time I feel the itch to hunt up a father, I'll have a place to start." Georgia stood and brushed away cookie crumbs. A few days ago, Stockard couldn't get rid of the box fast enough. Now she was stalling. Why the change?

In the mudroom, Stockard hung her garden tools from hooks and began unbuttoning her coveralls. "Give me a sec."

Georgia continued to the dining room past a round oak table scarred by years of casseroles and dripping mugs. Heavy Victorian prints papered the walls. Red blossoms vining across a navy blue background should've felt gloomy, but light filtered through stained glass and silk lampshades gave off radiance like light in the forest. A display of framed photos above the sideboard stopped her. Georgia lingered on her favorite, Stockard as a young girl standing in a field wearing an ankle-length dress with black braids falling to her waist. Behind her, straddling a row of spinach, stood her father, Albert Swanay, half Cherokee, his large hand on her shoulder.

Ten minutes passed. Georgia heard the fits and starts of a telephone conversation, and then Stockard bustled into the room.

"Did you get lost?"

"Huh-unh. Just called an old friend at the court house, he's putting together a packet. And taking a chance I called the Sauvie Island School. If you hurry you can catch Jonathan Kovac before he leaves." Stockard stepped toward the front door.

Georgia checked her wristwatch. "He's probably at lunch. There's time. Let me grab the box."

Tinged with mildew, the cool basement whisked away August heat. Stacks of cardboard boxes atop palettes lined one wall. A Christmas garland dangled onto the rusty handlebars of a fat-tire Schwinn. Stockard shoved aside luggage and opened a path.

Georgia sat on the second step from the bottom. "When you suggested I help Gilbert, did you suspect murder?"

"No, not that, but it was bound to get complicated." Stockard rubbed her forehead where the skin was creased like old tissue paper. "And I knew you could help. You have a knack for seeing through people. Even more important, you trust your instincts. Not everyone does."

The compliment unsettled Georgia. Yes, she could tell saints from sinners, but what of those nights when she melted into the darkness with a strange man, when in spite of the knack, a restless urge obliterated common sense?

Then it came to her, where she'd seen the red roosters; last year they'd hung as curtains in Stockard's kitchen window. "Why'd you start sewing on those God-awful pockets?"

"Here, I'll show you." Stockard tugged out a scuffed Samsonite case and placed it on Georgia's lap. "I couldn't recycle these, all the memories. Go ahead, open it."

Georgia unsnapped the locks. Odds and ends of children's games tumbled out—action figures, small metal cars, even a set of wind-up chattering teeth. Three marbles rolled in different directions across the cement.

"My collection," Stockard said. "When I began working with children, I was surprised that a piece of plastic could be so comforting, but my clothes lacked pragmatic pockets."

"You never gave me a toy."

"With that mascara smeared across your face, Barbie dolls didn't seem appropriate. Amuse yourself while I hunt up the scrapbook."

How, out of all her memories, had they arrived at this one—a fifteen-year-old girl huddled in her closet sobbing and shredding clothes?

Head down, Stockard groped through another box. "You've avoided my night calls before, and I don't blame you. The truth, I do check up on you, I tell myself not to, but then I'm dialing, and well, the phone's ringing."

"Believe me," Georgia said, "I've dealt with it. It's been months since I've prowled around."

Stockard unfolded a green lawn chair and settled in. "I worry. Until you honestly confront this, get to the bottom—I know, sorry, skip the lecture, but a good counselor could—"

"Nobody messed with me. I go out at night because I go out at night. Nothing more to it."

Stockard gave a last long stare. "You sure you want that box?"

More stalling. It didn't make sense. "I'm sure."

Stockard resumed her hunt, and Georgia picked a red Duncan yo-yo from the suitcase and hooked the string around her finger. After a minute the right stroke returned, and with tiny flicks she coaxed the toy up and down. Maybe it was the yo-yo, or the Schwinn bike, or the basement's mysterious smell, but she felt the thrill of whispered childhood secrets, building forts, games of hide-and-seek. Then she noticed the opposite shelf burdened with legal boxes, the same ones she'd seen in Stockard's office at Children's Services. Her yo-yo skittered to a stop. In one of those she'd be filed away, paper-clipped to a copy of her mother's death certificate.

The basement became clammy and tight, the mildew acrid.

"Here you go, memories." Stockard handed her a cardboard box.

Resting the box on her knees, she didn't move. Her mother had stuffed away photos, greeting cards, and one ragtag scrapbook. This box, a little over two feet square, contained her life until age fifteen. About one and a half inches a year.

*

Gilbert poured coffee, thick, hot and black. A cup for himself and another for Georgia. The way he fidgeted she'd prescribe Prozac not caffeine.

"One of those?" She pointed to the boxes stacked around the dining room table.

"Oh no, those are Theda's 'effects'. That's how her attorney referred to them, 'her effects.' Such a banal word for such an un-banal person."

"I agree."

"Our first day at school, I settled at the back of the room. Not Theda, front row center for her. By noon recess she had ten new friends. Me, I maintained my obscurity near the tetherball pole, shifting to the back of the line whenever I came dangerously close to playing."

The coffee had cooled and Georgia sipped.

"I wanted to belong," he said, "Just never got the hang of it." He stared at the boxes, but Georgia couldn't identify which one held his attention. "Everyone called us Theda and Gilbert, never Gilbert and Theda."

"Where's the box you wanted me to see?"

The phone rang. For a moment he looked confused then left for the living room. Georgia tried listening in on Gilbert's whispery chatter but had no luck, so she butt-swiveled on her chair and opened a drawer of the gargantuan hutch. Left unsupervised she was honor-bound to snoop. Instead of place mats and silverware, she struck the mother lode of spectacles, each with an ear attached to one stem. Tossed in with assorted matchbooks from restaurants and bars, the glasses looked sad and funny, like a crowded sale bin in a novelty shop.

She couldn't turn away. Something was wrong. With her

nose an inch above a silicone lobe, she got it. It wasn't what she saw, but what she didn't see. Through a lens, the print on the matchbooks should bloat out of focus. She lifted one pair of glasses, then another and another. Every frame had been fitted with flat glass, clear as a window pane. Gilbert might not be guilty of anything more than bad luck, but like a highway sign that warns, *slippery when wet*, she had to remain cautious. He was not a reliable witness.

Again she listened to the rhythm of his phone conversation. A burst of short sentences might mean he was tying things up. She pushed and the drawer jammed. First impulse—rattle loose. When that didn't work her fingers fumbled until she found an ear trapped under the lip of the drawer. She wriggled it free as Gilbert entered.

She turned to face him. He placed a green box on the table, and she pulled back the flaps. Although he'd described the contents, she stiffened. Her fingertip traced the ragged outline of each ear, nose, and mouth.

"When you found the box," Georgia asked, "did you notice anyone loitering around outside?" She imagined a presence waiting for Gilbert's surprise, savoring the moment much as the killer might have watched Theda's frantic search for her EpiPen,

"I'm sure no one was around," Gilbert said. "It was almost… wait a minute..."

"Don't over-think it, just tell me."

"A lawnmower. I heard a lawnmower."

"Where? Whose?"

"Bud Grant or maybe his wife. I can't remember her name, he always calls her by some annoying endearment like *biscuit burner* or *my better half.* It drove Theda crazy. 'For God's sake,' she'd rant, 'can't the dickhead remember his own wife's name?' Sorry about my language. A direct quote."

Georgia sensed his delight at telling naughty stories on Theda.

"See, there's Bud now. He's always tinkering around outside.

The perpetual quest for a perfect lawn. Theda claimed he snuck out at dawn and measured the grass blade by blade."

"I'll go talk to him."

"Shouldn't I come with you?"

"Relax. But no more coffee."

When he saw Georgia crossing the street, Bud Grant doffed his baseball cap in an awkward gesture. "Peterbilt" was stitched above the bill. Noting his antique decorum, Georgia suspected he might relish helping a woman. She flashed her PI license.

"Your neighbor, Gilbert Kovac, hired me. This morning an unmarked package was left on his front porch. Have you seen any strangers around?"

"What was in the package?"

"Can't say, confidentiality, I'm sure you understand. Anyway, did you notice anything out of the ordinary?"

"Was it a bomb?"

"God, no. Did you notice anything odd?"

"Nope, nothing unusual. Strangers on the street, didn't see a one, and I always keep a look-see, neighborhood watch, you know." Bud, a barrel-chested man, gestured with his weed eater. "I keep a sharp watch, just ask the little woman."

"So you saw nothing unusual, say, sometime before noon?"

"Nope, nothing—wait... Nope, nothing." He whipped the weed eater in a circle. "I think the wife mentioned something. I remember 'cause for lunch she made me a sandwich. Didn't even warm it in the microwave." Bud laughed and stared across the street where a mailman stuffed envelopes through a slot.

"Please, ask your wife what she saw."

"Are you sure Gilbert didn't confuse what happened? It might be nerves. Traumas affect the way you look at things. I know about stuff like that; I listen to talk radio. We wanted to tell him, the little woman and me, we were real sorry to hear about his sister." The weed eater buzzed again and then went quiet. "You wouldn't mean something official, UPS, maybe?"

"UPS on his porch?"

"Might have been yesterday. But nope, I'm sure it was today. I was getting some Maalox in the kitchen, acid reflux you know, and I saw someone like that on Gilbert's porch. That's all." Bud's thumb moved to restart the contraption.

"Please," Georgia said. "Please describe everything. Any detail might help."

"A person wearing brown, that's why I thought UPS."

"Male or female?" Georgia asked.

"You know it's odd, the clothes were real baggy and the person wore a baseball cap. I only caught a glance, but I'm almost sure they had on glasses, could have been sunglasses. Anyway, dark lenses. But it was cloudy at the time, I remember wondering about rain, and thinking sunglasses don't make much sense, so probably it was those glasses that darken up in daylight. Ruthie's glasses are like that."

Before Georgia left she told Bud Grant to thank Ruthie for her concern for Gilbert's loss.

*

Georgia crossed the Sauvie Island Bridge, dodging at least ten cyclists before she pulled into the parking lot of the Cracker Barrel Market. She stepped onto gravel and stretched. Multnomah Channel sheltered strings of houseboats, and under the bridge a pleasure boat scattered shimmering waves. Her GPS located Sauvie Island Elementary School on Reeder Road. It promised to be a long day.

Driving west she slowed for another group of cyclists in beaked helmets. As the flock approached the school, they shifted position, a flutter of blue and green Lycra intense as peacock feathers. She parked, and by the time she gathered her belongings, they'd taken flight around the next corner.

Sneaking into school felt ass-backward. When she opened the front door, her shoulders tensed, and she imagined a principal bellowing, "You, Miss Lamb, where are you off to?" Growing up, she'd bounced from school to school and never bonded with the adults. She almost believed that teachers, not unlike bears, hibernated each summer until roused by the September scent of chalk dust.

Next to the trophy case, a map of the school identified Jonathan Kovac's classroom in the east wing. A sign warned: All Visitors Must Wear a Pass. *Not a chance. We don't need no stinkin' badges.*

Behind the office window she spotted Luke Quist, perched on a desk chatting up a middle-aged woman. Must be his mother. The woman's dyed black hair and blood-red lips didn't match Georgia's picture of a ginghamed farm wife. This woman would not be amused by Georgia dallying with her sons when there were pastures to plow and pigs to butcher.

Luke's back was to her, and Georgia began a brisk saunter. Two girls stepped into the hall, and the one carrying a basketball bounce-passed it to the other. Luke glanced up, and Georgia ducked below the window. When the tallest girl pointed, Georgia pantomimed searching for a contact lens, crawling and patting the floor until she passed the office. She balanced the imaginary contact on her finger, tipped back her head, and inserted it. Blink, blink, blink.

Old linoleum had been waxed and buffed into reflective swirls, and open doors exposed rows of desks with chairs balanced upside down. Every classroom, every hallway, and surely the cafeteria and johns had been painted green. Somewhere a company must churn out rivers of soothing green pigment then sell it cheap to institutions.

Kovac wasn't in his room. A coffeemaker gurgled on a counter, and wide shelves displayed bottled animals and dead insects. That odor, both pleasant and unpleasant… what was it? Morbid fascination snagged Georgia, and she studied a fetal piglet, pink and curved, floating in a jar. When she turned to footsteps in the hall, she imagined the pig's membrane-covered eyes piercing into her back.

Jonathan Kovac had been a tow-headed kid; pale eyebrows and eyelashes gave it away. She envisioned a skinny blond boy wearing wings, teetering on the barn, thinking jump, jump, jump.

Georgia offered her card. "Your cousin Gilbert hired me."

"I'm fixing coffee," he said, "teacher room sludge. Pour you a cup?"

"Sure. Bring it on."

"Powdered cream, sugar?"

"Straight." At last she identified the aroma, a blend of brewing coffee and formaldehyde.

Even when he smiled, annoyance pinched the corners of his mouth. He read over Georgia's card and his eyes crossed slightly. Although close-set, they were his best feature, the same color as Billy's, a golden russet. Like a lab assistant conducting a biology experiment, he compared mugs until he found two with the fewest brown stains. The coffee pot protested with spits and sizzles when he slid it off the stand.

"Exactly what does my cousin need investigated?"

"Theda's death. He thinks she was murdered." She meant to shock him, but not a twitch. With that docile face, she bet people cut him off in grocery lines.

"Murder by bees, it's absurd. The police ruled her death an accident, and I believe them. Why is Gilbert wasting money on an investigation?" He glanced over Georgia's shoulder.

"You don't seem upset by your cousin's death."

"What? You expect a gnashing of teeth? Theda alienated people, especially family."

Georgia took her first sip and fought back a grimace. "I've discovered things that need explaining. Did you know that pranks have been played on Gilbert?" Georgia waited. No answer. She considered asking the bottled pig, "Well, have you?" With all the possibilities—pies shoved in the face, a horse's head spilling blood on a pillow—she'd have to be gagged not to ask, "What pranks?"

"And you believe everything Gilbert tells you?"

He squinted at the wall again. Every classroom she'd been in had a white-faced clock with big block numerals. She bet one was behind her. Did the same company that whipped up the green paint manufacture these clocks?

"This will sound silly, but I hate spiders, and on the second shelf of your display case, there's a tarantula. Sure, I know it's dead, but can we change seats?" She shivered. He obliged and they swapped chairs. Now try to check the damned clock.

The steel band of a wristwatch peeked from his shirt cuff. He leaned back and stifled a phony sneeze. With all the subtlety of a pubescent boy using the old stretch-and-yawn to cop a feel, he stole a look at his watch. She almost asked, "Got a hot date?"

"Have you talked with Billy lately?"

"If you mean that fuss about Miss Heath, yes, he confided in me. But he's often confused."

"What you call confusion, I might call insight. He'd make big bucks if Northwest Metals bought his land, right?"

"All this fighting over property, it's absurd."

If Georgia hadn't visited the assessor's office, she might've believed his evasion. His shirt, frayed at the collar, looked secondhand.

"If you think it's so absurd," she said, "why warn your uncle to keep quiet? Do you have an interest in the sale?"

For a heartbeat he looked startled. "I have no idea what you mean. And it's not the first time Gilbert's blown things out of proportion. Such a tedious life."

"Lives turn dreary for all of us. When that happens I play guitar or rent old movies. Gilbert reads. What do you do for kicks?"

"You're the detective, use your deductive skills."

Of course he meant the butterflies. The north wall was

devoted to them, dozens of framed cases displaying radiant, dead insects.

"You're wasting my time," he said. "I'm sure you heard that Daniel Quist tried to run Theda down. Question him."

"Has there always been animosity between the Kovacs and the Quists?"

"First the Kovacs, now the Quists. Is this a fishing expedition? If you want to hook the big one, try Theda's ex, Ted Brody."

An instant ago he was ready to throw Daniel Quist to the lions, now he was defending the Quist family and tossing out new names. Hey, pick a side.

"We're done here," he said. "I've been generous with my time, but school starts soon, and my prep time is precious. This interview is over." He broke into a long, slow smile, the kind you give a dentist when he decides not to drill.

To avoid Luke Quist and his mother, Georgia escaped out a back exit. Along the breezeway she admired a student-built habitat garden and walked down an elevated plank that stopped in the middle, a short bridge to nowhere—an appropriate symbol for her interview with Jonathan Kovac. He'd won this round, but his twitchy clock watching suggested he had plans. She drove down a side road, swung around, and parked. Through a stand of birch trees she watched the school. Now let him try and skip out.

While she waited, she dialed Financial Aid at the University of Oregon. "Hello, this is Lois Houston, reporter for *The Scappoose Scope*." Georgia assumed the role of journalist so often she now considered it her legitimate minor.

"Yes?" The woman's voice, cautious, tilted up.

"Your coaching staff told me you'd help." Georgia guessed the head football coach had more clout than the university president. "One of our hometown boys, Luke Quist, starts, no, *started* for your football team. We're mighty proud of him back here in Scappoose."

"Luke, of course." The voice warmed.

"Now that he's injured, well, the town's organizing, working on a fundraiser to help with tuition. In the strictest confidence, does he have any other means of support besides the football scholarship?"

"That information isn't—"

"I'm not asking for numbers, but Coach thought you could give me a nudge in the right direction, anything like work studies? Just a guide to help us set a target."

"A partial academic scholarship, that's the most I can say."

Jonathan Kovac flew by in a rattletrap Subaru.

"Sorry, got to go. Pileup on Highway Thirty."

She crept out behind him, sped up and zipped past a garden center, Blue Heron Nursery, the name she'd seen on the truck that had honked at Luke yesterday. At long last a connection. The Subaru slowed, and she scouted for turnouts. A perfect stand of trees came into view, but Jonathan, that son of a bitch, wheeled left and stole her spot. At the next curve, she pulled a U-turn, headed back toward the Subaru, and ducked into the first empty driveway. Clustered like a tiny village, a collection of mailboxes obscured Jonathan's view. Damn. She could be stuck here for hours. All her paraphernalia—cameras, disguises, and most important, a big plastic cup for peeing—was stashed in the trunk.

Her stomach rumbled, one of Mother Nature's cruel tricks: quit smoking and your appetite becomes orgasmically aroused. She shoved aside the cardboard box from Stockard's and rummaged through the glove compartment. Not much. Gas receipts, a creased cigarette pack, and three fossilized French fries. One fry snapped in half, obviously its expiration date had passed. When she yanked back the cardboard flaps of the box, the musty reek of Stockard's basement overwhelmed her. She cracked open a window then sorted through odd photos.

God, what she'd give for a couple of puffs. She shook open

the cigarette pack. Grainy tobacco sprinkled onto her lap like flakes falling in a snow globe. Her hankering deepened into the stuff of country western songs. *My teeth are all twinkly, my breath is pristine/I don't miss the stink, it's that damned nicotine.*

But Nashville would have to wait. Jonathan leaned forward. His neck craned left, right, then left again: he was on the hunt. A black-haired woman in jeans began loading plants onto a wagon. Georgia clucked her tongue, *patience, Jonathan, patience.* The woman finished, came around the corner of the building, and lit a cigarette. Mystery woman had the makings of a new best friend; they'd sneak smokes behind the bleachers. The woman shaded her eyes with her hand and Jonathan crouched down.

Georgia noticed a photograph on the floorboard and picked it up. It must have flipped out of the box. If someone had asked, "Do you have a picture of your foster family?" She would've said, "Shit, no way." But there she was, lined up with the Hazlets, all spit and polish, and ready for church. The whine of a car starter alerted her, and she looked up to see Jonathan easing onto the highway. She tucked the photo into the box and laced the flaps closed.

In the city she'd allow two, maybe three cars between herself and her prey, but out here without any traffic an unbroken line shot from her to Jonathan Kovac's rearview mirror. She had to rely on curves to shield her, braking early and letting him pull ahead on open stretches. A big-wheel pickup spinning up dust rocketed out of a driveway. Music, Metallica, boomed back at her, and she hunkered behind the truck for cover. When she gunned out of the last bend, Jonathan had vanished. She eased her foot off the gas and coasted, searching for turnouts and exits. Houseboats lined a moorage in Multnomah Channel. Down a long access road his Subaru was snugged in behind a giant dumpster. Had he seen her? Was he hiding? Georgia punched past and rounded a curve. Gravel pinged as she swerved onto the shoulder, stopped, and jumped out.

In the trunk she pushed aside a plastic tarp and orange highway cones until she uncovered binoculars and a rumpled khaki shirt. She gave Luke Quist a silent thank-you for reminding her that Sauvie Island, with its cranes, sparrows, and loons, was a birder's paradise.

Worried that she might miss something, she ducked behind a stand of skimpy shrubs, snapped away obtrusive twigs, and fiddled the binoculars into focus. Jonathan had also been busy accessorizing, and now wore wraparound sunglasses, a brown nylon jacket, and bulky, probably canvas, gloves. When he elbowed back the dumpster lid, his shoulders jerked at the clank. A man with wispy, blond hair carried a hefty vacuum cleaner onto the deck of a houseboat. His glance brushed across Jonathan.

Jonathan reached into the dumpster, lifted a maroon shopping bag, and peeked inside. After he dropped the bag, his fingers fumbled toward his mouth and pressed the butt of a half-smoked cigarette between his pursed lips. Not bothering to light the damned thing, he stuffed it into his pocket. The way his arms moved, sorting and setting aside, Georgia guessed he was hunting for a specific treasure. After a minute or two he scooped up something flimsy and white.

God, let it be a handkerchief.

When he burrowed his face into it, she shuddered. One last snuffle and he tucked his find into the left pocket of his jacket, next to his heart. Even in a romance novel, the next-to-the-heart bit would've been corny, but Georgia caught the look on his face, dreamy like a baby listening to a lullaby. How damaged was this man?

She waited in her little briar patch until Jonathan returned to his car and sped off. Again she popped the trunk and swapped binoculars for sunglasses, then worked restless fingers into latex gloves. She grabbed a clipboard and snapped in a page labeled Signatures. There'd been five names scribbled in, but she'd repressed her raunchier junior-high side and erased Harry Butts. A bogus ID badge pinned to her shirt completed the new ensemble.

She meandered toward the dumpster, jotting notes about Jonathan's little scavenger hunt. A slotted aluminum mailbox stood at the head of the gangway. Above each slit, clear plastic protected numbered paper tabs with the last names of houseboat owners printed on each one. Down the columns, past Jennings, Osler, and Hickle, she came to a stop at "Quist 18." Could this be Judith Quist, the biblical sibling of Luke and Daniel. But in small towns, old families multiplied like rabbits, so she'd better double-check the family tree.

Careful not to let it bang, she pushed aside the lid of the dumpster. An overripe smell rose, and she held her breath high in her throat. A flurry of gnats buzzed her face while she lifted and rummaged around. No maroon bag. Certain that Jonathan hadn't taken it, she thrust aside a clock and fragments of a broken mirror. Reflected in spidery-cracked glass she saw her face, determined. Upending a scummy piece of plastic released the stench of putrid meat, and she choked back bile. Once she found the maroon bag, she sliced it open with a shard of mirror. Food scraps and cigarette butts spilled out, the filters smudged with lipstick. Flipping aside wads of spaghetti and potato peelings, she searched for a bill or receipt, but every paper scrap had been shredded. An hour spent following Jonathan had come to this: mystery woman wore bronzy lipstick.

Behind her someone coughed. God, please not Jonathan.

"You don't belong here."

Georgia turned and faced the bull-necked man she'd seen hauling a vacuum. She peeled off her latex gloves, tossed them in the dumpster, and offered her hand. "I'm Ms Ledbetter, friends call me Lulu." She snatched up the clipboard and pressed it to her chest. "I represent Houseboat Owners of Oregon Today, HOOT for short. We're a budding organization, but energetic. And you?"

"Hickle."

"Pardon."

"Rex Hickle. What are you doing in my dumpster?"

"All aspects of houseboat ownership interest my organization, especially environmental concerns."

Wind off the river stirred his thin, blond hair. "Ms Ledbetter, that doesn't answer—"

"Lulu, call me Lulu. You've heard the expression, eyes are the window of the soul?"

He shrugged.

"Well, we believe garbage is the window of recycling."

"Hmm. Never thought of that."

Neither had she. "It'd be a better world if more people did. We encourage our members to be environmentally responsible, and this is our little way of checking. Happy to announce that for the first visitation your marina did exceptionally well."

He grinned approval and hooked his thumbs under his belt. His stomach erased any waistline and instead of letting things dip below the equator, he hoisted his shorts nearer Honduras.

She brushed her nose then swatted at air. "Mind if we talk on your deck away from these flies?"

"I guess that's okay."

Beside his front door a plaster seagull perched on a chunk of driftwood. Along the deck terracotta pots brimmed with a hodge-podge of flowers, some she even recognized: spiky blue salvia, red geraniums, and yellow puffs of chrysanthemum.

"Excuse the mess here," he said.

"What mess?" Georgia followed his gaze to the welcome mat and eyed a sprinkling of dirt.

"Potted up those flowers this morning, but my broom's useless, and I haven't vacuumed out here yet."

"I didn't notice—in fact, I wanted to talk here because your deck is so meticulous, no more than that, inviting. Love, absolutely love the seagull."

His broad smile exposed a gap between his front teeth. "How can I help you?"

"As a proud houseboat owner, what are your concerns?"

"Concerns?"

"An example, that houseboat next to you, number eighteen. It's so, so… untidy."

"Well, Lulu." He smiled. "I've tried giving that tenant suggestions, just being a good neighbor, but she rebuffed me."

"And your suggestions?"

He seemed lonely, aching to talk, but remained suspicious.

"I want to see if we're on the same page," she said.

"First, those vines, messy, messy. It's so jungly." Rangy purple flowers and half-dead vines tumbled from knee-high pots on either side of the neighbor's door. Gnarled roots twisted from the drain holes. "My neighbor works at a nursery. You'd think she'd know how to control vegetation."

"And her name?"

"You need that?"

Shift gears. "Part of our mission is finding a less sterile term for houseboat. Any suggestions?" Poised to take notes, Georgia licked the tip of her pencil.

"Well, I've never told anyone, but I refer to this as my floating home sweet home."

"Ah, personal, yet poetic, mind if I write that down?" She scribbled nonsense and surveyed the other deck. "Any trouble with your neighbor's pets?"

"So you noticed the bowls of pet food? Here's the shocker, she doesn't own an animal. Another neighbor told me it's for feral cats."

"All that food must attract raccoons, possums, and you know what that means—rabies. We often send our literature to errant owners, beautifully colored brochures, it inspires them to spruce up their floating home." She smiled. He smiled. "If I had her name, I could send pamphlets, anonymously of course."

"She doesn't listen. Like I said, she's a private person."

"Does she have children?"

"Nope, single."

"Ah, late-night parties, men traipsing in and out."

"Pretty much a loner, except for her brothers."

Georgia winked. "This is in the strictest confidence, but there've been other complaints about Judith Quist."

"What complaints?"

"Like I said, confidential, but you weren't far off when you noticed the excessive pet food. Thank you for your time, it's been—"

"I'd like some pamphlets."

Georgia patted herself down. "Busy, busy morning, gave them all out at John's Landing."

"Maybe you left some in your car. I saw you earlier with binoculars. Were you spying on someone?"

Georgia lowered her voice and stepped closer. "We try to avoid inciting panic, that's in our mission statement, so if you repeat this, I'll deny it." She had no idea where this was leading. "But migrating north along the Willamette... promise not to tell?"

"Promise."

"Stern rot."

"Stern rot?"

"Level four, pushing five."

"But that doesn't explain why you—"

"Are you a birder?" she asked.

"No. Of course I can tell a finch from a blue jay, but—"

"Certain species flee during stern rot infestations, can you blame them? Up the road I saw a spotted masked booby. Very encouraging."

He nodded along with her.

"But I've searched all afternoon..." She scanned the shoreline and trees.

"And?"

"Not a single three-toed widgeon or marshtit warbler. Rex, I'm deeply troubled."

Let him try to Google that.

7

Jonathan Kovac

Nymphalis antiopa cracked the shell of her chrysalis and struggled to free her head and thorax. Jonathan Kovac twisted his shoulders in involuntary mimicry. If he placed his butterfly in the killing jar before she was ready for flight, her wings unexposed to damage, he was assured a perfect specimen. But he always allowed his butterflies a half-hour of life.

The phone unplugged to bar interruption, he paced then tugged back the front curtains. Even in sunlight his home was dreary, clean, yet nibbled down—carpet, corduroy couch. Drab, all drab except for his butterflies. He closed the curtains.

When seven minutes remained, he soaked paper towel strips with ethyl acetate and the fruity aroma of ripe bananas saturated the room. He pressed strips across the bottom of the killing jar then fixed perforated cardboard over the poison. Using forceps he picked up *antiopa* and lovingly placed her in the container and tightened the lid.

He never watched the death process, and the moment her eyelash legs shuddered, he shoved himself away from the table and switched on the desk and floor lamps. Sheets of glass covering his display cases doubled and tripled the reflections. Butterflies of the Lower Columbia River, genus by genus: his collection was almost complete. Another year and then what? He leaned back and shut his eyes.

Jonathan marked a red X on his calendar after each encounter with Judith. The last time he'd talked to her had been Monday, when he helped her recycle. He pictured her in the kitchen reaching for a glass in the cupboard. Her rumpled T-shirt had lifted, exposing her navel and the white skin above her jeans. Each summer working at the nursery, her face and arms tanned, but he preferred her skin winter-pale, a stark contrast to her black hair. Once or twice over the years he'd caught her sleeping. Her eyelids, like a child's, had blue veins sketched close to the surface.

Would he always be the voyeur? Could she care for him? He knew he wasn't handsome. He never liked his face, except for his eyes; Judith told him he had nice eyes.

It was time. His blunt fingers gracefully maneuvered the forceps as he placed the creature on a spreading board. He resealed the jar and pushed his chair back. Despite perfect symmetry, the intricate curves of each wing seemed separate and unique, black lines streaking from the thorax to a gold edge.

He often fantasized about confessing his feelings to Judith. In most of these daydreams they were on a beach, it was summer, and he dared kiss her. Last Fourth of July sitting behind his house at the river's edge, the setting had matched his fantasies, and he tried to tell her. The possibility of rejection forced him to stare at the granules of sand flecking her shoulder. He brushed the sand away and said, "I love you."

Strands of black hair stuck to her lip and she wiped them free. "Don't be an ass, Jonathan. My old dog was good company. That doesn't mean I wanted to…"

He shut out her final words and pinned the butterfly to the board with sharp, exact movements.

8

A berm of thriving grasses split the parking lot of Blue Heron Nursery into two long aisles. Georgia found a patch of shade and cruised to a stop opposite a long, low building. The cooling breeze off Multnomah Channel had died, and thick air settled under the oaks. She rummaged up a roomy purse to go with goggle-eyed sunglasses and a floppy straw hat. New ideas settled in. Jonathan Kovac was stalking Judith Quist. Love, lust, or something more lurid? And did Judith know?

A pigtailed little girl bobbed through hopscotch squares chalked on the sidewalk, and Georgia detoured around her. Double doors opened with a pneumatic sigh.

"Need any help?"

"Just browsing." Over the top of her sunglasses Georgia examined the red-haired clerk. Too young, an eager coed. "Wait, yes, where's the restroom?"

The clerk steered her past stacks of ceramic pots glazed cobalt, scarlet, and jade. Arrows pointed to display gardens in back where gravel paths vanished into a wall of green. A quiet swoosh and glistening umbrellas arched from sprinkler heads along the path; Georgia imagined sizzles as the water evaporated before hitting the ground.

She ignored the restroom and opened the next door marked *Employees Only*. Yep, a cafeteria table with newspapers piled at one end and a coffeemaker on the counter. Break room. Of more interest were the lockers and the bulletin board with a work schedule pinned to it. She snapped pictures.

"Hey, you don't belong in here."

"Sorry, lost, confused, new meds. Thanks for finding me, I was calling for help." Georgia held up her phone and nudged past the clerk.

She loitered near the front, browsing through seed packets. The woman Jonathan had watched maneuvered past, towing a balloon-tired wagon piled with bags of compost. Judith Quist. Inches shorter than Georgia, compact rather than petite, she filled her jeans nicely and moved with ease to a customer's car. She clutched each bag at the corners and humped it into the trunk with a knee boost, a smooth circular motion pleasing to watch. Was this the woman who captivated Jonathan Kovac and whose sass perplexed Hickle? She had something, whether she knew it or not.

Quist stashed the empty wagon with others in a row and walked to a red Mazda, where she grabbed a cigarette pack from the dash then vanished behind the building. Stepping from the shadows, Georgia found her on a bench hidden in a stand of bamboo. A whiff of tobacco smacked her; why was life crammed with self-denial?

"Hi, mind if I sit here? Lamb, Georgia Lamb."

The woman said nothing, but obliged, sliding over to make space. Her eyes, the same vivid blue as her brothers', appraised Georgia top to bottom.

"You work here?" Georgia wasn't used to being broken into fragments then studied piece by piece.

"Hmm."

"Knew it." She leaned closer, sucking up nicotine. "Say, I'm thinking of moving here, to the Island, that is."

"Hmm."

"But I heard the place is becoming a dump, wells all poisoned. True?"

"Cut the crap. You've been poking around, first my brothers, now me."

"Busted." Georgia handed over a business card. "Gilbert Kovac hired me."

"Ah, a private dick, what a terrible waste of imagery. Gilbert's so Old World I'm surprised he hired a female." The woman's laugh had a low-down edge.

"You're Judith Quist, right?"

"You decide."

Feint, parry, thrust. Georgia knew the moves. "And your brother tried to run down Theda Kovac."

Judith's cheeks flushed, and she hissed a stream of smoke into Georgia's face. "On your business card, that number, it's your PI license isn't it, in case I decide to file a complaint?"

"Yep."

"Now, why did he hire you?"

"His sister's death. He's devastated and asked me to look around, rule out possibilities."

"Cut the melodrama. We're all knocked out by Theda's death, but accidents happen, and this is stupid. I mean, murder with bees?"

"Certain things don't fit."

"Like what, besides the murder and the bees?"

Georgia let the silence grow. "Did Theda have enemies?"

"Don't we all? But this would be a special kind of enemy, wouldn't it? Someone willing to kill. You must have an idea, a leading suspect. Care to share? I'm all ears."

"Were the two of you friends?"

Judith shrugged and seemed to relax. "When we were kids, she was like an aunt, a bossy aunt, but she'd listen."

"What happened?"

"Stuff. Once upon a time she came back here to live, even brought the new hubby. Getting back to the land, she said. Explain something—why do these New Agey types think if they find their inner primitive the world will be better? Makes no sense. A little hard work and all that romantic BS melts away. Anyway that summer I was young and bored, so I hung out with them." She brushed imaginary long hair away from her ear. "Now it's your turn, whisper your secret. Who done it?"

"I can't say, but I'm almost ready to go to the police."

"If there was proof, hard proof, the police would be asking these questions, not you. My guess is you're late on a car payment and stringing Gilbert along because he's vulnerable. We need to protect him from you."

We? Jonathan? Billy? Why this sudden concern for Gilbert? Rather than jabbing back, Georgia described the dog turned loose in the bookstore.

"Oh, come on." In a quick motion that almost hid her trembling hand, Judith lit another cigarette. "Everyone knows about Gilbert's phobia. Some customer left the door open, a dog wanders in, Gilbert flips out. Anyway, he's dreary, Jesus H. Christ, who'd want to hurt him? Did he tell you how he lost his ear?"

Georgia nodded.

"I'll take a wild guess. In his version, Theda saves his life, right?"

"Right."

"Didn't happen that way."

"Okay, tell me."

"I was only five, but some things you never block out. Theda's no hero. In fact, I blame her. She tormented Jonathan like always. At fourteen she should've known better. Jonathan snapped, jumped her, and Gilbert tried to break them up. Jonathan's dog, a half-wild thing, knocked Gilbert down." Judith stopped and turned away from Georgia.

"And?"

"Jonathan's dad almost always tucked a pistol into a little holster. He ran out of the barn, grabbed the dog by the collar, and kaboom. Gilbert's mangled ear, the dead dog. Blood and brains everywhere." Judith threw down her cigarette and shredded it under her heel.

"Shit."

"Look, chatting with you has been charming, simply charming, but this is stupid." She flicked Georgia's card into a waste can.

In the parking lot Georgia checked Judith's car. Nothing much. An ashtray jammed with butts, a few clothes tossed on a large drawing tablet.

"Hey, get away." Judith, arms crossed, stared Georgia down. Georgia flicked a pebble into a hopscotch square.

Judith, Judith, mad at me
Couldn't make a cup of tea
The only potion she could brew
Was wishy-washy mouse-tail stew

*

Georgia swung into the drive-through of Dot's Burgers and spoke to a box. Astronaut-scratchy, a microphoned voice repeated "Chicken nuggets." Back on the street, traffic was cranky. Cars zipped in and out for a precious ten-foot gain. A bus braked in front of her, and no one budged. She munched hard on fried globs of potato and sinew. After five minutes of idling, the Toyota's air conditioner died. Hot air fanned her face, a mechanical raspberry. Sweaty and frazzled, she yearned for a shower.

On paper Ted Brody had the most to gain from Theda's death. Without opposition, he'd earn a huge commission brokering the land sale. He hadn't returned her calls, but he couldn't hide from her smiling face at his front door.

She opened her phone. If he didn't answer, she'd get an early shower; if he picked up, well, a long day grows longer. She keyed in *67 and dialed.

A male baritone voice came on the line. "Brody residence."

She clicked off. He was home, an obvious invitation.

As she turned south on Macadam, Georgia hit speed dial for Stockard. After half a dozen rings, Stockard answered.

"Stomping on lots of toes?"

"Not enough. I'm headed to Lake Oswego, the Brodys. What can you give me?"

"Where to start?"

"The beginning, what attracted Theda to him?"

"Ah, Ted. All the blank spaces in his life surprised her. He'd never camped, never gone to a political rally or attended a poetry reading. And tacos, for God sakes, he'd never eaten a soft-shell taco. Theda joked that he'd escaped from witness protection. You know how she thrived on projects: saving whales, spotted owls. Ted topped the list. And at first he tried, I'll give him that."

"But what won't you give him?"

"He imagines himself a great lover, too much for one woman."

"Was lover boy all that?"

"Theda claimed he was sexually attentive, but never broke a sweat. She'd rant, 'If he loved me, he'd stink of BO.' God, I miss her. Then she caught him cheating."

"With wifey number two?"

"Younger. Theda said, 'I've got bras older than her.'"

When she hit the woodsy corridor between Portland and Lake Oswego, Georgia lowered the window. The air, pure and baptismal, replaced gassy traffic smells.

"I'm almost at the lake. Describe the new wife."

"Dawn's to the manner born."

"Ah, money."

"Buckets. Generations of timber barons. Ted's a social climber, but the joke's on him, Dawn's not about impressing people. Theda called her 'flowered Melmac amongst the bone china.'"

9

The trap was set.

Sitting on her bed, Judith Quist stroked polish across each toenail three times: left, right, center. She stretched her leg and noticed several marks, dots like pinpricks of blood, on her big toe. Usually she separated her toes with cotton balls.

For a moment she considered giving her herself a manicure, but why bother? Manicures rarely lasted more than a day. She was sure to snag a fingernail, besides they drew attention to the permanent green stain on the first finger on her right hand. She'd tried wearing gardening gloves, but they were clumsy, and she missed the sensation of gripping weeds and yanking them out, or burrowing into the soil to calculate moisture content. Besides, she liked the contradiction of pristine toes and scrubby fingers.

Unsure which sound or movement alerted her, she screwed the top onto the bottle of polish and waited. The white, feral cat she'd lured onto her deck peeked past the door. She'd left an unwashed sweatshirt under the bowl of kibble so her scent wouldn't alarm him. Neck outstretched, belly low to the floor, he slunk across the bedroom. His limp was worse. She dangled her arm over the bed, and when she sensed a slight breath on her fingertips, she gave an approving purr that tickled her lips. The cat, a Persian mix, jumped on the bed and yelped before settling into a furry white comma. His easy trust indicated he hadn't been feral long. While she stroked his skull, she felt two scabby lumps.

"So, my pretty boy, you don't run from fights."

His purr was more vibration than sound. At the base of his left front leg she fingered a knot of matted hair, not the festering wound she'd feared. It might take days before she could snip away the entire painful clump. This was their first date, and she wouldn't press for too much familiarity. "That's the price you pay for lush fur."

The cat's ears perked. Her neighbor, Rex Hickle, knocked on her open bedroom door then stuck his head around it. His deep-set eyes reminded her of raisins thumbed into dough.

"Leaving your front door open," he said, "is asking for trouble."

"No shit."

His brow furrowed. Her sarcasm had zipped over his head.

"I'm concerned about your safety."

"What? You think McCavity here is part of a cat gang?"

His giggle was high-pitched and bubbly.

For months Hickle had worked to connive an invitation. Last week he even pretended her newspaper had been delivered to his houseboat by mistake. An hour earlier she'd watched him creep onto her deck and snatch it.

"I've been sworn to secrecy," Hickle said, "but thought you should know there's a pending infestation of stern rot."

"And how did you obtain this earth-shattering information?" When Judith sat up the cat leaped to the floor and dashed past Hickle.

"A woman from HOOT, Lulu Ledbetter, told me. She seemed concerned with the state of your deck, all those dying vines and the left-over kibble."

"You let someone inspect my kibble?"

He blushed. "Well, not inspected, more like eyeballed."

"Let me guess." She put a finger to her temple and shut her eyes. "This Lulu, she's a few inches taller than me with reddish-brown hair. And a dimple on her left, no, her right cheek?"

"That's amazing. Do you know her?"

"Our paths have crossed."

10

Georgia Lamb

The Brody's front door, ridged steel, looked part prison, part art. Georgia leaned left and peeked through a side window. She couldn't hear music but guessed somewhere in there a love song played. A bosomy blond cuddled a coffee cup. Her fanny pitched from side to side, and an unfastened orange robe kept slipping off her shoulder. Bleached hair blossomed around three gigantic rollers.

At the third ring the door opened, and a violin-smothered chorus floated around them. Georgia offered up a business card.

"Come in, come in. I'm Dawn Brody."

A massive wall of glass framed the lake, but the furniture was cutie-cute, Frank Lloyd Wright seduced by Holly Hobbit. Three empty curls still held the shape of the rollers. Where had they gone? Georgia scanned the room and spotted them under the sofa.

"Is your husband here?" Georgia asked.

"Oh, he's here, just not here, here. He's out back fertilizing this, snipping that, squirting bug-be-gone."

The skimpy rhododendrons along the front driveway hadn't prepared Georgia for the rush of flowers out back. A man squatted by a rosebush and inspected leaves, the bill of his cap shadowing his face.

"Gilbert Kovac hired me to investigate his sister's death."

"Murder? Is that what he thinks?"

"We're not sure."

"I'm all agog, a real fan. I don't mean a fan of you, how silly since we just met, but a fan of detective novels. And now, here you are, a real live PI working on a murder. How exciting, oh, I don't mean Theda being killed, I mean meeting—but I thought

Theda was stung by bees. No, no, don't tell me. There was this pinprick that the police think was a bee sting, but you suspect someone injected her with a poison that tests like bee venom, am I right?"

Tempted to answer, *Spot on, Sherlock,* Georgia said, "Not quite, but I have plenty of questions."

"Can I keep this card? Proof I met a real detective."

Georgia pulled more cards from her pocket.

"For me?" Dawn waved them as if drying the ink, then stuck them inside her robe.

"Look," Georgia said, "I have loads of questions, so let's dig in."

"We have plans for tonight, but don't worry, Ted tells me things start an hour earlier than they do so we're always on time, but I know his little trick. Where's my head? Sit, please, sit down."

Georgia sank into a couch, speckled and plush like a marshmallow rolled in pink coconut, and angled herself for a better view of the back yard. "About a week ago Billy Kovac called a meeting at Theda's, and you were there, right?"

"Oh, yes."

"Did you ask about her EpiPen?"

"EpiPen? It sounds familiar, but I don't always listen to what I say."

"Did anything strike you as odd or out of place?"

"Not really."

When Dawn sat, her robe gaped open and exposed the business cards nestled in her cleavage.

"Was that the last time you saw Theda?"

"Yes, of course."

"You're sure you didn't drop by her house?"

"Absolutely."

"A witness described a blond arguing with Theda on her porch."

"Nope. Not me."

Most people embellished their lies. Dawn told her lies in crisp, declarative sentences, saving the bells and whistles for the truth.

Waiting through an unexpected block of silence, Georgia noticed that the wheelbarrow was gone. Ted must be cleaning up.

"Did your husband ever talk about Theda?"

"Here and there, now and again. He complained about her moral superiority, always hated it when she insisted he eat organic. And he especially hated the way she bullied Gilbert, wouldn't even help save his bookstore, but Ted never really badmouthed her like you'd expect in a proper divorce."

"How frustrating."

"Exactly. That's what I told him, but he doesn't get it. Wouldn't it be wonderful if ex-wives gave references? You could ask the important questions, like what drove you crazy? With Ted, it's the way he smells—oh, God, I don't mean he stinks, it's just that he sniffs everything, like his socks. Every night he takes off one sock, smells it, and then here's the killer, he takes off the second sock and sniffs. I mean if one stinks, the other will."

Georgia felt like she'd been dropped down the rabbit hole behind Alice. No, this was different. She reminded herself that Dawn Brody had asked Theda about EpiPens. The woman directed the conversation, answering when she wanted, distracting when she didn't. Not so ditsy, are we?

Georgia glanced around as if checking for hidden cameras, then leaned forward, her voice low. "Just a few more questions."

"Let me take a peek outside, make sure Ted's still busy." Dawn plopped back into her chair. "The coast is clear."

Dawn was obliging, maybe too obliging. Was there any question she'd refuse to answer? "The night Theda was murdered, does Ted have an alibi?"

"Now let me think, his hours are odd, and I only ask him,

please, don't bore me with business talk. I could check his, what's it called, his Blue, no, BlackBerry, would that help?"

"God, yes."

"I can't promise when. He doesn't sleep with the damn thing under his pillow, but he keeps it within reach."

"Why would you do this for me?" Georgia asked.

"With murder the first suspect is a spouse. No spouse and the next best thing is an ex-spouse. I want Ted suspicion free."

Maybe she did love her husband.

Uneasy laughter bubbled up. "It's Daddy. I've avoided him ever since Theda died. He's sure to kick up a fuss about Ted's ex dying. I can hear him now, 'I told you not to marry that leech.' I'd never forgive Ted if Daddy's right."

Surprise. Dawn wasn't protecting Ted, just playing out old family dramas.

"Whenever I have to choose between Daddy and Ted, it feels like betrayal."

"Why betrayal?"

"Go on, dear, why betrayal?" The baritone. Ted Brody flipped his cap onto the couch then dipped in a half-assed bow. The gesture underlined his fastidious masculinity: thick eyebrows over pale-blue eyes, perfect hair except where it shagged over his collar, and a close-cropped beard meticulously shaved to accentuate his cheekbones.

"Theda was part of your family," Dawn said, "so that makes her like my ex-wife-in-law, don't you think? This is Georgia Lamb, a real-life PI, she's investigating Theda's death. I'm thrilled."

"You dress, dear, I'll finish outside."

He left by the back door without a nod, as if Georgia were investigating a faulty sewer line instead of a dead ex-wife.

"It's been wonderful talking," Dawn said, "but I have to change, and like I said, I've always wanted to meet a detective, that and Princess Di. Didn't your heart just break for her? Now you go grill Ted, we both know that's the real reason you're here.

Toodle-oo." Dawn dashed down the hall, flinging off her robe before she disappeared into another room.

Georgia stepped onto the patio. Had Ted ducked behind a trellis or crouched under a shrub? She crossed the lawn to a large steel sculpture. When she walked around it, the form dissolved and reasserted itself as entwined bodies, abstract yet erotic. An arm circling a crotch became a fluid, sensual line like that burst of freedom before a couple falls back into self-consciousness. She'd seen something like it recently, but couldn't remember where.

"Ollie ollie oxen free!" She hadn't yelled that since her hide-and-go-seek days. To hell with him. The sun angled orange and intense, and she followed the sound of trickling water to a pond.

"Your eyes are your best feature. Not brown, not green, like moss on bark."

Georgia bit her lip to keep from laughing. Flashes of gold and silver broke the water's dark surface, and a speckled koi darted beneath a feathery plant. Ted must've stepped closer; she felt his breath on her neck.

"How often are you laughed out of bars?" she asked.

"Never."

"So you believe that women, I'm not talking the rubber blow-up kind, but breathing, unlobotomized women, buy that bullshit?"

"I prefer them fully functional."

"That's what they all say."

"Let me give you the grand tour."

His touch was light at her elbow, but sure strides added confidence. She slowed, forcing him to match her pace. While he bragged on about the garden, she checked his pits for sweat. In this heat, half-moons should stain his long-sleeved shirt. Except for a vague sheen at the hairline, he was dry. Theda had been right, he didn't sweat.

"I like that sculpture," she said.

"Tell my wife. She prefers cottages that glow. Art should be uplifting. Daddy's idea, and since he's a patron of the Art Museum, he must know."

"I've seen a piece like it, smaller, at Theda's I think."

"Good eye."

"And Dawn doesn't understand it?"

"The one thing she understands is detective novels. She's ecstatic you're here."

"And you?"

"I have nothing to hide. Fire away."

"How'd you and Theda hook up?"

"At first, physical attraction."

"Geez, you're making me giddy. If that's all, why marry?"

"Her money? Is that what you expect? Doubt you'll believe the real reason."

"Try me."

"Theda saw through me—my need to be the center of attention. Despite that, she accepted me."

Being loved for yourself, yes, that could be powerful. Would he 'fess up to cheating? "So why divorce?"

"I'm sure you've noticed I have my share of male ego. I've always regretted my transgression."

"You mean fucking around?"

"It wasn't planned."

This was too tempting, right up there with red-cape bull-baiting. "When did you first notice that you were naked in bed with another woman?"

"I thought she'd forgive me. Stupid, stupid."

"Who'd you cheat with?"

"A gentleman never tells."

"I know it wasn't Dawn, or at least she wasn't the one Theda caught you with."

"Move on. I have nothing to say. Theda swore me to silence."

Odd. Theda is hurt by a cheating husband, divorces him, then protects the other woman. Georgia stuck a mental asterisk by his answer.

"Billy said you and Theda kicked up a ruckus in Theda's kitchen. Picking at old scabs, or was it something new?"

His fingers made a nervous twisting motion. "We did make a scene, but not what you think."

"I don't get it."

"When our divorce was final, Theda bought champagne and crystal goblets. Laughter always came easy to us. Anyway, we toasted the judge, the decree, even our friendship, and smashed glasses in the fireplace. At Billy's meeting, a glass broke. Picking up pieces, we remembered the celebration and laughed our heads off. That was the ruckus. No eye scratching. No fur flying."

"I know you have plans for tonight, I'll hurry this along."

"A little secret," he said. "I always tell Dawn the wrong time so we're never late."

"Aren't you a clever rascal?"

"All these questions, they're ridiculous, why would someone murder Theda?"

"There's money."

"Did she leave a will?"

Had he been waiting to ask? Gilbert inherited everything, but why not have a little fun? "Theda spoke to her lawyer about a change in her will, and we've searched everywhere—sorry, I've said too much."

"No kidding?" His eyebrows shot up.

Gotcha. Although her lie stank of Nancy Drew, he bought it. Like most bullshitters, he was gullible.

"Theda had money," Ted said, "but strong convictions are expensive."

"Ah, the Abraxas Group. You must know Marci Heath."

"Heath? Theda's assistant?" He smiled sweetly, trying to manage her. He smiled a lot. "Miss Heath's one of those girls who sat in the corner during high school dances after stringing crepe paper. She told me a story once about her unhappy childhood."

"Please tell me."

"It's too personal."

"Cross my heart, I won't blab."

"Growing up, her father was cruel and teased her, he said on her tombstone they'd inscribe 'Returned Unopened.'"

First Dawn and now Heath with daddy issues. Maybe she was lucky not to know her father. "Any boyfriends lurking in Heath's life?"

"Why?" he asked.

"Just tossing out shit, seeing what sticks."

"Exquisite image."

"A gift."

He pinched off the blossom of a white lily flecked with pink and presented it to her. "It's time to check on Dawn."

Dawn was dressed and dressed and dressed, as if she'd tried different outfits and forgot to remove the unwanted pieces. A frayed pink ribbon cinched her waist, and even Georgia, who had the fashion sense of a warthog, yearned to pluck away the threads unraveling across Dawn's stomach. La pièce de résistance, the bag slung over her shoulder, looked like a threadbare Mexican rug. That clinched it for Georgia: Dawn Brody was the blond on Theda's porch. But why was she lying?

In one hand Dawn held a tomato and in the other a saltshaker. A seed stuck to her chin.

"You're dripping, dear." Ted snatched the tomato.

Dawn licked juice from her fingers, then clapped her hands. "Princess, oh Princess Di! Come here, pookie pie."

A yellow Labrador wriggled past Ted. Dawn bent and slapped her knees. Her skirt rose in back and revealed veined white thighs. The dog galumphed over to her. "Ted grows tomatoes but Di gobbles them off the vine, so I knew, just knew having this dog was serendipitous. *Serendipitous*, isn't that the loveliest of words?"

Georgia knelt and knuckled the space between the dog's ears.

"Okay, sweetie-poops," Dawn said. "Do me something cute."
Princess Di rolled on her back and kicked her legs in the air.

*

Georgia watched a cloud of sparrows, chattering then quiet, vanish into the boughs of a fir tree. Now all she wanted was a shower and bed. A white Ford hatchback hung back and let her pull out of the Brodys' driveway. At the first stop sign, she made a right along Lakeview Boulevard. The Ford rolled through behind her. A hodgepodge of McMansions followed the contour of the lake, decks jutting above the beach. Late sunlight flared off the water.

A spark of light, dazzling and prismatic, snagged her attention. She checked the rearview mirror. There it was again—a twinkle from the hatchback's windshield, maybe a gleaming chunk of crystal spinning where teenagers once hung fuzzy dice. Past the stables on Iron Mountain Road, she hit a long woodsy stretch and jabbed the accelerator. At sixty-five she flashed brake lights and downshifted for the next residential speed zone. The white car, headlights bobbing, paced her through downtown Lake Oswego and north toward Portland. For the first time since becoming an investigator, she was the followee, not the follower.

Who had she pissed off? Most everybody. She punched the CD button and Son House growled out "John the Revelator." On home ground she could slip the tail, but hell, first she'd match a face to the car.

She crossed the Sellwood Bridge and hung a right off Tacoma Street. Wheeling left, she circled the block and came to a halt, her signal blinking for a return to Tacoma. The white hatchback, trapped in traffic, hung back and waited for Georgia to pull in front. Blinded by headlights, she couldn't see the driver or read the plates. Open space stretched from the hatchback down the length of Tacoma and impatient drivers began to honk. Unable to wait any longer, she waved a thank you and wedged in front of the follower.

More turns. This procession thing was becoming a goddamned bore. She eyed parking areas, any old place to call home, and came to a rocking stop next to a child's Big Wheel.

The hatchback idled at the curb. Georgia snatched her new purchase, the Louisville slugger, from the back seat and opened the door. In three long strides she was across the parking lot, wielding the bat above her head, "Eeeyyow" splitting the night. The white car screamed backwards toward the intersection, then stopped, waiting and anonymous, the engine pulsing. Georgia thumped the center stripe of the street with her bat. Come on, SOB. Try it, and you'll go home without a windshield.

The engine throbbed louder. Rubber bit asphalt and the hatchback lunged toward her. This time she'd get the number, and when the car swerved away, she'd whack it. But it came on, straight at her, the license plate a muddy blur. She tumbled toward the curb and came to her feet in a crouch. The baseball bat clattered into the gutter. Georgia retreated from the street and ducked behind an aluminum light pole. Jeez.

The car skidded into a U-turn and came again. The right tires on the street, the other two popped up across the driveway apron and rode the sidewalk. In a cockeyed tilt the car rocketed at her. Inches from the pole, it turned sharply to the street, and rounded the corner.

She retrieved the bat and waited, leaning against the car to catch her breath. No heads appeared at windows; no light flicked on. Going apeshit had quenched her frustration and almost killed her. She keyed the ignition, and Son House hit the final refrain on the CD: *Don't you mind, people grinnin' in your face.*

*

A paper cup rocked through the pond into the moon's shuddering reflection. Georgia had dumped her bag at the apartment and followed the dog to the park, all the time checking for a white car. Because the tail had begun at the Brodys', she assumed it was someone connected to this case. But that's all she had.

The dog curled beside her, inching his head onto her lap. She stroked his shoulder, a rhythm that calmed her agitation. The grass had lost its heat, and dark clouds slid across the moon. If only she could lose herself in that weightless mass.

Her phone chirped then made a full ring. The readout said, "Number unavailable."

"Hello?"

Heavy breathing. Was the caller asthmatic or a nasty tease?

"Hello? Hello?"

The breathing switched to short, excited huffs. If she hung up, the caller would think mission accomplished, I scared the bitch. "Damned glad you're getting off on our little chat," she said. "Don't have time for this horseshit. Now, and I'm speaking from the bottom of my heart, be a stranger." She clicked off. For no good reason, except having been followed, her instinct placed the caller nearby.

The dog stood and his ears perked.

"Any idea who that was?" The dog nuzzled her hand. "Let's list the possibilities. For enemies, start with cheating husbands. Add strangers I've picked up in bars and strangers I've rejected. Throw in drivers of white hatchbacks and anyone with a grudge against Theda. Add them together and you have assholes queuing up into infinity."

The standoff had released something in her, a twitchiness so familiar that it had its own place low in her gut. Had she inherited the pick-up-a-stranger gene? Or had she been conditioned by those lost afternoons when her mother dragged her to local taverns? It wasn't all bad. Her pockets lumpy with quarters for pinball, she'd gobble French fries out of red plastic baskets lined in paper translucent with grease, while she watched her mom dance with any man bold enough.

Across the water where ducks nested, a squawk reminded Georgia, time to go. "Come on, dog." He sniffed their route home, pausing at every inanimate object for a damp donation. She remained alert.

Uneasy with her uneasiness, she roamed the apartment, snapping on lights. Sudden rain pelted the windows. Only a fool would go out in this. She flipped through TV channels. Reruns and reality shows. Nothing suited her mood. Noodling around on the guitar usually lowered her blood pressure and nudged her into a quiet zone. Her forefinger brushed the engraved pick guard and traced the outline of a hummingbird. She strummed once, twisted a tuning peg, and strummed again. Good. After years of playing restrung closet guitars, she'd saved enough to buy this Gibson. A quick run through scales to loosen up and she tried to work out a new version of "Richland Woman Blues," but the twanging strings snagged her fingers like barbed wire.

The rain had stopped. Water gurgled through the gutters, and she stepped onto the back porch. Wind ripped threads of water from the overhang. She retreated inside. The door closing sharpened the sound of her phone ringing.

"I've been waiting, chewing my nails. Where have you been?"

"The bookstore."

Oops. She recognized Gilbert's I-need-to-apologize voice.

"I have concerns about Marci Heath," he said.

Of course. "I'm listening."

"She phoned, said she's pressuring the lawyers, but it might be a week before—"

"I know, I know, the check's in the mail."

Silence. Maybe he'd hung up. "Did you tell her I was at Billy's? That he locked himself in the bathroom to escape from her?"

"It, it slipped out. She feels awful, just awful that her intentions were misinterpreted. Anyway, I said I'd talk to you."

Goody, goody. Now he's Marci's little minion. Frustration

pinched her voice. "Gilbert, next time your phone rings, check caller ID. If it's anyone on that list you gave me, don't pick up, call me instead."

"Sorry, but I was flustered. These days I'm often flustered."

"If you need to talk, call Stockard." Comforting was a skill Georgia had never acquired. "Sleep well" was all she could manage.

Her toe nudged the box from Stockard. She lifted the scrapbook onto the bed, and a report card and several photos slid out. She opened the card. Her seventh grade teacher, Miss Fandy, had written: *Georgia is willful and resists following rules.* Georgia laid the card aside and studied an old photo. Back then her freckles were more prominent, spattered in a saddle pattern across her nose. In this close-up, with eyes crossed and tongue thrust out, she typified the poster child of willfulness, proof of Miss Fandy's insight.

She hunched over the photo of her foster family. Who had taken this? She tilted it, studied shadows, then remembered Ben Hazlet explaining his new Polaroid camera to the neighbor lady.

He'd arranged the whole crazy-sad family for an Easter portrait. His arm around his wife, Kate, they stood behind the children lined up according to height. Georgia and her foster sister *donned*—that was Kate's word, *donned*—white gloves made of an elastic material. Georgia, admiring this stretchy attribute, pulled and thereby doubled the length of her middle finger. A second before the camera clicked, Hazlet instructed, "Smile." She'd obeyed; grief had curbed her impudence.

Hazlet stripped back the black flap on the Polaroid. "Before we posed, I told everyone to use the bathroom, and from this photo it's obvious Joey did not obey my instructions. There's no time for another picture." He flicked the photo into a bed of daffodils. Georgia lagged behind and snatched the picture. Joey, the glare of sunlight reflecting off his glasses, had crossed and clamped his legs together.

In the kitchen Ben cleared his throat, a signal. "No one uses the bathroom until after breakfast. Joey, go to your room and leave the door open."

What did he think, Joey would pee out the window?

After breakfast Ben led the family into Joey's room and told him, "Drop your trousers." Joey obeyed and Ben examined his underwear. No wet spots. Georgia said nothing, and the intolerable silence that followed still echoed for her.

From the floor, the dog scratched and made a half moan, half bleat: *I want up.* They both knew she'd give in, and she patted the bed. She slipped the loose photo into her scrapbook. Ben Hazlet had insisted everyone address her by her legal name, Georgiana. The name fit some spunky do-gooder in a Disney movie. Georgia flopped down beside her new roomie, her nose inches from his muzzle. He smelled old and comforting like a damp sweater.

When she moved into this apartment, she'd asked the manager if she could keep a pet. The answer was, "Only if it's aquatic."

"Hey you, anyone asks, your name is Turtle."

Her need to escape came like a crushing weight. The hatchback, the call from Gilbert, and old memories had revved her up. From the closet she snared a halter-top. No sense kidding herself, she was headed out the door. The bargaining had now commenced—*I won't go out; well, I'll go out but not to a bar; well, I'll go to a bar but just listen to music; well, while I listen to music I can talk to one guy…*

"Sorry, Turtle, I'm out of here."

After Georgia flicked on the porch light, her lies began unspooling—*but I won't hook up with a stranger.*

*

Another burst of August rain drummed against the car's roof. After Georgia parked, the shower softened to mist, a film caressing her skin. Her sandals slapped along wet pavement. At the end of the block another set of footsteps, a harder echo, matched hers.

The wind kicked in and flattened a Taco Bell wrapper against a brick wall. She lingered in front of a shop window, half hoping her slutted-up image might nag her into going home. A grocery cart chattered along the sidewalk, and she expected the reflection of a homeless person trundling possessions. Instead a man in a suit stopped behind her. Their eyes met in the reflection, and she walked away.

If she charted these barhopping binges by poking pins into a map, the cluster would circle her apartment like the crime scenes on a police map. To avoid trouble she rarely returned to the same bar. Tonight she'd driven across the Ross Island Bridge, an extra precaution, turned down Fifth Avenue, and ducked into the first bar she saw. When she was in this mood, she'd sit by a window, the outside view offering an escape route that reassured her. She ordered a beer.

Her phone rang. "Georgia Lamb here." She waited through the first seconds then recognized the concentrated silence at the other end. "Can't a girl step out for one lousy beer?"

No answer.

"A point of etiquette, when I say hello, you respond. Now one syllable at a time, let's practice remedial greetings: hell-o, hell-o. Sorry, don't have time for your crap."

A couple at the next table stared at her.

"Regis Philbin. He keeps insisting I've won a bazillion dollars."

A man approached. Under two minutes, close to a record.

"You alone?" he asked.

He reminded her of a sturdy James Dean, and she pictured him riding a Harley.

"Sorry," she said, "I'm meeting someone."

He shrugged and moved on. She gave herself a good-conduct

gold star. Yes, she'd finish one beer and tomorrow wake up clean—no hangover, no man.

A cloudburst flailed against the windowpane. Under the streetlight, rain looked like water streaming from a showerhead. Two more sips and another guy hit on her. This must be her lucky day, or did the charged weather goad horny guys into roaming the streets? This one, a blond with baby-sweet cheeks and dimples, must be all of seventeen. Way too young.

He asked if he could sit with her.

"Sure." Why not a little talk before she tossed him back into the pond?

"It's Peyton, right?" he asked.

She'd used that alias before.

"Remember me? I'm Austin."

"And we met here?"

"That's right."

God, she should take snapshots of these men and mount them in a rogues gallery.

A plump waitress brought over a pitcher.

"I ordered for us," Austin said. "I remember you like Hefeweisen. A confession, I've been dropping by here, hoping I'd see you." His voice twanged and he grinned in a loose cowboy way. A cigarette poked out of his shirt pocket. The black tip told her he'd lit it before. He tilted his glass and made a big deal out of pouring his beer. "You don't remember me, do you?"

"You look awfully young."

"Twenty-seven. I can show you my driver's license."

"Not necessary. I have this agreement with the Liquor Commission, they don't police my pickups, I don't card their customers."

When he laughed his eyes narrowed and revealed crow's feet. Maybe she had slept with him. Whack-shit-a-doodle, what a wonderful little life she'd carved out for herself.

"Here's a test," she said. "Multiple choice. If I ask, where on my person do I have a birthmark shaped like a boot, is your answer A, my thigh; B, my imagination; or C, you don't give a rat's ass and I'm referring to the shape of Italy?

"C, definitely C."

"Go ahead, finish your beer." He offered another pour, but she capped her hand over her glass. "I have a new roommate and promised not to be late."

"Come on, the night's still young."

No shit, he actually said "the night's still young." Bet he brimmed with romantic clichés.

"What's your roommate's name?"

"None of your beeswax." She had a box-load of her own clichés.

"And your roommate story, it's true?"

"The varnished truth, you won't get better from me."

"You never told me what you do for a living."

"I'm a chanteuse."

"Chanteuse." He spoke the word as if it invoked a sweet memory. "Let me guess, you lounge across a piano and collect tips in a brandy snifter."

His description mimicked her imaginary depiction. Careful, he's not as vacuous as she'd assumed. She guzzled her beer. "So long, I'm out of here."

"At least you owe me an explanation."

"I owe you?"

"Here we go. Why did I bother with you again?"

"Probably for the same reason you gawk at car wrecks."

"Let's start over, please?"

The peculiar way he puckered his mouth, and the way he said "please" kicked in memories of her mother's simpering. Negotiating, forever negotiating.

"Choose a persona," she said, "nice guy or not nice guy. Think, hmm now, what gets me laid?"

"It'd be easier if you'd tell me. Kidding, kidding. Honest, I just want to talk."

"And me and my vibrator are strictly platonic. We both know why we're here. Let's cut the BS."

"You've got me all wrong."

"Ah, so we're engaging in an existential exploration." She imagined Peyton and Austin keeping a joint diary to show their grandkids.

At the next table a woman with hair the same tawny-gold as her mother's, laughed. It was a good laugh, but lacked the proper build-up. After some guy told a lame joke, her mom would start with a heaving in her shoulders that expanded into full, rippling hoots.

"Is something wrong?" he asked.

His question struck Georgia as hilarious. Tears filled her eyes; her shoulders shook. Austin stared, fueling her laughter, and it kept rolling out, warped and full of gasps. An ugly realization jogged loose. Somehow she and her mother had arrived at the same place.

"What's the matter with you?" he asked. "I hate it when you act all crazy."

The phrase echoed in her head. Someone else had used those same words, *hate it when… hate it when…* "Please, repeat what you just said."

"I don't understand why—"

"No, no, your exact words. Repeat your exact words."

He shrugged. "I hate it when—"

"That's it."

"What's it?"

"Someone had used that phrase? But who? *Think, think.* She tossed a five-dollar bill on the table and was out the door.

*

Outside smelled cool and clean; city lights reflected bloated rainbows off the wet pavement. The traffic gods smiled on Georgia: red lights switched to green, dawdling cars settled into the other lane, and when she pulled into the AM/PM, a parking space waited at the front door. All good omens. But whatever had been stirred up in her was not going gentle into that good night.

Hated it repeated like a jingle that turns up on every TV channel. Who said it? What did it mean?

She turned left on 19th into the parking area of her complex. She'd almost bought a pack of smokes at the AM/PM to go with the bottle of Thunderbird wine she didn't buy. She scooted onto the warm hood of her car and leaned back against the windshield, sorting possibilities.

The answer came like a spear thrust. Dawn Brody had used that phrase, said Ted "hated it when" Theda manipulated Gilbert, refusing to help save his bookstore. Ted could only have learned this tidbit from Marci Heath, the same gossipy Heath who assured her that it was all "hush hush," just between the two of them. Obviously Ted and Heath were more than nodding acquaintances. It explained so much: Heath sucking up to Gilbert, Heath refusing to hand over documents, Heath intimidating Billy. Was there more? Had Heath driven the hatchback? Had the two of them schemed to kill Theda? Georgia stared into the darkness.

The killer had delighted in tormenting Theda and Gilbert with their personal fears. Was the murderer playing out a vendetta? As far as Georgia knew, Heath harbored no grudges. But Ted might. Georgia rolled off the car. Turtle, he's waiting.

No porch light.

A shaft of light angled through Georgia's kitchen curtains and illuminated the hedge on the opposite side of the walk. Earlier she'd switched it off. She groped in her purse and found the can of pepper spray.

Burglary, home invasion, a serial rapist murderer? Who had a key? Stockard. But she would've called first. Had the apartment manager discovered Turtle? Georgia retrieved the Louisville Slugger. How had she survived all these years without it?

Hidden in shadow next to the building, she raised her head above the lip of the back porch. Quiet. The door was ajar and a sliver of light fell across the sidewalk. Bat in her right hand, pepper spray in her left, she tiptoed up the three steps, nudged the door open, and peeked around the jamb. The lamp in the dining room was still shining. No movement. The usual shadows.

Staying low, ready to dodge in any direction, she leapt into the kitchen then bounded from the hall to the dining room. Her right foot came down on a CD and slipped from under her. Landing hard on her hip, she rolled to absorb the impact. The bat flew out of her hand, and she bounced to a stop, spread-eagled on the floor, arms extended, hands clutching the pepper spray. Georgia wedged herself up, first to kneeling, then standing. She was alone.

Wires dangled from the CD player, its innards twisted and ruined. Beyond that, books were strewn around the front room. At least her computer was still intact. She checked the file cabinet, safe, but the locks were gouged where someone had tried to force them open. Whoever did this hadn't found her gun.

Turtle, where in the hell was Turtle? The bedroom? She rushed then slowed and flicked on lights down the hall. Everything tossed. On the bed she found her beloved guitar, the Gibson Hummingbird, sprawled like a gutted fish, strings broken, the top ripped outward from the sound hole. Behind her a noise. She jumped into the closet.

Scratching. From the bathroom.

She twisted the bathroom doorknob and slammed the door open. Turtle cowered, making himself small behind the toilet bowl. Hand extended, Georgia knelt and he leaned forward to sniff her fingers.

"Come on, big boy, you're safe, we're both safe."

Fury grew in her gut, and fierce tears in her eyes. She called 911. No, she wasn't in danger. No, she wasn't hurt. Yes, she'd be home tomorrow between ten and noon.

Face or boobs? Make a choice, face or boobs?

Dawn Brody snapped open her compact, centered it on her lap, and hovered above the mirror. Her cheeks sagged; the parentheses around her mouth deepened; baby jowls waggled. Gravity. Dawn cursed the merciless bitch. She held the compact above her head and tilted back. Much better, all the fleshy bits smoothed away. That magazine was right, lying on your back during sex flatters the face. To hell with variety, she'd finagle missionary position then let the fireworks commence. She clicked the compact shut and apologized: sorry, boobies, tonight you sprawl like eggs hitting the frying pan.

She heard the bathroom faucet and then Ted gargling. He must've started his dental hygiene, flossing alone might take five minutes. One night, impatient with his bathroom preparations, she'd peeked in. Romantic fantasies shriveled while she watched him snip nose hair.

Usually she scrubbed her face then slathered it with night cream, but tonight she'd retire in full battle makeup. After their boring banquet, Ted had excused himself for a business meeting, and she'd rushed home. When was the last time they'd had a good roll in the hay? She'd soaked in a bath brimming with bubbles and oils. Hot to trot she had no one to trot with.

Moisture cream stung the corner of her eye. The pale film made her eyelashes look skimpy. She smoothed a dollop of foundation across her forehead, nose, and chin. Applying what beauty magazines called 'a feathery stroke,' she gave her eyebrows a higher arch.

Nope, not enough. She brushed on a spidery layer of mascara. She heard the soft swallow of the toilet flushing. Dawn scolded herself, don't listen, don't spoil the mood, picture something else. Peignoir, a delicious word. Like an aging actress who insists on Vaseline smearing the camera lens, her mother had slept in peignoirs so that layers of chiffon veiled all her flabby parts. Ted scoffed at peignoirs, said it was like thrashing through drapery. Tonight she'd chosen red for an extra boost, and he understood that red meant playtime. Once a keep-the-lights-on man, Ted now darkened their bedroom before sex. Well, tonight if she had to handcuff him and hang a spotlight from the ceiling, he'd stare down onto her face. Ted entered all shiny and tan. He sat on the bed, slipped off his BVDs, and scooted under the sheet.

Stay on your back, she coached herself, don't budge. During his kisses she remained rooted. He groped under the chiffon, and that's when it happened. He rubbed his eyes and said, "These lights give me a headache, mind if I switch them off?"

You bet she minded. "Whatever you want, dear."

Dawn rolled over and flicked off her lamp, but when she heard the snick of his light, she seethed. She was pissed for not saying "I mind like hell," pissed at Ted for assuming he had a right to the I-have-a-headache excuse, and pissed that her mother had taught her, *to please a man you must eat your words*. All her efforts felt trivial, like the wife in a detergent commercial thrilled by white laundry.

A squirm here, an "ah" there. If this had been American Idol, he'd be packing his bags. He groaned his last groan then made a throaty sound, a cross between a purr and a birdcall. More predictable than an egg timer, in three minutes Ted snored away. Dawn heard Princess Di scratching at the door. "Believe me, old girl, you didn't miss a thing." After sex, an atom bomb couldn't wake Ted. She knew she was going to cry and raced to the bathroom.

Dawn flicked on the vanity light, tinkled, then re-examined her reflection. Hell, she'd gone to bed *all gussied up*, a phrase her father used, and now Maybelline Great Lash Mascara blackened her eyes. She wiped away eye gunk and tossed the tissue into the toilet. *What's that floating in the water?* She clicked on the overhead light. In the bowl, teeny red stars and gold glitter glinted back at her.

Dawn faced the full-length mirror, hitched up her peignoir— *exposing the good china*, her mother's phrase—and thrust out her pelvis. Like a lewd wink, her who-hah twinkled back. She knew where her nether region had been, and at no time had it made contact with glitter. Transference of evidence. She'd read enough crime novels to spot it.

She opened the door to the hall. Princess Di stretched across her path, and Dawn hiked up chiffon and stepped over her. Where was it? She'd just seen it a few days ago. Di snuffled along behind, and Dawn thought this clever, reminding her of a bloodhound. In the top desk drawer, shoved behind a tennis ball, the electric bill, and three used sparklers, she found the clip-on reading light that had been a gift for a magazine subscription—*House Beautiful* or *Architectural Digest*, she couldn't remember which.

Crouched next to the bed, she shook Ted's BVDs then aimed her light inches above the rug. Metallic specks glimmered. Dawn inched under the sheets, took a deep breath, and skittered the light over Ted's thighs. No sparkles, but she needed a proper look.

She re-emerged from the sheets and nudged Ted. He snorted. She made a fist and jabbed. "Ted, you're snoring. Move over." He rolled and relaxed, stretching his legs.

Back under the sheet, her feet dangled off the bed, and the peignoir bunched around her neck, tickling her nose. She tunneled the light up his leg and stopped at a scatter of spangles. There was no denying this evidence. Confident he could fool her, Ted had arranged a rendezvous with another woman, and then the dumb cluck hadn't bothered to shower. A moan crumpled out of Dawn. She coiled tighter until her knees touched her chin. Afraid she'd jar loose more pain, she pretended the blue sheets were water, and she was snorkeling in the Caribbean.

New questions struck her. Did Ted know about his lover's glowing kootchie? Or had she turned off the lights and tricked him? He, of course, would have told her he no longer slept with his wife, but she'd know better and scheme to make her presence known like a brazen tattoo. No, like a neon light—*he's mine.*

Just as her father had predicted, her marriage was a flop. Passion and honesty all gone; even their playfulness had fizzled. During the honeymoon Ted gave his twenty-first appendage a special name, Willy. She'd enjoyed their naughty secret and laughed when Ted lisped, "Willy wants to visit," or "I think you wore Willy out." She joined in the game. "Does Willy want to go night-night?" Five years of this silliness had become hair-pullingly irksome, and she quit talking to Willy. Ted never noticed. Now when Dawn thought of Willy, she imagined a sock puppet.

Sitting on the edge of the bed, she pressed the pillow to her chest and rocked. God, how she yearned to wake Ted and confront him with her tinseled fandango. She grabbed the remote, thinking she'd whack him on the head, but instead she flicked on the TV. A blue, lunar glow illuminated Ted's dreaming face. And then she heard a voice, a voice she'd expect from God if he got chatty. No, not deep enough; her father's voice. "Get him where it hurts."

Dawn gripped the pillow until her arms quivered. Her Daddy would not be disappointed. She was Lorena Bobbitt, hide-the-kitchen-knives mad.

Sunlight burrowed through Georgia's eyelids, and she tugged the sheet higher. Her hand dropped free over the side of the bed.

Warm and wet. Warm and wet.

What the hell? She smelled Turtle's breath, moist and beefy, and opened one eye. He licked her wrist then shifted back on his haunches. When she opened both eyes, morning light amplified the wreckage in her apartment. She checked the clock. Six thirty-five. Damn. Late. She remembered setting the alarm but not punching the last button. Double damn.

A tether from the porch rail to Turtle's collar gave him twenty feet and five minutes to roam along the fence and take care of business. Her Levis bordered on gamey, but would have to do until she eked out laundry time.

By seven AM her turn signal blinked left for the approach to the Ross Island Bridge. Up the length of Powell Boulevard all she could see were cars jammed nose to tail. A blue Ford hatchback zipped by, then a green one. If she waited long enough, would the right white hatchback whiz past? The light at Twenty-First went red and traffic opened up.

Once over the bridge, cars backed up again. She checked her reflection in the rearview mirror. Her ponytail flopped above one ear like the plume of an exotic Mayan bird. Scraggly hairs had knotted around the rubber band and, anticipating pain, she ripped it off like a Band-Aid in one swift yank. No sense even looking for a comb; with the heel of her hand she steamrollered over a hump left by the ponytail. Instead of circling the block to find a parking space, she pulled into a pay lot and hoofed it, dodging through traffic. She could still beat Heath to the office.

Georgia's mother had lost apartment keys as often as she'd

lost boyfriends, and by age twelve, Georgia had mastered picking locks. She flexed her fingers while climbing stairs to the Abraxas office. Did she still have the touch?

Though office hours were nine to five, the door was open. Shit, Heath had beaten her. She peeked inside. A young guy, dreadlocks wriggling from under his rainbow-striped cap, zipped a box closed with packing tape.

She tapped the doorframe. "Where's Heath?"

"What's that?" He stood and pulled iPod buds from his ears. "What'd you say?"

"Heath, is she here?"

"Nah, not now." His smile got lost in the thicket of his beard. "I met her here like at six this morning, she left a few minutes ago."

Georgia stepped to the center of the room. Breuer chairs stacked in one corner, the Persian carpet rolled up in another, packed boxes—in a few days the place had gone from penthouse to warehouse.

"What's happening?"

"Moving, I guess. Yesterday at lunch Ms Heath dropped by the shelter, said she needed a laborer. Did everything except check teeth and pinch biceps. So, eye of newt and wave of wand, here I am." He popped open a flattened cardboard box, folded down the flaps, and taped the bottom so it stood on its own.

"Have you had breakfast yet?" she asked.

"Nope."

"Tell you what, I'll cover for you, go grab a bite."

He looked at her, shrugged, said "Sure", and he was gone.

"Hey." Georgia rushed to the door and leaned into the hall. "Do you need a few bucks?"

"Ms Heath said she'd spell me, but took off. Guess she figured I'd scrounge something."

Georgia slapped a five into his open palm.

Half the shelves in the file room had been stripped, the contents likely stuffed in those boxes. Against the opposite wall, the worktable was clear, except for a computer. Since finding Billy locked in his bathroom, Georgia had craved a tit for tat. She pictured this room in ruins, a duplicate of her apartment. Nope, couldn't do it. This was still Theda's space.

She punched the power button on the computer and tapped her toe waiting for the hard drive to spin up. Didn't the woman use passwords? Georgia found mailing lists and working files to sort through later. Though the donor lists were public record, she copied everything to her flash drive. There must be papers in here worth hiding. The brass nameplate had vanished from the big desk. Georgia pulled out every drawer, dumped the contents and ran her fingers around the edges. Beyond the odd paperclip, staples and a few slivers, she found nothing, not even an envelope taped to the bottom. Heath was thorough.

Georgia plunked into a cushy leather chair, swiveled to face the windows, and propped Heath's laptop against her knees. Scrolling through files revealed little. Had Heath nested private files inside others like Russian dolls? Sometimes haphazard worked better than systematic. She began opening individual folders and keyed in a search for Northwest Metals. *No results found* popped up. Under Sauvie Island she found two strange file names, both pleading for a password. She stared at the machine, tempted to flip it against the wall.

"Forget to say open sesame?"

She spun around. The homeless guy was back. His eyes tilted down at the corners and, smiling, he achieved an inverted symmetry.

"This isn't what you think," Georgia said.

"Didn't peg you as a bullshitter."

"Now you've gone and made me feel all guilty. This is exactly what you think. Name's Georgia Lamb. I'm an investigator."

His forehead bunched into a frown. "Cop?"

"Private."

He relaxed, but the silence stretched between them as he

studied her.

"Okay," he said, "payback for breakfast. Try *rburke*, one word, lowercase."

She typed the password, and alakazam. Heath had saved two emails, both from Roy Burke—*amount kept under ten million* and *set up appointment*. Cryptic, yet suggestive.

"How'd you know?" she asked.

"Shoulder surfing while I packed up in here. People think 'cause I'm homeless, I'm illiterate. Happens all the time, I disappear into the background like a dog or a pigeon. But look at that, odd don't you think, an environmental bunch mixing with a developer like Burke? The man leaves no tree standing."

He was right. She remembered Stockard's story about Theda chained to a threatened oak and stopping the construction of a strip mall; the police report listed Burke as the contractor. "Did you see anything about a Ted Brody?"

"Ah, so that's it."

"What's it?"

"If you want to curl your toes, try *teddybear* on the other file."

A calendar popped up. "Teddy Bear" and "Chickadee" hooked up on Tuesdays and Thursdays. The text below memorialized cyber-romance at its raunchiest, the cooing and billing of digital lovebirds. Ted and Marci sitting in a tree, no big surprise. She was more interested in Heath's vicious side. Besides terrorizing Billy, she was stringing Gilbert along. Let the masks fall.

Georgia scanned down to a more businesslike entry listing Brody and Associates, copied it, then studied the man. "Listen, I have a problem. I intend to leave Heath a little memento. Actually, a juvenile gesture."

"That's the best kind."

"But I don't want her to give you grief."

"Not to worry, when I'm done here, it's out the door. Wintering in southern California."

"And then you'll be back?"

"Most likely."

"At times I can use someone with your talents. How can I reach you?"

"I'll be back in the spring, just like a swallow to Capistrano." He wrote out his name and a phone number on one of Georgia's cards. "The ex-wife. I keep her informed."

"You better get out of here before Heath returns. How much was she paying you?"

"Forty today if I last till noon."

Georgia emptied her wallet, seventy-one dollars. "This year skip the freights, take Amtrak."

"Fortuitous, meeting you has been fortuitous." He savored the word and loped down the hall.

She rummaged through her purse, found one of the brochures that had terrorized Billy, and centered it on the desk.

Georgia heard the clickity-clack of high heels. Shit. It could be Heath. She jogged out the door to the stairwell and climbed to the third floor. No footsteps. Her phone rang.

"Is that you? Is that you? It's me, Dawn." Intensity crackled out of the phone.

"What's wrong?"

"Ted's a dick. He's cheating. I found proof, it was, and, his, his—"

"His?"

"His crotch, it sparkled. Horrible, just horrible."

Sounded pretty horrible. "Slow down."

"I followed a trail of glitter from Ted's undies, up his leg, and then nesting—like I said, it was horrible."

Georgia imagined Dawn, all braids and dirndl, holding Hansel's hand while she followed sequined breadcrumbs. "And you called me because—?"

"I want to hire you. Follow the bastard."

"When?"

"This minute, now, tomorrow, soon."

"It might be days before I—"

"Then soon as you can."

Georgia sensed a hang-up and blurted," Did you check Ted's BlackBerry?

"BlackBerry?"

"You said you'd check his schedule, find out where he was the night Theda died."

"Oops, slipped my mind. Lots of slippage in my memory." Dawn gave a brittle laugh. Her answer sounded rehearsed, a line she'd used before to wriggle out of tight corners. "He's in the shower—yeah, big whoop, *now* he showers. I'll try to sneak a peek."

"Let's cut the crap," Georgia said. "I doubt I can work with you."

"Why not?"

"Dawn, 'fess up, you haven't been straight with me. Who was the blond on Theda's doorstep? When you figure that out, call me."

Dead air. Not the hang-up of a patient woman.

*

Louise Tubberman, the manager of the apartment complex, churned up dust storms as she swept the walkway. The square of cement outside Georgia's window must've been filthy and required a full ten minutes of Louise's attention. Georgia blamed herself: she should've closed the curtains after the young cop knocked on her door.

Bright and friendly, patrolman Lewis was not a bit helpful. Nothing was stolen and he thought this fact, like a mother's kiss on a boo-boo, made it all better. She would have preferred kids stealing laptops to fund drugs. This was personal. Ravaging her apartment, sure, that was a bitch, but destroying her guitar, that was more. Stockard had once explained the German word *schadenfreude*—taking delight in another's pain and misfortune. This was chock-full of schadenfreude. When she told Lewis she'd left everything untouched, he seemed obliged to walk from room to room, not out of interest but as a point of etiquette.

"Do you have enemies?" She didn't answer. "Maybe if you think about it, you'll come up with a name."

A name. Hand me the frigging phonebook, I'll highlight fifty-nine possibilities. But she decided dishonesty was the best policy. Let him believe no one would harm her sweet little ass.

The front door closed behind Lewis, and Turtle crept out of the bathroom, his new sanctuary. She slapped the couch and he huddled against her hip. His eyes strayed to her face. "I know, I know, might as well get used to me lying. But just between us, I can't name all the possibilities."

First choice, someone connected to Theda. Payback for knocking on doors and sniffing around secrets. And now, drum roll please, the second group of suspects, faceless men she'd bedded once or pissed off. Baby-faced Austin would be the newest addition. Not knowing whom to blame left her suspended, legs kicking air.

"And you." She ruffled Turtle's topknot of prickly fur. "Get that tail-wagging under control."

Might as well face off with the apartment manager before she comes knocking.

Louise Tubberman opened her door. The broom leaned against the jamb, a ready excuse to snoop. Tubberman's black hair puffed out in unpredictable places like the absurd hair balls on poodles. The woman's short arms and eyes set deep in a fleshy face reminded Georgia of the Queen of Hearts. At any moment she might bellow, "Off with her head!" Instead she rambled on about last night.

"So, let me get this straight," Georgia said. "A neighbor phoned you, said he heard things crashing in my apartment, and ever vigilant, you waited fifteen minutes because 'Dancing with the Stars' featured a tango, and you've always been partial to anything Latin. Then you creep over to my apartment and hear what you think is a dog. Right?"

"Right." Tubberman's sweatsuit slouched over her more like bedding than clothing, and her breath smelled of menthol and lemon. She drew a hanky from her sleeve, snorted into it, and wagged the cartilage of her nose. "I almost didn't check, it was late and I have a cold. Besides, keeping a dog is a violation of your lease."

Georgia opened her eyes wide. "No shit."

"There's no need to swear."

"Then you don't live my life."

"Mr. Sanchez, the owner, trusts me to honor his rules."

The way Louise said *Sanchez* made Georgia think he was included in Louise's love of all things Latin. "And he wouldn't mind you ignoring the savage sounds of my belongings and his property being thrashed?"

"I did come over."

"Oh yeah, that's right, after the tango. I suppose that includes the commercial break and the judges' scores." Hold your horses; if you want to keep the dog, back off. "I'll be honest. Like me, you're a single woman living alone, so I know you'll understand."

Louise's nose wrinkled with a suppressed sneeze. Georgia stepped back in case it exploded.

"I'm a compassionate person," Louise said.

"That's how you strike me. A couple nights ago, I think Friday, my doorknob rattled, someone trying to get in."

"Friday night?"

If you're going to lie, why be half-assed? "Friday was the first time. I wasn't a hundred percent sure until Saturday. The rattles were louder, braver. Then I heard scratching at my window. Well, I can tell you, I slept with one eye open."

"I always check the back seat before getting into my car."

Her cell rang. Dawn again. Georgia flipped open the phone. "Decide to fess up?"

Louise stepped closer. Her black hair reeked of chemicals stronger than a dye job, maybe a new perm. Georgia turned away.

"Meet me for coffee and I'll tell all," Dawn said.

Georgia whispered. "Can't we settle it now?" Wasting time with Dawn irritated her.

"Name the time and place," Dawn said.

"Noon, Papa Haydn's on Twenty-Third."

"See you there."

Georgia rolled her shoulders, told herself this is for Turtle, and faced Tubberman. "Women like us living alone, we need to stick together. When I told my friend, that was her on the phone, she insisted I borrow her dog, you know, until I felt safe. If I can't keep the dog a little longer, I'll have to tell everyone here they're not safe, and of course by everyone, I mean Sanchez." This might buy her enough time to find a new apartment.

"I'm not sure—"

"And I'll cover expenses, a door was ripped off and a kitchen cupboard kicked in." She almost included an imaginary hole in the ceiling, but decided against being overzealous. "Hey, if you think Mr. Sanchez would prefer paying..." She dangled him like a baited hook.

"I'll have to think about it."

Georgia felt Louise nosing after her.

"I wouldn't want the other neighbors to know I let you violate the lease."

"Look, this goes against my strict principles, but if anyone asks, I'll lie. Tell them you didn't know about the dog, okay? And here." Georgia dug a twenty out of her jean pocket, her last-gasp emergency fund. "A doggie deposit."

*

118

Georgia drew a steno pad from her bag and turned the corner onto Northwest Davis Street in Old Town. Though she was sick of chasing the damned paperwork, she gauged its importance by Heath's attempts at secrecy. And what about her link to Roy Burke?

A blue awning opened over a brick arch. Chattering water echoed in a passage lined with shops, and at the back she discovered a hidden grotto. The glassed-in elevator stopped at the third floor with a jerk. Decorated in lemon and apricot, Burke's office contained three desks, assorted cabinets, and two chairs. A pale woman, jowly as a basset hound, studied Georgia. The nameplate read Teresa Brambly.

"Yes?"

"How are you? I'm Georgia Lamb." She offered her hand.

The woman stared over her glasses.

"I'm here for my interview with Mr. Burke."

"And you have an appointment?" Brambly checked a desk calendar. "I don't see, what is it, Lamb? Like the farm animal?"

Georgia considered bleating. "He didn't mention it? I thought this might happen. We talked at Commissioner Fry's, and Roy, Mr. Burke, said today—"

The woman shushed her. "I'll check. Mr. Burke's a busy man. Wait over there, please."

"I have a deadline."

"Please."

A door opened at the back of the room, and Roy Burke emerged, shorter and stouter than Georgia had imagined, but she recognized his puffy lips from billboards around town, and wondered if collagen made them extra-pouty.

She wedged past the secretary and stepped forward, hand extended. "Mr. Burke, Georgia Lamb from *Willamette Week*. We talked about a profile, Chamber of Commerce Man of the Year. A few quick questions?"

Georgia shrugged off Brambly's hand.

"I'm sorry, Mr. Burke," the secretary said, but he waved her away.

"Quite all right, Ms. Brambly. My door's always open to the press, especially when the reporter is so engaging." A Masonic ring cut into Georgia's knuckles when he shook her hand. She noticed the heavy gold bracelet beneath his starched cuff.

"Your car's waiting," Ms. Brambly said. "Everything's ready, sir, here's your case."

"Good, good." He led Georgia into the hall. "Let's talk on the way down. I'm flying to Seattle, corralling backers for Riverwood Estates. Picture this, after a day of golf on Sauvie Island, sipping cocktails, the Columbia River in the foreground and, in the purple distance, mountains rising, both St. Helens and Hood. Shame I can't move Rainier."

Georgia wanted to reply, *Picture this, great blue herons dead. Cottonwood stands heaped into slash piles.* Instead she asked, "Isn't Sauvie Island a protected wetland?"

"Well, yes, parts, but there's lots of room. You watch, I'll have the variances, it's all falling into place. Is this okay? Am I quotable?" He looked pleased as a pond-full of ducks.

"Eminently." On her notepad she drew a stick man with a bulbous head. The elevator door opened, and he ushered Georgia out with a proprietary hand on her arm.

"My editor wanted me to ask about location, we heard Ted Brody was negotiating—"

"Brody. He thinks he has a slam dunk, but I have more friends on the island than he realizes."

"Marci Heath, she's acting all hush-hush. Where does she stand on your proposal?"

When he scowled his forehead remained Botox-smooth. "At first, she was helpful, persuasive with the right people, but something's changed. She's become, what's the right word, secretive, more intense. No, distant. That's it." He looked pleased, and then his smile sagged. "You won't print that will you?"

"Not if you don't want me to. Off the record, is Ted Brody more intense?"

"Let's just say Ted's easily distracted."

"Women, I've heard the rumors. And Mr. Brody's ex-wife, Theda Kovac, before her death, wasn't she fighting to preserve the island?"

"We had our differences—it's all so sad. But look at the positive, since her death the community supports her ideals, and I say hurray for that. Toxic waste next to my eighteenth green would never do."

Sounds like Theda's death boosted his bottom line. Georgia added to her doodle—plumped-up lips spewing feathers.

"You getting all this?" Burke leaned over to peek at Georgia's notepad.

She put him off with a wag of her finger, but imagined a well-placed knee to his assets. "Are you saying Riverwood Estates might be a done deal?"

His brow almost furrowed.

"A promise," she said. "Again, off the record."

A uniformed chauffeur stood beside a silver Lincoln Town Car and held a door for Burke who turned back to Georgia. "Hmm, now listen, little lady, you come back tomorrow, and we'll definitely have something to talk about. But until tomorrow mum's the word."

*

Dawn signaled Georgia with a yahoo and a wave, two cups of steaming coffee had already been poured. She smiled big then pushed aside a salad plate, empty except for one exhausted and slightly nibbled spinach leaf.

Cream rejected, sugar accepted, Georgia jumped in. "Go ahead, I'm all a-twitter."

"I checked Ted's Blackberry. He wasn't home the night that… well, that night. His schedule placed him at the office."

"You mean the night Theda died?"

"Uh-huh."

"And where were you that night?"

"Me?"

"I have to ask."

Dawn laughed. "I've been waiting for that. Princess Di and I were at home waiting for him."

"How late did he get home?"

"I'm an aggressive sleeper, so he might've come home at any old hour, I'd never notice." Dawn brushed at air as if shooing a fly. "I thought we'd enjoy lunch before—"

"I've eaten and my day's packed. A quick question, where's Ted this afternoon?"

"The Schoenfeld Estate up in the West Hills. Hah—at least that's what he told me."

"Please, I need a favor."

"Sure."

Georgia slid a napkin across the table. "Would you draw me a map to this Schoenfeld Estate?"

"I'm very good with directions." Dawn completed the map and presented it to Georgia with a flourish. "I doubt you noticed, but my mind doesn't work in straight lines. It needs lots of elbow room. Now where was I going? Oh, I know. When I first met Ted, Daddy had him vetted, so I knew he'd cheated on Theda. Besides he's a man. The only reason men don't act like pigs all the time is that they want to get laid. How well do you know Marci Heath?"

"We've met."

"Has she confided in you?"

"She's been annoyingly evasive."

"That wasn't an evasion," Dawn said. "The poor dear is shy."

And poor, dear Dawn must not realize she'd stumbled onto her husband's mistress. "Tell me about shy Marci." Sarcasm seeped into Georgia's voice. Dawn didn't seem to notice.

"I swore not to tell, but now that Theda's death is suspicious, it's my duty."

"Absolutely."

"Marci said she can't trust men because of the way she lost her virginity."

The phrase rankled Georgia, and she pictured an umbrella misplaced in a closet of raincoats.

"Imagine, twenty-six before her first man. After weeks of whispery explorations in the supply closet, she agreed to sneak off with her boss and was shocked to discover that men were so, so bristly. That's a direct quote. When she told him she was a virgin, he rammed, again that's her word, rammed into her and said, 'You'll never forget the first one.'"

"Jeez."

"It gets worse." Dawn signaled a waitress and ordered cheesecake; Georgia refused.

"Please, go on."

Dawn waved Georgia silent. "I lost track, let me think."

"Her boss told her—"

"Now I remember. Her boss, that beast, folded back the bedspread and framed her blood like a prize for the maid to find. See, pigs, just like I said, all pigs."

Poor little virgin with an old man nipping at her heels— what kind of thrill did Heath get from telling this story to her lover's wife?

Dawn slurped coffee. "And me, I've been walking around with blinders on ignoring Ted's little piggy signs."

"What signs?"

"He's started working late, even joined a gym. He's always preferred a little air down below, but now he's switched from boxers to briefs because he thinks they look sexy. So maybe a week or two ago, I figure he's cheating, and Theda's name popped into my head."

"Why Theda?"

"You need to understand Ted: he always chooses the easiest

way. Always." Dawn folded her hands on the table so that her fingers pointed at Georgia. "For breakfast he loves Lucky Charms, but if Shredded Wheat is closer he grabs that. To get a little on the side, what's easier than an ex-wife?"

"So you were the blond on Theda's porch?"

"Yes, it was me."

"What happened?"

"Soon as she opened the door, I said, 'Are you bonking Ted?' She of course said, 'No.' It was very civilized."

"That's not what my witness said."

"Okay, okay, I screamed, 'Quit fucking Ted!'" Dawn's facial muscles hardened, and Georgia noticed that her pink lipstick had bled into the tiny wrinkles around her mouth. "Theda said I was crazy, but believe you me, I know the power that Ted has over women."

"And you went inside to talk?"

"I tried, but Theda refused, said she had a cold. What kind of an excuse is that?"

"Is Ted capable of murder?"

The skin below Dawn's left eye twitched. "If Theda's throat had been slashed or bullets had ripped her apart, then I'd be sure."

"Sure of what?"

"Ted hates messes. Pricks his finger on a thorn and the big baby can't apply his own Band-Aid. Once I thought, how sweet, swooning at a spot of blood. But dropping a hive down Theda's chimney would appeal to Ted. He's resentful and always blamed Theda for the breakup."

"He cheated, not her."

Dawn sipped coffee. Only her neck stretched for the cup, like someone following a scent. "I know, but Theda caught him. Ted didn't want a divorce, just a little extra. He liked being married to her. She ruined the marriage by insisting on a divorce, so it's her fault."

"That hardly seems—"

"There's more. I've been saving the best for last. I don't know the exact details, but Theda was screwing up a big land deal, and Ted was furious."

"Whatever you do," Georgia said, "don't let Ted know that we talked."

"I've worked everything out, and I can handle Ted." Dawn smiled as if having a plan gave her power.

"And you really think he's capable of, that he'd go—"

"If Ted murdered someone, that's how he'd do it. After dropping a beehive down her chimney, he could walk away, leave it to fate like flipping a coin. Heads, Theda lives. Tails, she can't screw up his business. Either way it's her fault, and better yet, it'd be all neat and tidy. Now me, I don't mind a little blood."

13

Dawn cradled the rifle as if it was a baby whose head needed support. Her first inclination had been, 'don't touch', but when she lifted it, the seductive heft of wood and the cold certainty of steel illuminated the silly male fuss over guns.

"Anything here tickle your fancy?" The man behind the counter had a chubby face and a Friar Tuck fringe of hair.

"I'm Dawn Brody." She stroked the rifle. "I was here last week, remember? I might have filled out the form as Mrs. Ted Brody, but I'm almost sure it's under Dawn. The thumb print smeared, guess I was nervous, and you had to retake my prints."

"Five, ten women a day walk in here. Used to be maybe one a week. Rape, you know." His voice was soft but exuberant. Dawn imagined him adding a "Praise the Lord." "Interested in that rifle?"

"Oh no, I'd like a, what's it called, a handgun. Nothing too bulky."

She handed him the rifle, and he laid it on the counter. For a moment Dawn stayed rigid—he reminded her of someone, not the hair, it was that smile, cherubic but still alarming. While Dawn strolled to the next counter, the man inched along with her, and she snatched the memory: Mr. Tompleton, her Sunday school teacher. She'd hated him because he made fun of her when she'd requested her favorite hymn, the one about animals, "Gladly, the Cross-Eyed Bear."

"Now, ma'am, please spell your name."

"B-R-O-D-Y."

"Give me a sec, I'll find your application."

The gun in the tiny holster attached to the back of his belt appeared harmless as a toy. Maybe she'd ask about those

Rambo rifles with the metal gizmos like a spear. Guns, knives, bayonets—anything here could be hers.

"Your permit checks out." He returned waving papers. "Haven't robbed any banks lately, have you?" Before he laughed he gulped air like a child preparing to burp. Mr. Tompleton had laughed like that. Dawn almost asked, "Are you Presbyterian?" But if he answered yes, he'd cast a pall over her good mood. No pall-casting today. She felt elated, as if adventure, not the ghost of a hated Sunday school teacher, were standing in front of her.

Dawn inspected the guns in the glass case and admired one with a mother-of-pearl handle. It was a sentimental choice, Ted had given her a mother-of-pearl compact for their fifth anniversary.

"This one." She tapped the glass above the pretty little gun. "What's it called?"

"Saturday night special."

"Saturday night special… What would you recommend?"

"The gun's for your protection, right?"

Was this a trick question? Was answering it mandatory? "Well, ah, yes." If he suspected she was lying, could he block her purchase?

"Lady, you okay?"

"Fine and dandy."

He retrieved another small gun from the display case and spun the empty cylinder. "I'd recommend this, a .38 caliber Taurus, always popular with the ladies. Easy to use, double action."

"Double action? What's that?"

"You don't have to cock it before you fire." He extended the gun.

She hesitated. Would she need that extra second? "I'll take it."

"What about a handbag?"

"A what?"

"Handbag." He lifted a baby-blue leather purse from the

rack behind him. "See?"

Dawn heard the scratchy rip of Velcro as he opened the side of the purse and revealed a secret pocket. "This way no one knows you're packing."

She reached out, nestling her hand in the leather pouch. "Don't wrap it. I'll wear it home."

With the purse slung over her shoulder and gun and ammo sequestered inside, Dawn strode to her car. She was in a smiling mood, a nodding, luminous mood, but the people she passed didn't notice. How could they miss it? Her radiance was neither soft nor helpless, and it came from her, yes her—sweet, dithering Dawn. Hah!

An unexpected pinch of guilt slowed her down. For dinner she'd cook pork chops and biscuits with apple butter. Ted's favorite.

14

Georgia Lamb

Although Georgia had grown up comfortable in chaos, settling into another person's rhythm calmed her. Three afternoons a week Stockard attended a yoga class, and if Georgia suddenly appeared, she would not be asked, "Why are you here?" A little thing, but she never took it for granted.

My gaggle of grannies was Stockard's name for the group; Georgia called it *yoga for old farts*. She angled folding chairs toward the glassed-in exercise room and set two coffees on the table. The women crouched into the lion pose, their faces cranked up like children working into a cry. That's how she felt—calm, then outraged.

Stockard waved, gathered her belongings, and left the group. She tore the lid from a coffee and inhaled steam. "You look tired. Any sleep?"

"Not enough. Shit, almost none." She peeked into Stockard's bag. "Is that financial mumbo-jumbo for me?"

Stockard dumped papers onto her lap. "One surprise before we get started. This morning Theda's attorney called."

A long pause, then Georgia said, "Not fair, no teasing."

"On Gilbert's recommendation I'm the first board member of the Kovac Conservation Trust. Theda's assets will be used to further her ideals. Not a dime goes to Gilbert."

"There's still the—"

"No, there isn't. I called to thank him, and when I asked, 'Is the bookstore closing?' Well, shocked would best describe his reaction. 'No such thing,' he said. He needs space for a collection he bought at an estate sale. No bankruptcy, hence no reason to resent Theda. His motive is gone."

"Don't go all Cheshire cat on me. I admit it, I was wrong

about Gilbert." Georgia held up the folders. "From the look of these, I still have viable suspects, loads. Why then Heath's dumb lie about a fight between Gilbert and Theda?"

"Distraction maybe, from Ted?" Stockard held up a finger and took a long sip of coffee. "Looks like Ted has an appraiser in his pocket. I cross-referenced appraisals against assessments, the numbers are wonky. I bet he finagles inflated loans then skims the surplus."

"So, bank fraud?" Georgia asked.

"Loads of cash have vanished down a rat hole and Ted's the rat. One phone call, I can get an investigation started." Stockard raised her eyebrows; the white hairs looked fierce.

"Let me shake things loose before we nail the twit. If backed into a corner, do you think Ted would've killed Theda?"

Stockard shrugged. "He's overextended and staring into the abyss."

"Can I add another name to the list?" Georgia asked.

"Of course."

Without sleep to cushion the caffeine buzz, Georgia's hand shook as she wrote out Roy Burke's name. Over the next half hour Stockard sorted through papers and Georgia's financial vocabulary swelled—*working the gap, shotgunning, appraisal fraud, lien stacking.*

"Marci Heath's name pops up all over the place," Stockard said. "On Abraxas documents, I'd expect that, but other properties are in her name. I'm not sure what to make of them, they appear to be leveraged against one another, stacked like a house of cards, one default and the whole thing collapses."

"Another of Ted's plots? Money motives multiply with this guy."

"Tug on this thread and his schemes might unravel." Stockard passed a printout to Georgia. "I got this from the state's corporate records website, the board members of Brody and Associates." The entry, *Marci Heath—Special Consultant*, was circled in black.

"You just gave me a way to roust the loving couple." Georgia began gathering the papers. "Ted's screwing Heath."

"Ted's a butt-head."

Georgia laughed. "I've been waiting years for my vocabulary to rub off. You advise me on finances, I'll tutor you on the nuances of *ass-wipe*."

*

Just as Dawn had guaranteed, her map was amazingly accurate. The road narrowed, and twice Georgia pulled to the shoulder so larger cars could squeeze by. Damned SUVs. Although high enough to avoid the heat building in the valley, her air conditioner labored. She turned it off and lowered her window.

The wealthy preferred the Heights, but why? Cars overheated in summer and in winter slid into ditches. Around the next curve the solid phalanx of evergreens opened to a panorama, and she pulled to the shoulder. Four snow-capped mountains and the shining ribbon of the Columbia River to the east. Yes, the view. Burke must be pissed that he couldn't plop a golf course up here.

An even narrower lane twisted past ancient maples to a Victorian mansion, gray from decades of weathering. The sweeping driveway circled down to a carriage house. She parked alongside a red Dodge Ram 4x4 pickup that towered over Ted's silver Lexus.

A century earlier this house, with its parapets, gingerbread trim, and widow's walk, must've been the grande dame of the Heights. Even now Georgia felt a stubborn order in the house, its top windows vigilant against encroaching row houses and the travesty of freeway overpasses, able to withstand everything except the ivy. Ivy smothered the front lawn, and roots, gripping the wood like tiny caterpillar legs, shinnied to the roof where new leafage dangled across the windows.

A burly gray-haired man stepped into the sunlight from the mouth of a brick tunnel that must've once been the tradesmen's entrance. Ted followed him, waving first one hand, then both as he yammered away. Dressed in Levis and a plaid shirt, Ted mimicked a lumberjack. No, scrubbed too clean, he looked more like an adman's version of a tall-timber logger. She bet he wore one of those musky animal scents from an organ she didn't want to think about.

Ted rattled on, the man shook his head. Georgia decided to eavesdrop and circled behind the truck through a thicket. Blackberry vines scratched her arms. When one whipped back and snagged her cheek, she almost cried "Ouch."

"You're sure?" Ted asked the man.

"Ted, I can't cut more corners, there aren't any left."

The man hopped into his truck and rumbled past. Georgia stepped back on the driveway. No doubt Ted and Dawn were almost history, but had he figured it out? Before he did, she'd use that knowledge. She stepped towards him; she'd been right about the scent. He preened and began reciting:

> I met a lady in the meads
> Full beautiful, a faery's child;
> Her hair was long, her foot was light,
> And her eyes were wild.

Pure bunk, right up there with *What's your sign?* A trick of intonation, the lilt at the end of lines, showcased his roguish baritone.

"I'm guessing Shelley or Byron," she said.

"Close. Keats."

"No faery child here, lack of sleep explains the wild eyes." She caught herself liking his deep, rumbling laugh. "Couldn't help overhearing, not good news, huh?"

"Renovating this place isn't cheap, but I got it for a song. You create opportunities. Enough shop talk, to what do I owe this honor?"

"Nothing special, clarification, dotting the i's."

"Sure."

He was too confident of his sex appeal. She decided to start with the big question, knock him off balance. "Where were you the morning Theda died?"

"You can't think—"

"Have to ask."

Ted was silent, calculating. "It's been crazy lately, nuts. Days fly by. Was I in town? Out of town? Honestly I don't remember."

"Doesn't your secretary manage your schedule?"

"I wing it, don't always call the office."

"How about Dawn?"

"Like I said, I don't always call."

One more poke. "Computer timestamps, a phone log? You must have a Blackberry. Anything solid you can give me?"

"What's with the third degree? My business is not your business. Theda's death was an accident. Sic the cops on me or get lost."

"Sorry, sorry, I get like a dog on a bone. Let's start over, no shoving, no cutting in line."

Ted took a deep breath. "Okay, okay. Let me show you around, you'll see the potential. The place was built in 1889 by Portland's biggest furrier. He lost it four years later in the Panic of 1893."

A sharp, moldy smell like old bread spiked with ammonia intensified as he led her deeper into the house. The entry opened to a great room with stairs curving to the second floor. Sunlight shone through the drooping ivy, and shadows shivered in the breeze. Coos and shrieks echoed from room to room. It was tough dodging the white piles of bird shit.

"You know, Ted, if you pull this off, you'll be called a visionary." If not, words like fool would describe him.

"Visionary." He relished the word. "It's all about opportunity."

"Suppose so. Is that the reason for the third mortgage? Making the most of opportunity?"

"You're a goddamned snoop. If I didn't like you… It's nothing, a temporary hitch in the cash flow, once the Sauvie sale goes through, I'll be good."

"Why not ask Dawn for help?"

"Daddy has her tied up tight in that pre-nup. The man lacks imagination. Like daughter, like father."

"How about Roy Burke? Both money and imagination."

"Burke? No, thanks. Turn your back on the man and he'll steal your shirt. C'mon, enough about business, let me show you the verandah."

Ted grasped Georgia's elbow and led her toward floor-to-ceiling French doors. He inched closer, she danced away, then he slithered in again. Doing his best raconteur imitation, he extolled the mountains' majesty, waving his arms until one hand dropped onto her shoulder and the other gripped her chin. He dove in for a kiss.

She backed off. "Geez, what is it with you?"

"I find beauty irresistible."

"Always that little head leading the big head. Why not focus more on business and less on getting laid?"

Ted's face struggled between amusement and anger. "Women don't understand."

"Not even Marci Heath?"

Now she'd grabbed his attention.

"Marci wouldn't understand either," he said.

"Dawn doesn't understand, Marci wouldn't understand, I don't understand. Must be time to explain."

"Why should I explain to you?"

"Because it will put me in a better mood. Maybe then I won't spill the beans about you and Heath. Dawn's definitely not a spilt bean picker-upper." With two long strides, Georgia was around him and squared off, her right palm flat against his chest. "Answers. How long has Heath been a special consultant to Brody and Associates?" Stockard would be proud.

"Hold on, we're branching into the nonprofit sector. We need her expertise."

"Hmm. Marci has picked up good-sized chunks of commercial property, but things are stinky." She wrinkled her nose. "With her salary at Abraxas, how does she cover the monthly nut? We're not even talking down payment. And stranger still, those outlandish appraisals. Sounds like a scam to me. Ted, Ted, Ted, there have to be better ways, even legal ways, to open the cash spigot." Who knew mortgages could be such fun?

He slumped onto the steps. "You're nothing but trouble. What do you want?"

"My needs are simple. Who was the other woman, the one who came between you and Theda?"

"We've been over this. My lips are sealed. That's what Theda wanted."

Georgia knew if she were the wronged woman, she'd go for the jugular. What had stopped Theda? "C'mon Ted, 'fess up. Will Heath be wifey number three?"

"Marci? Me?" He smirked. "She might entertain certain fantasies."

"Silly, silly girl, I'm sure that's another thing she wouldn't understand. I'm tired of misunderstandings. Set up a meeting, tell Heath to meet you in the Park Blocks, half an hour. Say you need the papers, and I mean everything."

"Go to hell."

Georgia held up her phone, "How convenient. Dawn's on speed dial."

"What time?"

"Half an hour." Any longer and he might have time to sabotage her plan.

"That's too soon. She might not be able to—"

"Hey, I've felt your magic, you can swing it." In Ted's world this was the equivalent of a double-dog-dare. "Do it and I keep my mouth shut. Otherwise I stop at the grocery and grab tomatoes, doggy treats, a pack of tissues. Dawn and me and Princess Di whiling away the hours, sharing secrets."

"Not a word to Dawn. Promise?"

When he finished the call, Georgia snapped a salute and turned toward her car. She tried stepping over the tendrils of ivy that snaked across the walk, but it was futile. No use being dainty, the stuff was unkillable.

*

Scalded milk and coffee hissed into a paper cup; Georgia paid the street vendor and thanked the universe for caffeine. Hidden among students idling on the patio of the Art Museum, she monitored the Park Blocks from under a massive elm. Even in the shade, sweat beaded on her forehead.

Her anger bounced from Heath bullying Billy back to Theda's death. Georgia sorted through city noises, discovered the quaver of a blues harmonica, and guessed it must be a busker on a nearby corner. The music helped subdue her rage, and out of habit her left hand formed chords along the neck of an imaginary guitar.

Tight black jeans hugged Heath's nonexistent hips. *Rebecca of Sunnybrook Farm Does Dallas*. Too bad the halter-top emphasized her jutting shoulder blades instead of her cleavage. Beneath the attempt at sexy, Georgia sensed the woman's corncob-up-the-butt sobriety. Years ago after a fatal car wreck up ahead of her, Georgia had been trapped in traffic. Images of scattered debris—a frilly gold shawl and half a dozen maps—were still fixed in her memory. She thought of Heath in this same way. Odd bits haunted her, but together totaled anonymity. Who was the real Marci Heath?

Ted's obedient lover clutched a stack of file folders. With luck, Georgia soon would have proof of Ted's financial sleight of hand. Tempted to swoop in, grab and be gone, she stopped herself. Let Heath's anticipation work against her. Georgia tucked Stockard's papers into her waistband and skirted a flowerbed of red salvia and luxuriant cannas then waited in the hot sun behind a bronze statue of Rough Rider Teddy Roosevelt straddling a horse. Heath paced, stopped, sat on a bench in the shade and tapped the folders, precisely aligning their corners. Coffee rings stained the top file.

"I'm baa-ack." Georgia flipped her empty coffee cup into a garbage can and settled at the other end of the park bench. "Mind if I join you?"

"Actually, I do."

"He's not coming."

"What are you talking about?"

"I forced him to arrange this meeting."

Heath hunched and glared.

"Lover boy's left you holding the bag, twisting in the wind, caught red-handed. I bet he's packing, even calling his travel agent. He's not coming."

"Someone like you could never understand. What kind of woman becomes a PI?"

Georgia beckoned Heath closer then whispered, "You're right, it's a sad, sad, tale."

Heath stood up, pressed the files to her bosom and rushed around impatiens glowing orange and red in the shadows.

Georgia followed. "Poor Chickadee. Too bad you can't escape, too bad Teddy Bear's leaving you behind."

"Get away." Heath's pupils dilated, black and glistening. "You left those brochures on my desk, didn't you? Do you enjoy being a smartass?

"It's what brightens my day. At least I don't get my jollies terrorizing people."

"Hah, you can't believe Billy."

"Billy? Did I mention Billy?" She turned to a student walking past. "Did you hear me mention Billy?" The girl looked

137

confused and hurried on.

"What's the big fuss anyway?" Heath asked. "His memory's shot, by now he's forgotten."

Georgia seized Heath's shoulder, felt an electrical satisfaction at the flinch, and imagined her hand reaching for Heath's throat. She hadn't realized she'd enjoy the adrenalin, the possibility of violence, the crackling rush up her arm. Her hand dropped. She'd lost all sense of boundary. Blood pulsed in her face. Revenge is a luxury, cool down. The files, focus on the files.

"I've learned a lot since we last parted. Your description of Theda bailing on Gilbert's bookstore, lies, all lies. Those two never fought about Theda loaning Gilbert money. You made up the whole thing."

"I don't know what you're talking about. Besides you can't prove a thing.

"And Ted's vision of the future, the Schoenfeld estate, right?" Heath flinched at Georgia's sweeping gestures. "One teeny-tiny problem—cash. Which of Ted's pals dummied the appraisals? Think, does Ted's name appear on the mortgages? Between neck nibbles and butt tweaks, did he slip you papers to sign?" Georgia smooched the back of her hand. "Now initial this, my little cabbage leaf."

Heath broke free. She tried to dodge brick steps but tripped, sat hard, and sprawled on the curb; one hand cushioned her back, the other was raised to fend off Georgia. Folders scattered. Georgia, sweating from anger as well as heat, stooped to collect them.

"They're mine. Steal them, I scream." Heath pushed Georgia's shoulders.

Georgia caught her balance. "If I need a court order, BFD, I'll get it. Here, take a look at these." She pulled Stockard's research from her waistband, thrusting papers at Heath. "See, your signature, not Ted's. And here, and here." Page after page littered the grass.

"Ted loves me."

Georgia quaked with frustration. Was the woman in a trance? "How do you think I found you? Two seconds and he gave you up. You're looking at fraud, add accessory to murder and—"

"You think Ted killed—"

"That wife of his blew his alibi. He can't protect you, hell, he can't protect himself."

"You know nothing about him." Her eyes took on an amused shine. "He does nothing, nothing, without checking with me first."

Georgia hesitated. What was she missing?

Heath rolled up a file, slapped it against the step, and walked off.

My God, was that it? Georgia imagined Heath in spiky boots and black leather. It wasn't a giant leap. She'd assumed Ted was using Heath. But what if Heath was in command?

Her phone rang. Out of habit she checked caller ID. Billy.

"Hello? Hello?" His voice buzzed with an urgent edge. "I need you here, now."

"Now?"

"Course now. It's that Heath woman, her car just drove by. That's the third time today."

"Billy, I was just with her, like a minute ago."

"Well, I saw her at lunch, I'm sure of it, and okay you caught me fooling with the time. But the bare bones of the truth is, she was here."

"I'm exhausted, maybe tomorrow—"

"I figured out about the bees."

"Tell me."

"Soon as you show up." He either laughed or coughed, and then hung up.

*

In a few days Billy had aged a decade. Georgia thought of a turkey—beak nose, wattles, and worst of all that vacant stare. A red clip-on tie hung askew from the neck of his blue work shirt.

"Are you going somewhere?" she asked.

"Why would you care?"

"I brought you a gift."

"Suppose then I have to let you in." He pushed the door wide enough for her to squeeze through. "It's dark in here," he said. "All this darkness irritates me."

When he tugged the curtain open, a blast of sunlight sharpened the smell of dog and bayberry. China saucers, at least one to a table, held squat, half-melted candles. A row of tomatoes ripened on the windowsill.

After he settled in the rocker, she flourished a prepaid cell phone in one hand, a bottle of tangerine nail polish in the other. She brushed two buttons bright orange and blew them dry. Twice he followed her directions, hitting the garish buttons in succession and laughing when her cell chirped.

"Hello there, Billy Boy," she answered in her huskiest voice. "Keep that in your pocket, and if anyone bothers you, call me. Now I need to ask a few questions."

"Ask away." Either the gift or playing telephone had made him less ornery.

"On the phone you said you knew something about the bees."

"You sure that was me?"

For now she'd skip the bees. "The Quists, have you been neighbors long?"

"Forever. But the families always fought, oil and water, even my dad couldn't mix with them."

"Why was that?"

"Back then we never had a regular church, and those Quists were natural preachers. Ezekiel would gather up a new flock of ninnies then scare them away with his hellfire." Billy laughed and thumped his cane on the floor like the tail of a pleased dog.

"Didn't he work the farm?"

"That was left to the boys, especially Daniel. Ezekiel, he'd sit on that porch baking in the heat like a lizard, even flick out his tongue. Always hoped he'd nab a fly. Now that's something to pray for. "

"What about Judith?"

"Most people forget her."

"Why?" Judith Quist had not struck her as forgettable.

"She's not much interested in people. An animal gets sick around here, people call Judith before they call the vet. She likes plants, too. But that's about it."

"And Jonathan? How does she feel about him?"

"Him?"

"Jonathan."

"Ah, Jonathan. They're the first Quist and Kovac ever got along."

"Are you saying Judith and Jonathan are close?"

"They could've been, but they missed their time."

"I don't understand."

Billy pointed to the window sill. "See those tomatoes? They're ripening up just fine, but you gotta watch for the right moment, miss it and they go bad. Jonathan and Judith missed it."

"Would Jonathan ever hurt Judith?"

"Not in a billion years, but if someone tried to hurt Judith, I don't know what he'd do."

"On the phone you said something about bees."

"That's right. Someone stole a hive."

"Stole them from where?"

"Me, from me. If you think I'm lying, go check outside by the orchard."

"That's just what I'll do."

When she reached the front door, Billy asked, "Did you bring any of it back?"

"Bring what back?"

"All you left me was candles and sheet music."

"It's me, Georgia, remember?"

"Sing me a song."

"Next time," she said.

"You'll come back?"

"Of course."

"With a song?"

"Yes, with a song."

*

Georgia found stacked white boxes, ten hives— no, nine—in Billy's orchard. One, a broken lid leaning against it, looked empty. No bees, no honeycombs, no nothing. At the base of the next box, a bee crawled through a square hole and waited on the ledge adjusting to sunlight. It zipped past Georgia's shoulder. She winced while another bee took flight.

Georgia smelled the cigarette smoke first, indulged in a deep breath, then turned. Water droplets shimmered on Judith's arms, and her cotton shirt clung to her shoulders and small breasts.

"Why are you snooping around here?" Judith dabbed her face with a towel.

"Billy asked me to check on something. You?"

"Skinny-dipping in our pond. The one pleasure I had growing up here." Judith blew a stream of smoke out the side of her mouth. Did she think it made her look tough or was she trying to be polite? "I see you're still chasing your murder-by-bees theory. Come on, I'll show you the equipment."

Georgia followed her through a meadow riotous with wild coreopsis and bachelor buttons to a shed hidden behind the barn.

"I'm doing this to show you I have nothing to hide," Judith said. "If you have questions, ask me directly, don't sneak around."

"Are you accusing me of something?"

"That's right, Lulu."

"So your neighbor tossed me to the wolves?"

Judith ignored the question and propped the shed's door open. She explained the smoker, the curved metal hive tools, and the hand-cranked honey extractor. Three sets of coveralls hung from pegs, but only two bee veils. Where was the third?

"Despite what you think, bees are harmless," Judith said.

"Yeah, Theda's death confirms that. Were the two of you ever close?"

"I wasn't completely vaccinated against Theda's charm. The annoying part—and of course there's an annoying part—was how she assumed the attention she got was hers by right because, after all, she was Theda."

"I don't understand."

"Billy's land. Jonathan is Billy's heir. But when Theda latched onto this cause—the land trust—she overwhelmed everyone. Jonathan no longer had rights."

"Did Jonathan tell her how he felt?"

Judith ignored the question, and Georgia repeated it.

"He's passive," Judith said, "and doesn't always stand up for himself."

Shy enough to rummage through your garbage.

Judith knelt and stubbed out her cigarette. "This has been stimulating, but I need to get home and change."

Judith cut through the field; her hair, still damp and slicked-back, gleamed like patent leather. On a whim, Georgia picked up the cigarette butt. Her exchange with Judith had been breezy, but the cigarette didn't reflect this mood. The brown filter had been pinched flat.

*

Georgia unlocked the file cabinet and wrestled out the metal box. Amazing that the intruder had left this untouched. She laid her Glock on the desk. Surrounded by obscene destruction, she let loose a frenzy of cleaning, sorting, and scouring. The neck of her guitar, broken strings twisted around it, protruded from a garbage bag. She wandered through the apartment with a camera. Though she needed the photos for insurance purposes, each one fed her passion for payback. After an hour of cleaning, Georgia collapsed on the bed fully dressed and fell asleep on top of the bedcovers.

Wind gusting against the window woke her. The air, acrid and electric, warned of another August storm, but instead of rolling over to look out the window, she unfastened the top button of her jeans and dozed.

Burke's voice blustered through layers of exhaustion. "Come back tomorrow. We'll definitely have something to talk about."

She told herself, remember, it's important, and drifted into a sleep without images.

15

Gilbert Kovac

The crowd drifted from booth to booth trying on leather masks, listening to Bolivian panpipes, buying corndogs, beaded necklaces, and pottery. Placards proclaiming "10th Annual Book Faire" hung limp in the heat. A downtown Portland block had been cordoned off, and under a giant tent booksellers and Northwest publishers displayed row after row of new titles and used first editions.

Most people wore shorts. Even Gilbert shucked off his suit coat and loosened his tie while arranging books. Despite bony knees and chubby calves, Theda would've worn shorts on a morning like this. Every summer the sun baked her one color, red, skipping all the honey tones that Gilbert saw on the people passing.

Today would've been their forty-second birthday. They usually celebrated with Billy, but for the last few years, Theda had pitched in and helped Gilbert during Book Faire. She'd pile books on the table, he'd sort and arrange. A woman in a pink sundress placed her lemonade on the table and leafed through a copy of *Winterkill*. Gilbert touched the moist ring left by her cup and dabbed his temple with the cool drops.

He turned to the bookseller beside him. "Could you watch my table for a minute? I'm thirsty."

"Sure. Take your time."

He stepped from the shade of the tent to the sidewalk, where the sun struck a metallic sheen off the buildings. For hours the pavement had soaked up heat, and warm air gushed up his trouser legs. A man in a tie-dye T-shirt tromped on Gilbert's foot, mumbled an apology, then melted into the crowd. The wince of pain felt more real than anything on the street—more than the children with painted faces, the homeless man in a long black coat, the packs of teenagers, the musician with an accordion strapped to his belly. Caught in the flow of people, Gilbert ambled toward the food booths.

Lemonade would slake his thirst, and he found the right line. In the next booth, an Asian man fried meat for tacos. Heat shimmered off the grill, and the man's face rippled like a reflection in water. Gilbert paid for his lemonade then stepped to the side and gulped greedily, his head thrown back, ice cubes bumping his upper lip. Sticky liquid dribbled onto his hands, and it seemed imperative that he wash up. He decided to cut across Pioneer Square and use a restroom in Macy's. At the corner of Broadway and Yamhill, a teenage girl in an orange vest held up a stop sign. The crowd pressed at Gilbert's back.

Forty yards away, up past Tenth, the Max light-rail train curved onto Yamhill. The silent white cars rolled down the tracks. He felt a hand on his back. Thirty yards. He scowled. *Don't be pushy.*

Someone shoved.

Twenty yards.

Gilbert wanted to scream, but decorum pressed over his mouth like a gag. Another shove. Someone swiped away his glasses, and he tumbled toward the tracks.

Ten yards.

At the same moment the breeze from the train tousled his hair. He felt himself yanked back. A hazy mass of people surged around him.

His glasses were gone.

He cupped his hand over his left ear to hide the scar and knelt by the tracks, wiping away tears and blinking to clear his vision. Oh God, let them be safe. Sunlight blazed off the rails into diamond points, and splinters jabbed his fingertips. A broken bottle, please be a broken bottle. He fingered a fragment of silicone, the texture familiar as skin.

The crossing guard squatted beside him. "You all right?"

Gilbert's breath came ragged. "I think so. Are you the one who, who—"

"You stumbled, and I thought, jeez, what a god-awful mess. Just imagine. But then like I grabbed your shirt."

"I was shoved."

"All I saw was you falling and the train—"

"My glasses."

The guard helped Gilbert stand. "No glasses here. You hurt?"

"Nothing serious." He knew she gawked at his hand cupped over his damaged ear. If only she'd leave. If only he could say he'd twisted his ankle, a dignified injury. "I'm fine."

"If you're hurt and in all this heat—"

He dropped his hand.

Seconds passed before she spoke. "No blood," was all she came up with.

Gilbert wandered away from her in a widening circle. More people, heat, the stench of frying food; he shambled into Pioneer Square. The lightness in his head expanded and his eyes watered. Mistaking his lurches for drunkenness, and not hiding their contempt, people cleared a path for him. He wanted to explain his condition, but knew his words sounded silly, even crazy.

Crowd noises receded into the drone of insects. After Jonathan's crazy dog chewed off his ear, all sounds had garbled together. Oh, God, was it happening again?

Gilbert stumbled from group to group, straining to tighten the trill of voices into words.

16

Georgia pulled to the curb. Elbows on his knees and head in hands, Gilbert sat inside a kiosk like a man with a headache, tired, waiting for a bus to take him home. She honked twice. He didn't look up, and she rolled down her window. "Gilbert? Gilbert! It's me."

He sagged into Georgia's car. On the phone he'd insisted she stop by his house for spare glasses. He adjusted this new pair and gazed out the window, and then turned sharply back to her.

"I don't remember telling you where I keep my spare glasses. How did you know?"

"That's a trade secret. Magicians aren't the only ones who use smoke and mirrors." Her absurd explanation seemed to satisfy him. "Tell me everything."

He described the hands on his back and then the push.

"I don't want you to be alone. You can spend the rest of the day at Stockard's. Sit in the sun, relax, whatever.

"The booth, I have to—"

"Let me handle that."

"Tomorrow morning I have plans, for, for Theda's—"

"Theda's what?"

"Her ashes."

"Anything you do, anywhere you go, first run it by me, promise?"

"Promise."

"I'm not sure when I'll pick you up. I need to track a few things and then head home and pack."

"Pack?"

"I'm staying at your house, sleeping on the couch."

"For how long?"

"Tonight. No, longer. Until it's safe."

*

Two trains flew by before the crossing guard returned, prattling in full-nasal valley girl and gnawing on a wad of gum. Georgia shoved aside her irritation and pictured a halo bobbing over the girl's bleached locks. After introductions, Georgia flashed her license. "My client fell onto the tracks. I want to thank you for saving him."

"No need, like I'm so, so glad. OMG, can you imagine?" While she talked, her waxy-glossed lips pursed as if coaxing out smoke rings. "Is he better? He was so totally upset about losing his glasses and tried to cover up his, well, you know, whatever that is where his ear should be."

"Someone pushed him, he felt hands on his back."

"How awesome. I mean, you know, awesome in a bad way." Her gum smacked like an exclamation point.

"Can you describe any of the people around him?"

"I saw a homeless man in a fedora, I know that kind of hat 'cuz I just bought a little straw one, lime green. I mean mine's lime green, not the man's. And some teenage girls, I remember thinking they coulda been me last summer. And then I think a skinny woman in sunglasses."

"The woman, describe her. Any detail helps."

"Downtown type. Old, like in her thirties. Straight brown hair and maybe sunglasses, yeah, for sure, sunglasses. But like I couldn't swear to it."

Georgia gave the girl her card. "Please, if you remember the tiniest thing, call me."

"And my friends think this is such a dumb-ass job."

*

Turtle pressed close and sniffed; his wet nose tickled Georgia's ankle. Last night falling asleep, an answer had come to her. Damn, what was it? Be patient. It'll rattle loose. Turtle jumped up and curled into the butt-dent of her garage sale couch. They'd become an old married couple with their own side of the sofa. Instead of brushing off some husband's cracker crumbs, she picked at stray dog hairs.

Georgia sipped iced tea and worked the phone, checking alibis. She told Brody's secretary that Ted had been a no-show for an appointment. The woman said he was unavailable today. Was he dodging her? Dodging Heath? For the call to Abraxas, Georgia pinched her nose and snuffled to mimic a cold. An unfamiliar voice said Heath would be out of the office all day. Maybe she was rendezvousing with Ted. After the fifth ring, Sauvie Island School picked up. "Jonathan Kovac is out with a cold." Georgia hung up. This unexpected epidemic of imaginary summer colds was a pure bitch.

Georgia sorted through the pictures she'd taken at Blue Heron Nursery. Yes, there it was, the work schedule posted in the break room. She blew it up. Judith Quist wasn't scheduled for work today or tomorrow. She saved Dawn's yakkity-yak for last. No answer. Georgia tried twice more. What she had least expected was happening: Dawn was avoiding her.

Georgia's thoughts skittered back to last night. What did she need to remember? She reread the list of suspects pinned to the corkboard.

The couple next door was squabbling again, and she shut the window. Her gaze stopped at Gilbert's green box. The simplicity of it struck her. In less than twenty-four hours, why had the assault against Gilbert escalated from a cruel joke to attempted murder? Something had changed. What? Answering that question took on new urgency.

A cigarette. Convinced nicotine would kick-start her brain, she dragged a chair into the kitchen, and from the top cupboard dug out her emergency stash: a hand-rolled cigarette, matches, and a tuna fish can crimped into an ashtray. The can banged to the floor.

Burke had told her, "Now listen, little lady, you come back tomorrow, and we'll definitely have something to talk about."

*

Georgia stood in the entry of Burke's office sipping coffee. Teresa Brambly ignored her. The office hadn't changed much, just more piles of paper and less courtesy. When Brambly acknowledged her, they glowered at one another, a High Noon showdown.

"You're not welcome here."

"I have to talk with Burke."

"Not going to happen." Brambly flipped her desk calendar closed.

Georgia could almost hear the ching-ching, ching-ching of spurs as she crossed the room. She set her coffee on the desk and leaned in, a hand on each side of the nameplate. Georgia's thumb and forefinger circled the base of her coffee cup.

"Burke's in danger."

"Well, Miss Reporter-Girl, I checked with *Willamette Week*, and they've never heard of you. You can leave now." The woman crossed her arms over the calendar.

"Listen, I apologize for any trouble, but this I time I'm not kidding."

"Sure, and I'm queen of the tooth fairies. Mr. Burke has more important things to do. Cry wolf somewhere else."

Brambly stood; her nose came even with Georgia's chin. She picked up the phone. "I want to see your backside going through that door, or do I dial security?" She thumped the receiver against her palm like a club.

Georgia clenched her hand into a fist, tightening until the lid popped off her coffee cup. A torrent of mocha erupted and splashed Brambly's sweater; the papers spread across the desk freckled with brown splatter.

"You klutzy bitch." Brambly jumped back swiping at the coffee trickling down her bosom then disappeared through a door.

Georgia dashed around the desk, opened the calendar, and slid her finger down the pages until she found today's entry: Zoning Hearing, 501 SE Hawthorne, Room 100, 1 PM. Clearly Burke expected to get the variances he needed.

"I told you to leave." Daubing her skirt with paper towels, Brambly raced to her desk and slammed the calendar closed.

"Sorry, like to help," Georgia said, "but I'm out the door."

*

A pair of motorcycles blocked the downtown approach to the Hawthorne Bridge, and helmeted policemen in jackboots waved traffic south along First Avenue. Georgia slowed and asked what was up. One cop mumbled, "Bomb. Keep moving."

Two lefts and she headed north. A white excursion boat nosed past the Morrison Bridge, and the center spans had almost dropped back into place. Waiting for traffic to move, she tuned the radio to the AM band and punched the scan button. Station to station it cycled through hip-hop, Nashville twang, and shock jocks without hitting one news bulletin. The gates on the bridge bumped upright and the light changed. Traffic surged forward and uncoiled across the bridge.

A white hatchback crested the top of the bridge. Georgia goosed her Corolla and leapfrogged from opening to opening until she was nearly on the hatchback's bumper. At the red light she jolted to a stop next to her quarry. A startled white-haired man, dapper in his big red bow tie, shot her a cautious smile and tapped an imaginary cap. A green pine tree car freshener hung from the rearview mirror.

Parked catawampus, police cruisers blocked the streets, a riot of light bars strobing red and blue. Restrained by barricades, crowds of onlookers piled into the intersections, and traffic trickled down Seventh. Georgia ignored horns honking behind her, waited for a parking spot to open, and swerved into a space next to Hollywood Costumers. A clown mannequin laughed at her. Impatience and immaturity kicked in, and she flipped him off.

"Hey," Georgia said. A young black patrolman turned toward her and pushed himself off the fender of his car. "What's going on?"

"A bomb threat, the county building." He waved in the vague direction of Hawthorne.

"Oh, my god," Georgia said. "I was supposed to meet my baby brother there. It's his first job, he's saving up for college. Please, what's going on?"

"Don't worry. They're out, everybody's safe. The bomb squad's doing a sweep. Ma'am, what room did your brother work in?"

"One hundred." Wow, there's a creative answer. "Ma'am" had knocked her off balance.

His eyes turned up, and she imagined him thumbing through his memory of the building layout. "On that side they would exit south, try the Burger King parking lot on Clay."

"Thanks a million." She trotted down the block.

Knots of people milled back and forth, smokers huddled in clumps, while others laughed and joked about extra break time. Georgia checked off faces. No Marci Heath; no Ted Brody. She spotted the Burger King. Just beyond she saw Burke's silver Lincoln Town Car. The driver held the back door, but Burke, his hands slashing in quick chops, hung back from entering the car.

When she broke from the crowd, Georgia recognized the baggy sports coat. Jonathan Kovac's slacks looked new but too tight over his hips, and one pocket winged out to show white lining. She ducked behind dawdling onlookers. Burke continued the emphatic gestures. Jonathan nodded. From Burke's demeanor, she'd guess they were adversaries, but then

Jonathan laughed. Oops. Co-conspirators.

A fire truck backed into Georgia's sightline, and by the time it moved on, so had Burke and Jonathan.

17

Dawn flipped the dishtowel over her shoulder and grabbed a whiskbroom, dustpan, and hammer. Through the kitchen window she watched Ted shoveling gunk around his precious roses—mulching or composting or fertilizing, one of those smelly garden chores.

Tonight was the night.

She slunk out the front door. Half an hour before dark and the streetlights had blinked on. Dawn stood at the end of the driveway, peering up and down the street. The coast was clear. *If you're going to do it, do it now.* She covered the car's left taillight with her dishtowel, drew back the hammer, and whacked. Bulls-eye. The largest plastic fragments dropped into the towel, and she swept everything else into the dustpan.

Ted already had his excuse, a business meeting tonight at eight-thirty, and that meant he'd leave soon. Should she change clothes? Her dress was almost new, but this morning she'd punched a new notch in the belt to cinch it tighter. Ten pounds gone—she was teetering on svelte, but Ted never noticed. Why bother? Besides, the blue-gray in this dress matched her new purse.

She heard Ted trundling his squeaky wheelbarrow to the shed. He'd be four, maybe five more minutes. Might as well try what her detective novels called a dry run. She darted to the closet, grabbed her paraphernalia, and opened the front door. Best time yet. Her breath escaped in short huffs. Ted came through the back door. Would he notice?

Hoopdee-doodle, he wouldn't notice if her nose spewed nickels.

When he stepped out of the bedroom, he was wearing his

new shirt, just as she'd predicted, a beige mixture of silk and linen. Were the pants new? One shade lighter than his shirt, the crease made his legs look longer.

He leaned over to kiss her. "Don't wait up." His cheek brushed hers, and musky cologne made her grip the chair arm.

"Drive careful," she said. "Feels like rain."

The second he pulled out of the driveway, she swung open the closet door and grabbed her purse, sweater, and umbrella. The brown Ford she'd rented was parked two houses down; she'd picked it, instead of the prettier gold Chevrolet, for its anonymity. By the time she hit the ignition, Ted's car had vanished, but she gunned the engine and sped to the corner. Three blocks to her left she spotted his missing taillight.

The weatherman had been right. Rain drops grew fatter, fell closer together, and pummeled the roof. A truck passed, and water thrown from its wheels ghosted across her windshield.

Where was Ted? He must've turned off. No, there he was, bipping along in the other lane. Rain, the kind she expected only at the ocean, lashed the car. Dawn flicked the wipers to high. Sh-tick, sh-tick. Her vision drew back from the road, and she concentrated on the hypnotic swipe. She surprised herself, pressed the gas pedal, lifted her hands from the steering wheel, and waited to crash. The car swerved, and she braked.

Nope, she wanted Ted to crash.

He drove past a gas station before turning into the parking lot of a flimsy motel that advertised hourly rates. No champagne room service here. She checked the mileage. Halfway between home and office, he could have the tires on his car checked while he got lubed.

She switched off the ignition but left the wipers on. Ted ducked across the parking lot and knocked on a door. With her sweater sleeve balled over her knuckle, she rubbed a peephole in the window's condensation then leaned forward, but she couldn't see who greeted him.

Five minutes. Ten minutes. It was time.

When she opened the car door, rain pelted the side of her face. She aimed the umbrella out the door and slid back the spokes. The metal base pinched her trigger finger, leaving a point of blood. Ted, the big baby, would've swooned.

She flung the umbrella over the car seat. With her purse snugged under her arm, she marched at a middling pace across the parking lot and knocked a friendly tap at number 16. Water surged through a broken gutter. She knocked again then pressed her ear to the door.

"Who is it?" Ted's voice, juicy as a plum.

She tapped a third time, louder. The door cracked open.

"In, I want in."

"Dawn, what are you—"

"In."

"This isn't the time."

She loosened the Velcro side pocket of her purse and, with what she hoped was a dramatic flourish, whisked out the gun. "It's time, Ted, believe you me, it's time." She smiled to show how little trouble she'd be and stepped inside.

Her face was dappled with rain. A stubborn drop clung to the tip of her nose, and with the back of her left hand she brushed it away. Marci Heath leaned against the headboard, her smile big and juicy like Ted's voice.

What was that woman doing here? A beanpole and not a bit pretty. Dawn expected better. Once more Ted had let her down.

When Heath yawned, her skirt hiked up her thighs. This immodesty seemed significant, the difference between wives and mistresses. If that was me, I'd tug my skirt over my knees. Now what? She'd thought everything through—buying the gun, following Ted, facing off with his lover—played it all in her mind, but had never gone beyond this point.

Shoot? Don't shoot? It seemed a point of etiquette, bad form not to.

Dawn shut her eyes and squeezed the trigger. Pow! The knob

157

on the headboard exploded. Even she was impressed.

"Jesus, Dawn, have you lost your marbles?"

"No, but you might." She lowered the muzzle and aimed at Ted's crotch.

Marci laughed, and in a sly gesture, pulled her skirt to an appropriate length.

She decided to spare Marci Heath. Her sweater sleeve fell over her arm, and taking aim, she shoved it above her elbow. Then a sign appeared that she interpreted as a message from God. A pee stain spread across Ted's pants and settled into the shape of Argentina.

Shooting him now would be redundant.

Outside, metal clanged against metal. Georgia grabbed the baseball bat and tore out the kitchen door. Nothing. She flicked on the porch light. Was she being paranoid? Stacked boxes crammed with broken scraps of her life said no. Tomorrow she'd call a locksmith and beef up security. She chucked toiletries, underwear and jeans into a grocery bag. Tonight, after picking up Gilbert, she'd stay as his house guest.

A flurry of knocks at the door startled her. Turtle's growl rumbled into a full-from-the-chest bark that left her mama-proud. She peered through the peephole, and the form untangled from the shadows.

She worked the porch light switch, on-off, on-off. Darkness. A can of pepper spray in her hand, she eased the door open. Daniel Quist? On tiptoe she tapped the bulb into flickers then tightened it. When a steady light blazed on, the figure morphed into someone taller, thinner. Luke, not Daniel. Where was his neck brace? Why was he here? Was he checking to see if the train had hit Gilbert? She anticipated someone might contact her, but hadn't expected him.

"Out of gas?" she asked.

"Had to come into town. Thought I'd stop by, you know, a whim."

The clamor she'd heard earlier, had Luke tripped while peeking through a window? Maybe, maybe not, but she'd bet the ranch he loosened the light bulb. She stepped onto the porch and snapped the door closed so Turtle couldn't erupt with a Lassie leap to the jugular. Luke shifted. The light must bother him. She advanced; he retreated.

"I'm going to be straight with you," he said.

"Yeah, sure."

"I get back from Eugene and find you messing with everybody, bugging Judith at work, and Jonathan too. Then Gilbert tells me my tuition money is your decision."

"Whatever he says."

"So what's the deal?" Luke asked. "I barely have enough pennies to cover books."

"Your athletic scholarship, that's your only income?"

"Sad but true."

"What happened to your academic scholarship?"

"How'd you—"

"Fair warning, your numbers better be spot-ass on, or you get nada, zip. Comprendes?"

"The other scholarship, it slipped my mind."

"Hey, these are confusing times, your body's changing, hormones buzzing. Glad to see you shaved off that wimpy mustache. Trust me, practice and you'll become a whiz with the razor."

He touched the nick of dried blood that flecked his upper lip. "I need a yes or a no, will Mr. Kovac help with my tuition?"

His formality and the even tone rankled her. No doubt he'd been captain of his high school debate team and student body president for sure, accomplishments that would twinkle on any transcript. And now, she bet, pre-law. Georgia's political aspirations had peaked as fourth-grade bathroom monitor.

She cleared her throat. "First and foremost, keep your dirty mitts off my light bulbs. Tampering with said item will result in immediate termination of all fiscal responsibilities by said client, Gilbert Kovac."

"I get it, I get it. But is he going to honor Theda's wishes?" His hand clenched and uncurled.

"Patience, patience."

Turtle pawed the door. Georgia eased it open and snagged his collar. "There's a lesson here, Turtle, see what being pissed gets you?" If she pushed, would Luke push back? Could he muster the violence necessary to shove Gilbert?

"Are you going to help me?"

"A word of sisterly advice, don't play suck-up and intimidator at the same time. They cancel each other out."

"You haven't the right."

"I'm Gilbert's protector. If he wants to, of course, he'll honor his sister's wishes. Expect a call tomorrow."

"I don't know what to say." He relaxed into the arrogant sneer, the same smirk she'd wanted to slap away when he teased his brother.

"Say 'Have a pleasant evening' to the nice Ms Lamb and then get the fuck off my porch."

"Thank you, thank you." Luke backed away and disappeared toward the street.

Turtle cut loose with a good-riddance growl. Affection swelled through Georgia, and she scratched up from his chest to his neck, settling on the space between his ears. Yes, he had a fine bark, fine as any dog. Did they sell doggy brag books like those baby books parents buy? A place to list all his firsts—first bath, first bark, first mounting of a guest's leg—she'd center it on her coffee table and write little narratives under photos: *Today Turtle amused himself by licking...* He muscled against her shoulder and she buried her nose in all his smells, the mix evoking seasonal memories: sun-soaked grass, autumn leaves, mittens stiff with snow crystals.

Exhausted and grimy, she'd earned a whole fifteen-minute shower. While the water ran she undressed, and her mirrored reflection faded in a flush of steam. Hot water battered her, thrashing the shower curtain as she soaped and rinsed. A balled-up spider that had survived the torrent stretched its legs and scuttled away from the drain. Let it live.

*

Plunk, plunk. The doorbell sounded like a dead piano key. Stockard opened up and asked, "How are you doing?"

Georgia mouthed, "Where's Gilbert?"

"Follow me. Dozing in front of the TV."

"This detecting," Georgia said, "it's like grabbing Jell-O. One minute, aha, here's a clue. I squeeze then, yuck, goo oozes between my fingers. Before yesterday each incident was meticulously thought out. I hate to say it, but there was a kind of elegance and sophistication. But something has changed. Pushing Gilbert in broad daylight has a risky and chaotic bravado that terrifies me. Right after I phoned you about the bomb, I saw Burke and Jonathan with their heads together."

"What an odd alliance?"

"That's what I thought, and I'm not sure what to make of it."

"Did you see anyone else?"

"I looked, but no. The bomb threat could've been called in from a prepaid cell phone, untraceable. I think timing's more important than place, but that's all based on airy theory, not proof."

"I followed up on your questions," Stockard said. "A friend at the county checked, and all meetings will be rescheduled, but she had no specific dates. I called Northwest Metals, said I was Roy Burke's assistant and needed clarification."

"Clever girl."

"My guess is they'd prefer to consolidate the existing dump with Billy's property, cheaper and more efficient. Ted's proposal is still the first choice. But I sensed impatience."

"How's Gilbert doing?"

"He worries me. All afternoon he confided delicate information, no, not just personal items, but downright intimate secrets. He told me how Theda regretted never having children. The Gilbert I know totes around a heavy brick of respectability and would never reveal such details."

Georgia imagined him chattering about private tidbits.

Nope, couldn't do it. If she tucked her skirt into her panties, pasted toilet paper to her foot, and stuck spinach between her teeth, Gilbert would pretend not to notice.

Stockard shook Gilbert's shoulder to wake him. He sat up yawning, his mouth agape, then stretched. On the way to the front door he checked his reflection in the entry mirror. A shock of hair stood up like a rooster tail, but he ignored it. As Georgia followed him to the car, the prosthetic ear on the stem of his glasses slipped a quarter inch. He ignored it. He had always sensed the tiniest shift of his fake ear, and this, even more than the personal revelations, alarmed her.

Quiet on the drive home, Gilbert waited until they entered his house to explain the alarm system. Dark clouds silhouetted the gingerbread woodwork along the eaves as Georgia made a full circuit of the yard. Most people wired spotlights to their homes, but Gilbert preferred short poles with soft lights that flared and vanished like pixies in a Disney film. Inside the front door, she found the control unit and reset the alarms.

The house lacked an elephant foot umbrella stand and potted aspidistra, but wingback chairs facing the marble fireplace seemed so very, very British. The only rooms used on the first floor were bathroom, study, bedroom, and kitchen. In other rooms the furniture, outfitted with dust covers, seemed to await their true owner's return. The upstairs was dark, vacant. Why had Gilbert opted for a downstairs bedroom, a monk's cell with an iron bed? Had it been his room as a child, or were those other rooms too full of family ghosts? He mumbled a goodnight before he deserted her for bed. Georgia watched him leave the room, certain that he'd align his glasses. When he turned down the hall, his ears were uneven.

Georgia checked the windows. Gilbert used wooden dowels vertically between window and frame to double security. After throwing the deadbolt on the back door, she activated interior motion detectors, leaving herself a clear path to the loo. She settled for a wing-backed chair instead of the stubby settee. The flashlight looked meek next to her Glock. She covered the gun with a doily that had adorned the brocade love seat. Martha Stewart would approve. Now, the vigil. Hooking her heel around an ottoman, she drew it closer.

Jonathan Kovac

Three in the morning and still no sleep.

Jonathan walked outside, sat on the back steps, and tried to clear his head by identifying the childhood constellations he and Judith had invented. God, he needed sleep. Even as a child he'd roamed at night. Most times his father didn't catch him, but if he did, he gave Jonathan what he called "a good walloping" with the leather strop he used for sharpening knives.

While Jonathan drove, he tried to believe his route along the back roads was random. Pure bullshit. He parked in his usual spot behind her dumpster. He couldn't see the river but still felt its dark flow. Passion had driven him to things he'd never imagined. Before he ducked behind a hedge, Jonathan filled his pocket with gravel from the parking lot. He lifted onto the balls of his feet and tossed pebbles at Judith's bedroom window. The blinds in the houseboat next to hers shot up. Shivery light from a TV blued her neighbor's face. Jonathan waited until the blinds lowered then tossed more gravel, underhand and precisely aimed. If Judith's nosy neighbor appeared again, he'd leave. But instead her porch light blinked on, and Judith stepped outside. Under the yellow light her black hair shimmered.

Nothing in the stretch of his life had foreshadowed such devotion. Each time he came here, he told himself never again, this game's too risky. But Judith's hold, fine yet sticky, was like the trail of a cobweb that tickles your face and can't be brushed away.

Something clicked. A door closing? A twig snapping? In the night air, the noise sounded concise. Judith turned, alert, and stood frozen as if she'd forgotten to breathe. Jonathan had only seen such stillness in animals that hunt at night.

The screeching alarm woke Georgia. Shit, caught napping.

She snatched the gun and flashlight then dropped to the floor. A quick slither to the hall. The alarm stabbed her ears and the motion detector's red light blinked vigilance. She poked the flashlight's strobe button twice and let the after-image burn into her retina. No shadows flitted down the hall.

At the front door she fingered the control keypad to cut off the alarm. Her heartbeat slowed and she noticed a steady light on the panel, a downstairs window was open. She ran through each circuit. No motion inside or out, the alarm must've frightened the intruder. Or could the intruder still be inside? As she went from room to room, she flicked on lights.

She peeked into Gilbert's room. On top of bedcovers, he slept fully dressed, snoring. His damaged ear rested against the pillow. Did he always sleep that way, or was he hiding the scar from her? And why hadn't he heard the alarm? A water glass and pill bottle stood on the night stand beside his false ear; she checked the bottle: sleeping pills.

Gun in her right hand, flashlight in her left, she slid back-to-the-wall down the hall to the staircase, shining her light into the corners. Curtains billowed into the room. Her hand felt for the wooden dowel before her mind registered: gone. Someone had smashed the window.

When she stepped back to search for the dowel, a shard of glass sliced her heel, and she giant-stepped over other fragments to safety. Under her sweatshirt, she poked her finger through a rip in her T-top, tore off a length, tied it around the bloody wound then hobbled down the hall. Her foot rolled over the loose dowel, her legs doing a crazy scissor kick before she found her balance. Someone had broken the window and set off the alarm, yet took the time to throw the dowel back into the room. Why?

In the deep shadows of the living room, every dust cover became a hiding place. She heard a creaking, stopped, and then heard another. Just floorboards, the arthritic sigh of an old house settling. Boldly, because she needed something to do, she jabbed each covered object with the weighted flashlight.

At last she sat on the lip of the bathtub, tweezered the barb of glass from her foot, and flushed away blood. Finding disinfectant but no Band-Aids, she ripped another strip of cotton from her shirt.

*

A lattice of shadow and morning light ribbed the floor of the living room. Georgia's head throbbed, but it was time to get up. When her feet swung off the ottoman and hit the floor a spike of pain from her slashed heel charged up her leg.

Quiet, she let the coffee perk. Gilbert must have plywood somewhere, or at least enough scrap wood to board up the broken window. On the way to the garage she stopped short in the entry. A white envelope extended like a flat tongue from the mail slot. *This Birthday Can't Be Missed* was written in bold letters across the front of the envelope. Gilbert's birthday? Theda's? Maybe Billy's?

"Is that for me?" Gilbert stood in the foyer, his hand extended. He ripped the envelope open and slipped out a card. A yelp and he dropped everything.

Georgia retrieved the card from the floor. A single red rose was embossed on a black background, but where the whorl began at the center of the blossom, someone had glued a dead bee.

Time to find a hide-out.

*

Room 17 was dowdy and dark, but Gilbert didn't seem to notice. The motel curtains gapped open, revealing a slender triangle of gray sky. Georgia had filled the boxy half refrigerator with milk, lunchmeat, eggs, bread, a packet of fresh-ground coffee, and a bottle of wine—all pilfered from Gilbert's kitchen.

He sat on the bed holding the birthday card. His face had changed, the tension lines around his mouth had deepened. A headache gathered between Georgia's eyes. She peeled plastic from a motel glass and filled it at the tap.

"Let me see that again." Georgia, careful not to touch the bands of yellow and black that bristled across the bee's abdomen, tucked the card into a plastic sleeve. "I will find out who sent this."

"When I hired you," he said, "you told me to be honest."

"And after a few false starts, you have been."

"You think the card upset me because of Theda's death, don't you?"

She nodded. His listless voice alarmed her, gone was the assertive Gilbert.

"Name one person with a grudge against me." He waited. "You can't, can you? Not because I'm wonderful, I'm not. Love, hate, revenge, I don't excite those passions. You never asked me about enemies, because I'm me. That's why, isn't it?"

She spoke as if guiding him through a narrow passage. "Gilbert, I'm sure—"

"It's not me they want dead, it's your investigation. This card, the push, the broken window has made it all too real." His eyes were shiny with tears. She recognized the expression, expectant and trusting.

She wouldn't argue with him, but she could think of one good reason why someone would want him dead. If he was gone, Billy would inherit everything, and Billy could be managed.

The clouds must've burned off; a shaft of sunlight invaded the room.

She wanted to tell him, "We can't quit." Theda had always made the decisions, and now he sat on the bed expecting Georgia to do the same. She pressed her headache against a cool glass of water. The calm in her voice surprised her. "You decide if we continue."

She stepped outside to the stairwell. After the door shut, Gilbert let loose a keening wail. Her first instinct was to return and comfort him. No, let him work it out. Though she couldn't see the freeway, she heard cars streaming by. The chunk, chunk of the ice machine startled her, and a man walked past carrying an ice bucket. "Howdy." His open robe exposed a beer belly and red bikini briefs.

Her cell rang and she picked up to Dawn. "I checked Ted's tax records, poor dope keeps his Visa receipts for, it must be years. He rents a space downtown, gotta be a love nest." She recited an address. Georgia repeated the location to seal it in her memory. Dawn didn't sound so Dawn-like. No dithering or slipping into tangents.

Georgia scrolled her call list and found a new text message. Marci Heath wanted to meet. Had she realized she'd better save her ass? Red bikini briefs, Gilbert falling apart, a rational Dawn, and now a showdown with Heath: it promised to be a great day.

When she returned to the room, Gilbert's sorrow had eased into uneven shudders. On the bed next to the card was a box wrapped in glossy white paper. "What's that?" she asked?"

"Theda."

"Theda?"

"Her ashes."

"We might be able to squeeze in enough time—"

"No, not you. Just me." His eyes still glistened with tears, but they didn't spill over.

In case they did, she looked down and fiddled with the motel key. "I don't want you skipping out. You have to promise."

He smoothed his hair without mussing the part. "Every time I see this box, I feel guilty. Like she, she's trapped."

"You can't go traipsing around on your own, not now. Too dangerous. Just remember that ashes don't come with an expiration date." This sounded glib, even cruel, but she was tired of tip-toeing. To change the subject she described Luke's surprise visit. While he listened, Gilbert traced the folded paper corners on the box with his thumb.

When Georgia finished, he retrieved a card from his wallet, and said, "Theda was grateful for Luke's rescue. She would have wanted to help. I'll call the bank now and set up a tuition fund."

He sat on one side of the bed talking into the phone, and she sat on the other side categorizing the threats to Gilbert. Column one: Turtle in the bookstore, rubber ears left on the porch, and now the birthday card—all creepy but not dangerous. Column two: bees at Theda's and a push onto the tracks—one deadly, the other meant to be. She imagined the killer ripping petals from a daisy and chanting, "I kill him, I kill him not, I kill him…"

*

Before this morning, she'd doubted that Heath would ever open up to her. What had changed her mind? Georgia reread the text: *Meet me my place, tonight 10:15, wait in car, I have papers.*

Why wait in the car? And why meet at 10:15 instead of 10:00 or 10:30? Did Heath have an earlier appointment? Was this a trap? Something hinky was going on, and the one person who might understand was Ted, but no one at his office had seen him. Except for shrieking birds, the decaying mansion was empty. So here she was at the address that Dawn had given her.

The building directory read: studio 215, T. Brody. How obliging, no one sat behind the desk guarding the panel of keys. Georgia strolled past the rolltop and snatched the key. At the end of the hall gray steel doors clapped together like a mouth closing. Through a wire-reinforced window, Georgia cursed the rising floor of the freight elevator she'd missed. Braced, she heaved a fire door open and climbed the steps two at a time. Fluorescent tubes flickered down the narrow hall, and she heard an electric snap and sizzle then the tap of a hammer. After a turn of the key and a whispered "open sesame," she stepped from darkness into a room charged with light. Walls painted white reflected the sky through clerestory windows. In the center stood a head-high maze of metal rods and wires, the armature for a sculpture. Draped burlap covered the bottom third of the modeled clay.

She lifted the burlap and circled the piece, perplexed by a confusion of lines, but sensing the same sensual bending of metal that she'd admired in the sculpture from Ted's garden. When she complimented that other piece, why hadn't he taken credit? Then she got it. In this room nothing was decorative. Here art was serious, not a seductive ploy.

Workbenches lined three walls, sketches pinned above them. Carving tools lay where they were last used. The far wall was blank except for a framed graphite drawing of a woman. The tranquility of the body contrasted with the agony in her face. Shadows scooped away the woman's eyes and lines suggested teeth clenched in pain. Where was the organic flow of Ted's sculpture? The drawing taunted her, dark and seductive, saying step closer, let go, and while she inspected the room, the eyes, hooded in deep hollow sockets, pierced her. Was this supposed to be Heath? The angles, sharp and elongated, fit, but Georgia sensed the artist more than anything else, the strength and determination. This new side of Ted's talent frightened and fascinated her.

A Chinese screen along the other wall half hid a cot with tangled bedding. Hard to tell when anyone had slept here. One thing for sure, this was no candlelit love nest. She sidestepped plastic buckets of slurry. In some, the water had evaporated and the clay hardened. A coffeemaker still held two fingers of scummed-over coffee. Here and there, clay studies stood on plywood squares.

"How'd you get in here?" A giant of a man, bearish in a black beard, his forehead hidden behind a flipped-up welder's mask, advanced into the room. A slag hammer shook in his right hand.

Georgia sidled toward a broom leaning against the wall, a weapon in case the bear rushed her. "I'm a friend of Ted's. He's been promising to show me his work, and well, things keep interrupting, so he gave me a key." Georgia knew she stunk at coy, her forte was brash.

"Doesn't sound like Ted. I've never seen anyone else here before."

"No one? How flattering to be the exception." Who was this jerk? "Are you and Ted friends?"

The hammer wavered. "I have the studio next door, and this morning I'm sure I saw his key downstairs."

"Hey, I haven't touched a thing. No wait, I confess. I've figured out how to tuck a two-ton sculpture under my shirt, and then you go and interrupt me. Let's give Ted a call."

"Why not? Hand over your phone."

She made a big deal out of patting herself down. "Oops, left it in the car."

"Sure. I want you out of here, and leave the key downstairs." As his footsteps lumbered down the hall, he yelled, "I'll be back" and a door slammed.

Georgia stared at the spot where the man had stood. For the first time she noticed dust veiling the floor and the bench; even the metal edges of the armature were softened to a fuzzy gray. On the windowsill the shimmering particles she'd disturbed began to settle. If Ted had been here recently, his tracks would show through the dust.

She searched drawers for a link between Ted, Northwest Metals, Roy Burke, or Jonathan Kovac. File folders, the same generic beige as those Heath carried, all held sketches. She lingered over two drawings, both nudes, tacked above the cot.

The first was a caricature of Heath—large nose, horsey teeth, and knife-sharp shoulder blades. Heath's clothes, a petticoat and flowery dress, puddled around her feet. One hand covered a boob. The exposed breast was no larger than an insect bite. Had Ted drawn this to parody Heath's tight-assed image? She doubted that Heath would laugh at the sketch, but the woman had fooled her before. In the other drawing, Georgia counted five lines. The eroticism of the woman, like a late Matisse, came from juxtaposition and simplicity. No signature, but at the top someone had slashed the word "Soon."

Using the broom, Georgia tried to rearrange the gray film and obscure her footprints. Why bother? The bear would tell Ted about her visit. But because his art was good, it seemed important to leave the room pristine. For her second Girl Scout good deed of the day, she rehooked key 215 behind the desk.

Dawn had once believed that daring would come on like gray hair, one strand at a time. This morning she tossed out that theory. After Ted peed his pants, she'd twirled the gun Annie Oakley style and tossed a hundred-dollar bill on the bed. "This should cover damages."

Now Ted wouldn't dare drop bees down her chimney. The phrase, *her chimney,* slipped out without thought. Yes, she'd have to sort out her pronouns. Yesterday she would've said "our chimney." This new-found audacity offered endless choices. Geez Louise, she could join the circus, become an actress, run for governor, but she X'ed two things off the list: moving back into Daddy's house and making up with Ted. She might let him stay until he found a new place; after five years she owed him that.

Dawn dressed and made the bed, her usual routine except for the karate chop she gave each pillow to crease it down the center. Afraid Ted might pounce on her, she scouted the hall then crept out of the room. Maybe he'd left for the office, fingers crossed.

Today was hot, summer's last gasp, and she flipped on the air conditioning. Sunlight blazed through the window, but the glass looked bleary like the plastic covers on old library books. Secretly, Dawn enjoyed housework. She'd imagine herself in a 50s TV commercial wearing heels and a polka-dot dress, and wax the floor until it gave off cartoony sparkles.

She wandered into the kitchen. Now why was she here? Her hand made a circular motion. Right, clean the glass. She dug out the Windex, returned to the living room, and sprayed sky-blue liquid onto the back window. There was Ted, gardening of course. She resented his effort, the implied partnership: what a good boy am I, see how I care for our home.

Horse pucky.

He stooped to pull a weed then waved and mouthed, "I love you."

Double horse pucky.

She polished the glass in large arcs. By the time she finished, Ted lounged in a lawn chair. From this distance she couldn't read his expression but knew if she snuck outside, she'd see a twitch of hunger around his mouth.

Money, twitch. Women, twitch, twitch.

He deserved a woman who laughed when his dangling manhood was threatened. Dawn squirmed with anger and sprinted out the back door. She'd forgotten to put down the window cleaner, squeezed the yellow trigger, and squirted Ted in the face,

His eyes popped open, and he sputtered; a line of drool hung from the corner of his mouth.

"Move in with your skinny little honey pot." she said. "I want you out, one hour tops."

When he wiped his chin with the back of his hand, cunning replaced surprise. His voice dipped into that bogus baritone. "Dawn, honey, we can work this out, Theda's death, it upset me, I wasn't thinking straight. We'll go away, Mexico, you've always wanted to go to Acapulco, sit by the water and listen to mariachi bands. This afternoon I'll call our travel agent."

Tears blurred her vision, and she dug her nails into her palms, willing the tears to stay put. She forced an even pace and returned to cleaning the windows. The next time she checked, Ted had disappeared. But where? Maybe he'd left for work, but his car was still in the driveway.

"Dawn, God, Dawn come here!"

She raced across the back lawn and found Ted. Bent over, he gagged and pointed at the garden shed.

Inside the door, Dawn slipped on vomit mottled with blood.

Princess Di's limp body lay on the floor, her lungs rattling as she worked to breathe. White granules spilled from an open pesticide box. Dawn had warned Ted, keep the shed locked. She could bear losing Ted, but this...

Dawn carried Princess Di to the car. Ted jabbered along behind her. "I know I locked the door, you've got to believe me, I'd never—"

"For God's sake, grab that box, the vet will need it."

"There's been an attempted murder." Dawn's telephone voice was barely audible.

"Are you okay?" Georgia asked. "What happened?"

"I can't believe anyone would poison—"

"Ted was poisoned?"

"Not Ted, Di, Princess Di. We're at the vet's. Meet me at my house soon, please, soon."

"Sorry, Dawn, it'll have to wait. Gilbert and I have errands—"

"It's just that after last night, well, I'm a hot, steaming mess."

"What happened last night?"

"I took a shot at Ted. God, it was wonderful. He peed his pants."

"I'll be there in fifteen minutes."

*

No one answered when Georgia pounded on the Brodys' steel door. She circled the house and called out again.

"I'm in here."

Georgia followed the voice. When she stepped inside the shed, the stench of vomit overwhelmed her.

"Thank God, you're here." Dawn stood next to a runnel of blood and foam. A red smudge splotched her cheek like a birthmark.

"How's the Princess doing?"

"They pumped her stomach, the vet says she'll be okay. See those granules? He thinks that's what poisoned her."

"What do you think?"

"Marci Heath. The meanest way to hurt me is poisoning Di.

And nothing could be easier. The key's on the nail outside by the door. Ted and Marci are, were, have, they've been fucking like crazed weasels." Dawn tilted her head and studied Georgia. "But you knew that, didn't you?"

"Suspicions."

Inside the house a set of red footprints marred the hardwood floor.

"And Ted, where's he?" Georgia asked. "Did you frighten him off with your gun?"

"Oh, you are a hoot. No, but he left the vet's before me, called a cab. You probably noticed his car's gone. I feel contaminated. Let me change."

A minute later, clothes piled in her arms, Dawn crossed the hall then returned to the bedroom. Georgia heard water rushing into a washing machine. Dawn returned wearing a ratty yellow robe and gold lamé slippers with veins cracked across the toes.

"How could anyone? This is a nightmare." She collapsed into a chair.

"When did you last see Di?"

Dawn eased the slipper off her heel and flapped it while she talked. "I don't remember, but sometime last night. The doggie door lets her out whenever the urge hits. I always check before bed, but last night with Ted and Marci and everything, I forgot."

"You still haven't told me about last night."

Dawn spread her hands. Her fingers were long and beautiful.

"Last night, hoopdee-diddle-doo, I followed Ted to a motel and caught them. This morning I told him to get out."

That meant Ted had spent the night here instead of comforting his lover. Georgia needed all the bits before her meeting with Heath. "What happened?"

"I scared the bejesus out of them with my gun." Dawn retrieved a blue purse from the closet and, slick as a cowboy, drew out a revolver. "See?"

"Hey, watch where you point that thing." Dawn didn't seem to realize her shiny new toy could blow a shiny new hole in Ted's shiny old forehead.

After flipping open the cylinder, Dawn dropped cartridges into her palm. "Now we're safe."

"Lock that up. Treat any gun like it's loaded. I hope you didn't fire that thing."

"Blew the bedpost to smithereens. Then, here's the good part, I aimed at Ted's crotch. He peed his pants, it was wonderful. But that Heath woman, the one I'd felt all sorry for, she's lounging on the bed, laughing, her skirt hardly covering diddly-squat. It made her, Ted, everything so sad. It's hard to shoot someone you pity."

"I'd imagine it is."

"You sit, I'll get us coffee. This morning I felt strong and sure, but now—" Dawn shrugged and left for the kitchen.

Echoing thuds racketed through the floorboards. The clothes in the washing machine must've bunched to one side. Georgia yelled, "I'll get it" and tore down the hall. When she opened the lid, moist, hot air bathed her face. Of course Dawn believed Heath had poisoned Di. And the cycle was right: a perceived wrong, brooding, and then personalized revenge. Something had changed since Gilbert was pushed, but not the way she expected. Instead of escalating, the violence had decreased. It didn't make sense. Burglars creep into empty houses before they invade bedrooms with sleeping families; serial killers mutilate cats then advance to hitchhikers and prostitutes.

This killer had graduated from pushing Gilbert onto the tracks to delivering a birthday card and poisoning Di. Georgia needed to re-evaluate motive. Yes, she still believed greed was a factor, but it wasn't enough. What could explain the killer's need to torment?

*

179

Georgia insisted she accompany Gilbert on his drive to the Quists, but had him drop her off at Billy's house. When he saw her through the screen door, Billy motioned her inside, and then disappeared down the hall.

He returned with his hand hidden behind his back and presented a pink tin, tossed the lid onto the sofa, and folded back gold foil. "I brought you a surprise. Almond Roca. Almost seventy-three and I still have my own teeth."

She examined his open mouth: silver fillings all the way back. "Impressive, very impressive."

Billy gripped the arms of his chair and sank onto the cushion.

She let chocolate melt against the roof of her mouth. "Tell me more about Jonathan's father."

Billy rocked back and his eyes shut like a tilted doll. She thought he'd fallen asleep until his mouth moved, chewing on a memory.

"Jonathan was a toddler, no older than five. Whenever his father slaughtered chickens, he made Jonathan collect the bloody heads. Said the world was a mean place, and Jonathan needed to toughen up. You can bet the world was a meaner place while my brother was alive."

"Jonathan's mother, didn't she protect him?"

"She died before, well, while I was still sharp as a tack. For years I lived next door, but a month after she died I couldn't summon up her face. Why couldn't I remember? Still bothers me." His voice grew rough, heavy with phlegm.

"Did you ever figure out why she faded?"

"Faded, that's the right word. Yeah, I figured it out, but it sounds foolish."

"I won't judge."

"No, I don't think you will. It's because I never really saw her, she was a sad, worn-out thing off in the corner, barely skin and bones. My brother made her disappear before she died." This time he leaned back and kept his eyes shut.

"Just one more question," Georgia said, "about Theda and bees."

There was a long pause. "You mean the time I found her stung and wandering through the orchard? My old blue pickup just made it to the hospital."

"No, later when Ted lived here."

"Ted, gotta give him credit for trying."

"Did he work with the bees?"

"Sure, we all did. My Dad taught me, and I taught the kids. Except for Theda." He went silent again.

"I'll go now, you're tired. And thanks, you've helped."

"Don't see how."

Georgia wasn't sure either, but knew it was true.

He swayed as he stood. When she clutched his arm, she felt his pointy elbow floating under loose skin. In the shadow of the porch, his cheeks resembled the concave bruises on an apple.

"Where's your car?" Billy asked.

"Gilbert has business with the Quists, he drove me out here. Billy, before I go, will you tell me something?"

He stepped to the edge of the porch and leaned over the railing. "I don't see Gilbert's car."

"He must've parked it behind the barn. Billy, please." She gripped both his hands and turned him to face her. "This is important. What is the secret between you and Jonathan?"

"Jonathan?" Billy's head swiveled left then right. "Is Jonathan here?"

"No, but you told me that the two of you have a secret, what is it?"

He peered down a row of sunflower as if checking for eavesdroppers then squared up to Georgia. "I'm not selling the farm to Ted."

"But why did Jonathan want you to keep that quiet?"

"He said something silly."

"What?"

"Said telling people might be dangerous. Told you it was

silly."

God, how she wished that Jonathan's warning was silly. So here it was, a tug of war—Northwest Metals and Ted on one side, Burke and Jonathan on the other. And caught in the middle, Billy.

*

Georgia hiked onto a dirt track that forked left from the asphalt, and followed the scent of water past cottonwoods to the top of the levee. Three generations of Kovacs had called this island home. For her, home had been an address recited to the school secretary, a closet of unpacked boxes, the jangle of house keys tossed onto the coffee table before she'd escape with her mother to a new furnished apartment.

Wind spilled out of the Columbia Gorge and drove the clouds ahead, their shadows pooling around hummocks and filling depressions. Theda had told her stories of the original natives, the Chinooks, men spearing salmon from canoes, and the story Georgia liked best, of women wading naked through the bogs, loosening tubers with their toes to harvest their staple food, wapato. Lewis and Clark had named this island Wapato.

On the other side of the levee, a gate blocked the entrance to the landfill, and a large sign read, 'Northwest Metals. Private. No Admittance.' The road ended in a round pad large enough for trucks to back up and dump. Heaped mill tailings reached the river, and dust clouds spun through dun hillocks and rust-red mounds. Engines grumbled as bulldozers shoved piles from one spot to another. Next year the cornfields that stretched beyond Billy's could look like this. She walked back on the two-lane blacktop. A snub-nosed dump truck loomed over her, its tailgate banging as she dodged off the road.

*

Georgia tapped on the front door. Luke appeared, and she mouthed, "Water, please." She hoped to merge into the blue hum of air conditioning, but the Quist house, oven hot, offered no respite, and she had to rely on the dribbles of sweat cooling their way down her spine.

Luke beckoned her and she followed. A peek into the living room revealed Gilbert and Luke's mother, the school secretary she'd seen, with heads together jabbering away. Luke led Georgia through the dining room past dark claw-footed furniture presumably inherited from previous generations. Daniel hadn't lied about the family photographs: two walls traced the history of the Quist family from a mule pulling a plow, to a Model A, to the John Deere she'd stood beside.

"Where do you figure in all this?" she asked Luke.

"Nowhere, count me out. With Gilbert's help, and yours, I can finish school never to return. Thank you, thank you." He gave her a quick nod and slight dip at the waist. Where was the menace from last night? The kid had politician written all over him; calculate what the other person wants, then reflect it right back, mercurial.

"I thought you planned to stay and help with the nature preserve, complete Theda's legacy?"

"Doubt that's going to happen. We need to cut our losses." Luke imagined a bright future, but only for himself.

Stepping in closer, she scrutinized the last row of pictures. One photograph of women in long high-necked dresses with wide collars and men in frock coats had been taken in this room. Of the eight matching chairs around the dining table, seven remained. Next was a family group taken on the front porch. Georgia could pick out Luke's mother and Judith behind her brothers. A bald man, pinched and sallow, stood apart from the family group. Exactly as described by Billy, he must be Papa Ezekiel, stolid in his misery, confident in his piety. Had Luke inherited that mindless certainty?

"Hey, it's been good." He reached out to shake hands.

"Kitchen's that way. Gotta make sure they don't cut me out of the will." He vanished, but his limp chuckle hung in the air.

The water tasted metallic as if from a garden hose, but Georgia downed a full glass. When she left she held the screen door so it didn't bang. Judith's car was now in the driveway squeezed tight next to Gilbert's car so that he couldn't open his door. Aren't we all passive-aggressive today?

Georgia started her search where she'd last met Judith, at the white beehives. From there she traced Judith's path to a stand of poplars. In Portland the air, stubborn and still, had hung over the city, but at the pond's edge cattails tilted in the wind. Her deduction was spot on. Judith sat on a red and white beach towel near the pond's edge. Her hair was still dry; she hadn't yet dipped into the water.

"Mind if I sit with you?" Georgia asked.

Judith scooted over and patted the towel. "I misjudged you. Mom and Gilbert, Luke's tuition. You've helped us."

Georgia toed off her sandals and eased her foot into the cool water—relief for the cut on her heel. Funny the effect Gilbert's money had. Keep her talking, sort the trash later.

"Have you and Jonathan ever been lovers?" Another zinger. How far could she push?

"Christ, no, why would you think that?"

"When I mention your name, his expression changes."

"We were close as children, almost family," Judith said. "That's hard to give up."

"Do you want to give it up?"

"No, never." Sudden tears made Judith's eyelashes dark and spiky.

The passion startled Georgia, but she squelched the urge to warn Judith about Jonathan. Save it for later, information was power. Poplars cast jumbled shadows across the water, and she turned to a breeze. It was cooler now, and she sensed the approach of autumn, a change coming over the world.

"Jonathan's a bitter man," Georgia said.

"He has good reason." Judith lit a cigarette.

"Billy told me about his father."

"For once Billy got something right."

"If you pause and view things from Billy's perspective, he often makes sense."

"He's right about Jonathan's father. A man like that would screw anyone up. Next to him, my father was Gandhi."

"Why did this land, everything, go to Daniel?"

"Daniel has a penis, and his dick is older than Luke's."

"Ah, irrefutable biblical logic."

Judith sputtered out a laugh, and Georgia dove in. "I know Luke resents it. What about you?"

"I never fantasized about inheriting anything." Judith's hand trailed in the water, and then withdrawn she dappled a rock with drops from her fingertips.

"Is Jonathan withdrawn around you?" Georgia asked.

"I've never thought about it, but I can be myself with him."

A fish broke the water's surface then darted, a silver blur, beneath a fallen branch.

"Ted said the same thing about Theda, that he could be himself with her."

"Sounds like Ted's bull."

"You don't like him?"

"Ted's Ted. He has a Y chromosome, doesn't he? Why expect more?"

"You having man trouble?"

Judith's cigarette hissed when she snubbed it against a wet spot on the rock. A bird trilled a three-note call. "Hear that? Meadowlark. I'm sorry about Theda, but shit happens."

"It nearly happened to Gilbert." Georgia described Gilbert being pushed onto the light rail tracks.

"Any witnesses?"

"A couple hundred." Georgia let the question hang. "And someone tossed my apartment."

"In your line of work, you must attract enemies."

"Hmm, a few, a few dozen or so, past, present, future."

"We all have skeletons. Hey, I have to get to work."

Their fifteen-minute bond had fizzled, and instead of skipping through the meadow holding hands, the march back was silent and brisk. Georgia had checked her photo of Judith's work schedule and knew she had today off. So why lie?

Jonathan Kovac

Jonathan Kovac watched Judith Quist climb his front steps. She knocked, but he remained silent and waited for her to saunter in. The knock wasn't a question, *Are you home?* but a pronouncement, *I'm here.*

Judith closed the door and tossed her purse on a chair. "Did I interrupt your dinner?"

"No, of course not." One glance at the coffee table and she'd see three pizza wedges in an open box.

"Men are such bastards," she said.

"All men?" He waited for her to say, "*Not you*," until the silence grew clumsy. "Are you hungry? We could go to a restaurant, my treat." He hated rambling, but she had that effect. He stared at the pizza. Grease stood out in drops on the orange, rubbery cheese. To keep his hands busy he closed the lid and slid the whole mess under the couch. How stupid, plain stupid. What must she think?

"Men, I mean they're never like I expect them to be."

Everyone noticed her blue eyes, but he loved her eyebrows best, the black hairs precisely angled, emphasizing her eyes' feline slant.

"How should men be?" he asked.

"Loyal. Instead they treat you like food. They're hungry, they eat. Then when they get tired of you, they don't come back for seconds. Instead they tell you crap like, 'I'd never promise a hamburger not to eat a hotdog'."

He laughed.

"You're the one person who thinks I'm funny."

He moistened his lips with his tongue. "Let's walk by the river and watch the sunset."

She led him through the kitchen. At the back door she grabbed his nylon jacket off a peg. "You're always cold, take this."

She was right, he was always chilly. Because his mother couldn't protect him from his father, they had united against an enemy they could conquer: the cold. The hangers in his closet sagged with quilted jackets, mittens stuffed into every pocket. In the evenings while watching TV, she'd knit scarves that muffled him until only his eyes peeked above the scratchy wool.

He followed Judith outside and ran his hand over the railing where worn paint had flaked away. Side by side they followed gray creases in the sand. The sun flared on the hills, and cooler air pressed in off the river.

"Tonight," he said, "you don't have any... you're not going—"

"Free as a bird. A sparrow, or do you think a vulture?"

"A blue jay." He wouldn't tell her the real reasons he chose a jay—the cunning and contempt.

Wind swept off the water, but instead of hunching her shoulders against the chill, she broke away from him and jogged to the water's edge. He gave into a hazy, deserted feeling, waiting for the rollercoaster ride: she's happy, she's sad, she's relaxed, she's frantic. He caught up with her, and they paused where the sand, dark and polished, curved around a log. Waves washed over a dead seagull, its breast feathers yellow like old newspaper. Another bird circled above them and made foolish cries.

"You're shivering," he said.

She stared at the bloated seagull as if she could bring it to life. "It's that bird."

When she trembled again, he dared put his arm around her. "Let's go back to the house."

His hand on her shoulder, they retraced their steps. He willed his arm not to relax and alert her to his touch. It must be she doesn't notice. It must be she's cold. It must be she cares.

Before they reached the porch, he removed his hand.

"I'm staying out here." She sat on the bottom step. "If you're cold, go inside and put on a warmer jacket."

Because that was exactly what he'd planned, he now decided against it. Was she testing his manhood? Before he sat, he gauged the proper distance between them—every possibility amplified, weighted with significance—then he ignored his calculation and moved closer. When he inhaled to catch her scent, he found instead the rotting smell of the riverbank, familiar and disturbing.

"I remember your father." She kicked off her sandals. "And the hard time you had. Did you ever think about my family?"

"What do you mean?"

"What I mean isn't the point. You examine each word out of your mouth. Quit groping for a magical combination to charm me. I crave spontaneity. The first thing that pops into your head. Anything else and I leave."

"I promise."

She tapped out a cigarette but didn't light it. "My family."

He remembered prayer meetings, sneaking into the Quist barn past hay bales in rows like church pews, then settling in a back corner where farm equipment rusted. There on the packed dirt floor, he'd lean back and rest his head on a saddle that smelled of sweat and Neatsfoot oil. Voices quivered over him, and even though he could not see Judith he felt her aura.

"Because I was the preacher's daughter, everyone treated me differently. Girls apologized for swearing, and the boys…"

"What about the boys?"

"I was a fragile object, that or a challenge, you know, deflower the Christian girl, score one for Satan."

"Your father seemed like a washed-out version of my father, both had dark centers. I never thought about your mother or brothers."

She lit the cigarette. He hated tobacco and allowed only Judith to smoke in his presence.

"You, Jonathan, were my safe harbor. All those times we'd sneak out at night and lie under the stars, inventing constellations." She stretched her legs and leaned back. Smoke curled from her lips. It wasn't dark enough to see many stars, yet she pointed north. "There, the Big Dipper. We called it Lance and Shield. I'd squint until the stars became elongated, almost connected. You never tried to kiss me. Why not?"

"I was afraid you'd stop sneaking out with me."

"You were probably right."

"Night after night we were together and then never again. Why?"

"If that's what you want to know, I'll tell you."

Now, after years of wondering, he'd find out why those summer nights ended.

"You're cold," she said. "For God sakes, go inside, grab a warmer jacket, I won't run away."

"I'm fine, please go on."

"I've never told anyone this. Remember the night my mother almost died?"

"Yes, pneumonia."

"I always thought she resented me—her marriage, her life so grim. She was grim." Judith scooped a fistful of sand and let it stream through her fingers like water. "You and me, nobody else on this island uses 'father' or 'sir.' They say 'dad' or 'daddy.' 'Hey, Pops, whazzup?' It's even weird as a joke. If I'd ever said, 'Goodnight, Daddy,' his heart attack would've hit sooner."

"And your mother?"

"We believed she was dying. I don't think she much cared one way or the other, but she got well, willed it, she got better to protect me."

"From what?"

"Fighting to stay alive, that was brave."

"You said protect, protect you from what, your father?"

"Not what you're thinking, not anything sexual, but yes,

protect me from him. I was barely thirteen and naïve, still, I would've sensed that."

"I'm confused."

"This has to come out the way it's coming out, I can't tell it in a straight line."

When he cupped his hand over hers, he began ticking off the seconds before she pulled free.

"That night, my father didn't read scripture. I knew he was up to something. I tried to get ready for bed when my brothers did, but he told me, 'We need to talk.' Jonathan, don't ever tell anyone this."

"I'd sooner die."

"Yes, I think you would."

She stood, and he wanted to scream, *Don't go, finish your story.* He followed a few feet behind and watched the strongest waves wash over her feet. Those nights they'd spent together weren't always wonderful. She'd frighten him, wading waist-deep, and then deeper. Her clothes wet and clinging, she'd say, "Now I feel alive."

He untied his shoes, stuffed his socks inside, and rolled up his jeans. A lover must feel like this, rushing to undress, afraid his partner will change her mind. He moved close to her, and their bare feet almost touched. With each wave, the sand under his toes skimmed away. He searched the river for a rhythm to calm him, like breathing, steady in the first moments of sleep.

"When he told me—"

"Your father?"

"I studied his hands. Hate came easier when I focused on parts of his body. His fingers had no shape. And his mouth worked hard, clipping each syllable, managing words the way he did in sermons. He told me things would change. My period had just started, still I was innocent, knew nothing. 'You'll be the woman of this house, cook, clean, take care of your brothers, have responsibilities like a wife,' and then he added, 'but not in every way.' Later I realized he meant sex. 'I won't remarry,' he said. 'Tomorrow you begin home-schooling. Pray for your mother to enter heaven. I'll set the alarm for five.' Have you ever played with an Etch-A-Sketch?"

"Years ago."

"That's how I felt, like someone shook me, erased me, then turned the knobs so just the outside lines showed. I was empty."

Neither spoke while they strolled back to the house, up the porch steps, and into the kitchen. Her confession left him lightheaded. Nothing must contaminate the moment.

Her arms fastened around his neck. "Poor, miserable Jonathan. What would I do without you?"

He experienced her one sense at a time. He touched her cheek. Warm. He'd expected cold. Reflected in the kitchen window, he watched his hand on her back. And like a voyeur imprinting a memory, he lowered his hand to her waist. Me holding Judith. He waited for her to cue his next response. She was not rigid, but tame like in his daydreams. It wasn't enough. Snatching the material at the back of her shirt, he yearned to rip away her control, but remained still, inhaling her cigarette scent.

"I need to go." She shivered, and he dropped his hands then followed her from the kitchen to her car.

"How tiresome," she said.

"What's tiresome?"

"You, me. Money, that's what I need. I'm going to marry for money."

"What about love?"

"Money doesn't rot and go bad."

"Have you found the man?"

"I need rest, Jesus, how I need rest."

"Who is he?"

"Doesn't matter."

"Do I know him?"

"Do you know a rich prince? If you do, this is goodbye."

Judith's lips parted, and he could see the tip of her tongue.

"There is someone, isn't there?" Judith's lies were never blatant, just misdirection sprinkled with nonsense.

"Now I've upset you, and you look so tired," she said. "Please, tonight for once, get some rest."

Did she know that he spied on her? Was she telling him to stay home and sleep? He watched her slip into her car and adjust the rearview mirror. She took his interest for granted and tapped the brakes to wave goodbye. Her taillights bobbed down the road.

Had he said too much? Not enough? He turned back to the house. Now he'd be up all night parsing meaning from each word, but he craved sleep. He shook the bottle of antihistamines. Half-full. Though the label advised one every four hours, he spilled a half-dozen into his hand. Maybe these would knock him out. He swallowed the pills without water, sat at his worktable, and unscrewed the lid on the killing jar. The fruity scent of the ethyl acetate swelled through the room and became memories—the ripe, almost black bananas his mother set aside. "Don't touch," she'd say, "Let them sugar up for the sweetest bread." For once she was in focus, vivid, abundant at the mixing bowl.

A slash of light twitched through the fringes of his eyelashes. He saw Billy wheeling a grocery cart to an empty space at the center of a supermarket. Doors slammed and Billy vanished. Fat-ankled women and men in white shirts that choked their farm-browned necks crowded around. Between loaves of bread and red-veined cabbage, children, asthmatic and misshapen, nestled in carts.

Ezekiel Quist proclaimed from a loudspeaker, "I will heal them, heal all the children."

The shoppers rattled their carts and raised their hands. Palms pressed air. "Praise him, Lord. Praise him."

"Spurn the devil, pitch him out. If you sin by deed, if you sin by thought, then—" Ezekiel's voice sizzled. "You will burn."

Lulled by the shush-shush of a garden sprinkler, Georgia had dozed in the shade of an old oak. She woke, startled. Where was she? Was it dawn or twilight? She stood and stretched waiting for reality to drift over her.

Gilbert had chatted up the Quists long enough. She started for the house, but a sweet call, not unlike that of the Meadowlark, distracted her. "Shit, shit, shit."

She tracked the call to the barn. Inside the door she found a tractor, the front wheels supported on metal ramps; a heavy chain dropped from a crossbeam disappearing into the innards of the thing. Relieved that Daniel, not Luke, crawled from under the tractor, at least she'd solved the mystery of the cursing barn. He sat up and smiled. Unprepared for the warm, fuzzy feeling that whacked her, Georgia warned herself, stand back, way back.

"Damned knuckle buster." Daniel held up a grease-stained hand. "Are they still negotiating?"

"Luke thinks they're signing the Magna Carta."

"And how's the helpless out-of-gas city girl?"

Georgia flopped down on a hay bale. "Sorry. Just doing my job. Can I get a second chance?"

"Heard you've been sneaking around, talking with Jonathan and Judith, your reputation's shot."

"Ah shucks, give a gal one more chance."

"Promise, no more lies."

"Of course." She extracted dried straw from the bale, nibbled at its nutty sweetness, then raised her right hand. "May lightning strike me down."

"Now what?" he asked.

"How about twenty questions?"

"Back on the job already?" He snapped a new socket on the end of the ratchet.

"Luke said the night you were drinking, you yelled about tree-huggers. Was he right?"

"Don't remember. Luke said it, so it must be true."

"Drunk or sober, I don't see you running down Theda."

"So what happened?"

"Luke. Was he your target?"

"If he was, why tell everyone I wanted to hurt Theda? Explain that."

"Luke convinced you, used your guilt. Give the boy an Oscar for saving Theda, he's the real actor. 'Fess up, you cover his ass and take the heat, right? Here's a promise, I won't screw up Luke's tuition, but for once, be straight about your brother. You've protected him for years. My God, you must be sick of it."

"You won't use it against him?"

"Pinky swear, that's legally binding in Oregon." The straw had lost its flavor and she selected another stalk. A small bird with blue wings and an orange breast dipped and swooped through the barn. "What's that?"

"Barn swallow."

"Why's it fly like that?"

"Catching bugs." He sat next to her on the hay bale, and his fingertip followed the scab on her cheek. "How'd you do this?"

Careful: stare into his big blues, lean in two inches, and you'll be rolling in hay. "Attack of the killer blackberry vines."

The mix of hay and sweat made a heady smell. He laughed too loud.

She wanted to believe professional ethics curtailed their moment, but in spite of all her hang-ups, fear of attraction had pulled her back. "You never explained how families are like chickens."

Elbows braced on his knees, Daniel stared at his boots. "Say a chick gets hurt and the flock smells blood, they peck it to death. Family."

"How do you stop them from attacking?"

"Separation helps, isolation."

"And more honesty? Come on, give it up about Luke. What does he really care about?"

Daniel breathed deeply. "Luke's first thought is always, 'What will people think? Will I look good or bad?' Understand, he'd never hurt anyone. Can't damage that Eagle Scout reputation."

She suspected Luke was capable of much more.

"Sure," Daniel said, "I let him get away with stuff. If I say anything, people think I'm jealous, and yes, well, at times I am."

Questions jiggled loose. Had Theda offered tuition money after the incident? The longer she thought about this, the more she believed Luke had decided to cash in on his heroics.

"Where does Judith fit in?" she asked.

"Fit in to what?"

"Family."

"Never thought about it, she's just our big sis. Almost six years older than me, she keeps to herself. Early on we learned to steer clear."

"How'd that happen?"

"Nothing important, family stuff."

"Not fair, I'm curious."

When his expression softened, Georgia guessed he was picturing Judith as a child. She managed a throb in her voice. "I never had a brother or sister, so sibling stories get me. How did she stop you from pestering her?"

"She always had her own room."

"That wouldn't do it."

"Okay, we'd sneak in and play, Luke and me. I remember a porcelain music box, a ballerina twirling to music. One day I wound the box too tight and the spring broke. Luke blabbed. They've always been closer."

Georgia wanted more examples of that bond, but Daniel was

196

engrossed in the telling, and she knew not to interrupt.

"I must've been six. I'd never seen her that mad. Right there, she bites her own arm until blood seeps into the tooth marks. She inspects it then rips off with a scream that hurt my ears. She told mom I'd bitten her. At least that time I stood up for myself. I'd lost my two front baby teeth, the imprint on her arm didn't match."

At the back of his neck dark hair looped into damp curls. Georgia fought the urge to touch them. "Were you punished?"

He shook his head and the quiet between them lengthened.

"One last question. If you sell the farm, what then? Getting away from family is one thing, but not farming, are you sure?"

"What's going on?" Daniel's mother stood in the doorway next to Gilbert.

Daniel wasn't hitching up his zipper; she wasn't fastening her bra. No one could think they'd been rutting in the hay.

"We were talking, Mom, nothing else. I'm not a two-year-old."

"What do you know about women like her? Explain that grease on her face."

He must've left a smudge when he brushed her cheek. Georgia didn't wipe away the grease. Instead her eyes fixed on the woman's snarl of red lips. Gilbert took Georgia's arm, but she jerked away. Wounds from another time opened. Georgia's mother had worn red lipstick the night she died.

"Gilbert," Georgia said, "I need out of here, now."

In the car, even before the air conditioning turned cold, Georgia adjusted the louvers so air funneled onto her face. The posted speed limit was 50, and they hurtled along at warp 53. Like most jack-shit drivers, Gilbert nosed into intersections, changed his mind, and tapped out stops and starts in a herky-jerky hokey-pokey. Georgia wanted to tell him, "Hurry up, I have an appointment with Heath," but knew if he sang Heath's praises she might start screaming. When they pulled into the motel parking lot, she thanked him for not asking questions.

Georgia entered the motel room first. Who knew what might greet them: tarantulas under the sheets, trick-or-treaters in the closet?

Gilbert sat at the edge of the bed. During the drive back, he must've squirreled away all his chatter, and now his words, usually so ordered and meticulous, tumbled out. "Continue on the case. Please, don't abandon me, and find out who killed Theda. And thank you for being patient with me. I know I've been rude, that's not really like me."

"I'm almost always rude, so we'll call it a draw. Know what surprises me most?"

"What?"

"I'm comfortable with you. Because of my mother, hell, because of lots of things, I don't trust men, ever." Bone-weary, this confession leaked out. She needed to leave. A minute late and Heath might change her mind.

"But you trust me?" Gilbert didn't wait for an answer. "Your mother, how old were you when she died?"

"Fifteen." Here was the talky Gilbert that Stockard had described. The fastest way out of here was to answer a few questions while she eased out the door.

"Not younger?" he asked.

"Fifteen." Please, not tonight. Even if they'd been sitting here all chummy and drinking hot cocoa, she'd resent this. "Why?"

"Just something Stockard said."

"What did she say?"

"When I asked about investigators, she recommended you, of course. And I hesitated. I told her I didn't want to impose on friendships. She said I'd be doing her a favor."

"A favor? I don't understand."

"Let me phrase this correctly."

Crap, why had she asked for an explanation? "Sorry, Gilbert, but I have to—"

"Stockard said I'd be a healthy diversion, said that she'd

discovered disturbing things, things no thirteen-year-old should face. Pathology, I'm positive that's the word she used, pathology."

Georgia's attention fastened on Gilbert. Stockard would not have confused her age. Never. If she'd been running crazy lately and trolling bars, Stockard's statement would make sense. But hell, in the last three months she'd practically reverted back to virginity. Then it came to her. Down in the basement Stockard didn't want her to take the box. Instead she tried to hurry Georgia out the door. Something about that scrapbook made Stockard nervous.

"Sorry, I don't have the foggiest what Stockard meant," she said. "Probably mixed me up with another client. Screwed-up teenagers, we come in six-packs. No big deal."

Stockard had nagged and nagged, "Keep the scrapbook at your apartment." But after a check for water damage, she'd turned reluctant, suggesting Georgia was too busy and it could wait. That afternoon in the basement, Stockard had shuffled boxes pretending she couldn't find it. What bullshit. Why stall? Only one reason. She hoped Georgia would grow bored and tell her, "Screw this."

A salty taste filled Georgia's mouth. Her forearms propped on her knees, she leaned forward. Through the open bathroom door she could see green and blue fish swimming across the shower curtain. Queasiness drifted from her mouth to her stomach. She clenched her jaw, but it didn't help.

"Are you all right?" Gilbert asked.

Despite watery legs she made it to the bathroom, collapsed to her knees, and choked through dry heaves and stomach rolls. Nothing to flush, but she flushed anyway.

*

Georgia buckled the holster tight so the Glock wouldn't shift and gouge her. She set her phone to vibrate and shoved it in her pocket. The sky was a deep indigo, the new soccer stadium a luminous bubble to the north. Perched in the West Hills she listened to the droning freeway below. The white cottage was dark. She switched off the car's dome light and waited for Heath.

Five minutes. Ten minutes. Had the woman fallen asleep? Doubtful. Heath couldn't be trusted, why expect anything else? More likely she was lurking in the dark, anxious for revenge. Georgia eased the car door open, taking time to size up the place. Tangles of brambles and ferns tumbling down the bank offered some cover. Nothing moved except bats chasing moths in the glow of a streetlamp.

A deck cantilevered over the abrupt slope, and uphill from the house a detached garage crouched in shadow. One twist of the handle and then another—the garage door was locked. Skirting a rock-lined flowerbed, she stared through a four-paned window, and the beam of her flashlight defined a brown Ford Taurus, the car she'd seen from Theda's roof.

Odds were Heath was home.

The phone jumped in her pocket. Sure, after watching her slink around and laughing the whole time, now Heath calls, thinking, *That Lamb bitch, what a sucker.* Georgia flipped the phone open, ready for Heath to cancel their meeting, but the display stopped her—number unavailable. Her anonymous phone friend. She stepped to the driveway. Not tonight, sweetie-pie.

She knocked on the front door and called Heath's name. No answer. She rapped "Shave and a Haircut" with a four-letter word thrown in for rhythmic variety. Still no answer. She finessed the knob, but the deadbolt held fast. A brick path disappeared around the house toward the deck. When she turned the corner, a row of floodlights flashed on. Dazzled, she flinched back into shadows. After a few seconds the lights blinked out, flaring again when she stepped into the open. Motion detectors.

White plastic chairs grouped around a matching table filled one end of the deck. A big gas grill and covered hot tub crowded the other half. French doors into the house completed the ambiance, and she pictured late-night soaking parties with Teddy Bear. Ugh. Beyond the railing an evening breeze rustled through a leafy canopy of maples and alders. One French door swung open when she tugged at it, and Georgia sidestepped into the house. She called Heath's name once, then a second time.

Her flashlight swept across a combined dining room and home office. No chairs overturned; papers stacked neatly on the printer; everything tidy. Guess this was meant to be an open house, welcome all snoops. She stuck her tongue out at the Hummel figurines frolicking on the bookshelves.

Spying with a flashlight was thorough, all senses funneled onto an illuminated circle, but nosing around under a crystal-dripping chandelier would be quicker. If Heath shows, Georgia would scold her for being a less than perfect hostess. She flicked a switch. Nothing happened.

Sure that a bulb had burned out, she circled the dining table and tested the switches on her way to the living room. No change. In the kitchen she found a wine glass and an open bottle on the counter but no light. Damned if she'd hunt up the electrical box and pop the main breaker. The floodlight lit up when she retreated to the deck. Yep, battery backup.

Stuck with the flashlight, she'd make this visit short. Shuffling through printouts, she found a few memos, environmental chitchat about chemicals in the Willamette River and future protests. She pictured the top file that Heath had carried: coffee stains from different sized mugs. Had two people hashed over the contents? And what did the splotch mean? Spilled coffee? Someone in a rush? Or distracted, nervous, even horny?

With the flashlight clamped in her mouth, she ransacked a drawer. File after file taunted her. Odd-sized pink and yellow papers crammed a folder headed Receipts; and a corner of stiff white paper poked up amongst them. She tugged it loose, a copy of a letter on Burke's stationery. She read it twice. A new proposal to Northwest Metals. She snapped a picture of the letter and placed it back in the folder.

Enough games. Where was Heath?

Georgia opened her phone, scrolled to Heath's number, and punched the button. Three rings and it went to voice mail. She heard an echo, her phone in stereo. The back of her neck prickled. Heath's phone had to be somewhere near, but she couldn't get a fix on the location. She hit redial and followed the matching rings through the living room. Redial led her deeper into the house, through the kitchen, and down a hall punctuated by three doors.

She cracked the first door, then toed it open. Her light exposed towels on a rack. The room smelled of lavender. Bottles and tubes and compacts flanked the vanity. Most of the cosmetics were in their original packages, unopened or barely used. Farther inside, a robe draped from the vanity onto a pink stool. Redial again, and the robe's pocket bleated three rings. She fanned her light from wall to wall. Condensation had drawn squiggly lines down the mirror. Under the robe a black cord trailed from an electrical socket across the washbasin to the edge of the counter where it disappeared into scummy water pocked with bubbles.

Jesus H. Christ.

Georgia snatched the plug from the wall and yanked on the cord until a hairdryer clattered out of the tub onto the floor. She dropped the flashlight on the vanity, where it cast a wobbly nimbus across the wall. When she leaned over the bathtub, the gun jammed her ribs. With both hands she lunged into murky water and bumped a body slick and soft. It flopped away from her, and then bobbed to the top smacking her chin. One hand supporting the neck, she lifted Heath's head clear of the water. Framed in the flashlight's halo, Heath's skin looked translucent like old mayonnaise.

*

Three minutes passed before Georgia heard sirens, just long enough to remember her mother's body.

Like the other boyfriends, Drew Temple had ignored her mom's tears and pleading. After shipping Georgia off to stay with a drinking buddy, her mother painted on garish makeup, a final mask, and swallowed everything in the medicine cabinet— sleeping pills, aspirin, Valium, even vitamins. Then, of course, she called Drew. As always, Georgia circled back to the same questions. How long did her mother wait for Drew to burst through the door? Did she ever realize, he's not coming?

Though alarmed by her mom's call, Drew phoned the friend instead of 911. Georgia picked up. She took a taxi home and found her mother sprawled across the bed, the sheets stained with makeup and vomit.

*

The sirens quit wailing. Medics and police stormed Heath's bathroom. Georgia handed over her gun and PI license then replayed the phone message from Heath. The forensic tech propped Heath's head on the lip of the bathtub. Hair slicked back with one strand crossing her cheek like a scar, Heath resembled a cracked mannequin. Georgia clutched at that image.

All the electric clocks read 9:48. The forensic team decided the time corresponded with Heath's electrocution. Georgia had been with Gilbert and she offered up the phone number to support her alibi. If she hadn't dithered at the motel, if she'd arrived at Heath's earlier, she might have interrupted this murder.

Drenched and reeking of lavender, she followed two detectives into the dining room. The older detective informed her that all bathrooms were deathtraps and delighting in describing every fall and broken bone he'd discovered in these most perilous of rooms. He seemed particularly incensed that

Heath had no bathmats.

She answered questions one baby step south of the truth, starting with Theda Kovac's death and Gilbert Kovac hiring her, but offered no new information. If they decided this wasn't an accident, Dawn and Ted would eventually top their suspect list.

The last three hours felt like ten, and she stepped from Heath's cottage expecting daylight, but it was only two AM. While she sat in her car, she stared at the phone, waiting for another call from anonymous, then rubbed her eyes. God, how she craved sleep to block out all the dead women: Theda, Heath, her mother.

There was a tap on the car window. Her shoulders tightened, then she recognized Dave Thayer, the homicide detective she'd dated. Relief at seeing someone she knew released tears. She wiped them away with the back of her hand and lowered the window.

"Hey, you okay? Saw your name on the computer with this address. Thought you might want someone to vouch for you."

What she wanted was to finish her self-indulgent-weep-your-eyes-out cry. She managed a steady voice. "I'm all right."

He crossed his arms, rested them on the window frame, and leaned in. The outside lights sparked on, and the scent of Juicy Fruit Gum on his breath replaced the lavender stench of her T-shirt. His smile dropped, the lines on his forehead deepened, but his eyes, like the gaze of someone smitten, stayed the same. She homed in on his pleasure at seeing her. Face it, she liked being looked at this way.

"Don't hesitate. If you need someone to talk to, well, you've got my number."

"Sure, thanks. I'll do that." What was one more lie?

Ted stood behind a laurel hedge and waited for Dawn to back out of the driveway. He'd guessed right. Last week in a dietary frenzy, she'd filled a trash bag with half a cheesecake, Twinkies, assorted candy bars, and her favorite—Nutty Buddies. Now the stress of Heath's death had triggered her sugar cravings. While she was off shopping to replenish her supply, he'd sneak into the house and pack.

He'd left his car blocks away and crept up the path through the garden. Three of his potted canna lilies had wilted, but he decided against leaving Dawn a reprimand with instructions for the sprinkler system.

In the living room the morning newspaper was draped over the coffee table with more pages spread across the floor, something she knew he disliked. Headlines screamed: *Woman Electrocuted in Bath.* He imagined the pop and sizzle of French fries plopped into a deep fat fryer. He wasn't ready for a police interview, not today, not until he'd worked himself into the role of grieving lover.

He made his way into the bedroom. Princess Di asleep on the bed ignored him. Over the last few days Marci's face had hardened, especially the lines around her mouth. He knew she was ready to give him up. Now she was gone. He felt a lurch of relief and scratched one of Di's ears. She tilted her head so he could accommodate the other ear.

Ted lugged a suitcase from the closet, heaved it onto the bed, and established a rhythm, dresser to suitcase, dresser to suitcase. In the bathroom he cleared his shelf of the medicine cabinet and dumped it all in an overnight bag. Not willing to waste time searching for a baggy, he wrapped the tooth brush in toilet paper. Dawn always teased him about his fastidious nightly rituals, and she was right. Each item in the medicine cabinet was familiar and had its own place, but on the shelf reserved for medications, he spotted a new prescription.

He tried to remember if Dawn had mentioned a doctor's appointment but hit a blank. What could he expect from someone who'd sneak out and buy a gun? The label read diazepam. Nothing bothered Dawn, so why the tranquilizers? Only one explanation: his departure must've traumatized her. Poor Dawn still loved him. Then he noticed the date on the bottle, three days ago. He shrugged, dribbled half the pills into his palm, and wrapped them in toilet paper.

26

Georgia Lamb

Please, no more cops.

In the Brody driveway Georgia spotted a dark sedan, the kind she'd seen at the police motor pool, the kind that had clogged Heath's driveway. Georgia continued driving and parked several houses down. Would Dawn try to avoid her? Ted had a solid motive for wanting Heath gone, but since he hadn't returned her phone calls, Dawn was her next best source.

She'd come prepared and dumped a dozen tomatoes on the passenger seat. Oval stickers identified each tomato as a tomato; a wise precaution in case some dumb-ass tried to slice tomatoes into an apple pie. She peeled off each pesky label. A finishing touch, she crumpled the grocery bag and refilled it with the vegetables. Or were they fruits? She could never remember the little red buggers' proper classification.

After a quarter hour the sedan pulled away.

Two knocks and Dawn opened the door. A good sign.

Georgia held out the bag. "For you, fresh from a friend's garden. She gave me a ton, so it's share or open a pizza parlor."

"Oh, I've been expecting you," Dawn said. "After all, who has a better motive than me for killing Marci Heath?" She beamed as if she'd won the state spelling bee.

"So, did you do the dirty deed?"

"Aren't you a hoot?" Dawn accepted the bag. "Of course, I'd never admit it, but come in, come in."

Dawn had a knack for setting her butt down and wallowing in the present. If essence of Dawn was contagious, it might elevate Georgia's mood.

Water gurgled in the kitchen, and minutes later Dawn reappeared toting a colander of drippy tomatoes counterbalanced by plates, saltshakers, and a serrated knife. A streamer of paper towels fluttered, clamped under her chin. She dumped the feast onto the coffee table next to a platter of maple bars.

"Did I tell you Di loves tomatoes and parties?" Dawn dashed off to the bedroom, returning with Di slung over her shoulder. She set her on a pillow-throne.

"How's she doing?" Georgia asked

"Very well, aren't you babykins?"

Dawn sliced a tomato and tossed it. Di stretched and snapped it up like a seal nabbing sardines.

"The police just left," Dawn said. "Daddy has a battalion of lawyers waiting in the wings. He'd be horrified. Not many people can keep telling the cops, 'You'll have to ask my lawyers.' What fun. Anyway, they think Heath's death was accidental. I considered straightening them out, but *c'est la vie*. Since we're all chummy, tell me where in the hell you got these." She held up a tomato.

"Safeway. That obvious, huh?"

"Definitely not homegrown. Besides, when I rinsed them, I felt sticky spots where the labels had been."

The woman was sharp; Georgia knew not to slack off—*Grandma what big teeth you have*. "How did you know I didn't tell the police about you?" Georgia asked.

"Your name never came up. Turns out Heath kept souvenirs—Ted's letters, movie tickets, even pressed flowers, imagine. So sweet, so sad, so stupid. Doubt I'll ever forgive the affair, but then death is a great leveler."

"The best."

"Speaking of best, last night I had the best sleep. I pretended I was a five-point star and sprawled, stretching my arms and legs into the points."

"So that's your alibi?" Georgia asked.

"I was taking care of Di. If only she could back me up. But ask anyone, I'm a dedicated nursemaid when the Princess gets sick." She laughed. "Bet Ted doesn't have one."

"How is your wayward hubby?"

"You just missed him. Earlier I ran a few errands, and while I was unloading groceries, the sprinklers came on." She clapped her hands. "I'd set a trap, and Ted took the bait."

"Please, please, tell me about your trap."

"After I kicked him out, I turned off the water and nudged a couple of flower pots into full sun. I knew if he saw wilted lilies, he could never resist setting the sprinkler."

"Brilliant. Who do you think killed Heath?"

"What you really want to ask is, do I think Ted did it? I still wonder why he lusted after that woman. He'd never chased a goody-goody type before, and she wasn't rich. Once I figure out their chemistry, I'll have a better idea if he offed her. But I can reveal one juicy tidbit." Dawn held the salt shaker tilted in midair and stared out the window.

"Well, aren't you going to tell me?"

"Of course, but don't you love dramatic pauses? Anyway, after that horrible, horrible night when I discovered his infidelity, I went to the doctor about my bedazzled crotch."

"I didn't realize that was a medical condition."

"Oh, you." Dawn flapped her hand at Georgia. "Anyway, she prescribed Valium, post-traumatic stress, she said." Dawn broke off a hunk of maple bar then sucked frosting off her thumb. "I've decided to let his garden die. Watching it shrivel is the perfect symbolic gesture, don't you think?"

"Inspired."

"After I turned off the sprinklers, I checked the bedroom. A suitcase and some clothes were missing, but I'd expected that. Next I searched the bathroom, and yep, he'd swiped my tranquilizers. Thoughtful as always, he only took half."

"You don't suppose he'd…"

"What? Suicide? Not Ted. He could never imagine a universe without his presence. But if he wanted someone else out of the way, well, pills are nice and tidy.

*

Damned nettles. Georgia scratched the rising red welts on her ankles. Settled on the hillside, she watched Ted park behind his tattered dowager. Sunlight blazed off the upper windows. A door opened to the widow's walk, and for long minutes, full of starts and hesitations, Ted paced the perimeter of the peaked roof, then gripped the iron railing and leaned out.

God, was he going to jump? She stood, ready to shout, but he turned and disappeared inside.

Above her, slow traffic passed along Fairmount Boulevard, and she slogged up the slope to her car. A red-white-and-blue mail truck stutter-stopped from mailbox to mailbox. The postman waved and she waved back. His gray ponytail fluttered in the breeze as he disappeared around a slow bend, and she caught a twinkle glittering through the trees. Her breath snagged in her throat. Could it be? She jogged to the corner.

A white Ford hatchback was parked ass-backwards into a turnout. A faceted glass pendant hung from the rearview mirror, throwing rainbows as it slowly turned. How many white hatchbacks were there in Portland? Plenty, but she'd bet only one had that charm.

Ted or the hatchback? Heads or tails? She ran to where she'd parked, drove to the top of Brody's long driveway, and plugged it with her Corolla, trapping Ted. No more playing coy. With the pistol stuck in her waistband, she hoofed it down Fairmont toward the hatchback.

Sneaky felt best, and she might catch the driver napping. She circled through a vacant lot, exchanging the smell of hot tar for the smoky aroma of decaying leaves, and duck-walked through a stand of ferns, dark and dense in shadow, until she felt the warm metal of the car's passenger door against her arm.

No driver.

Palm against the hood, she measured the engine temperature.

Not too hot, not too cold. The car probably arrived sometime after she'd gone down the hillside. The worn seat covers were frayed like an old straw hat, and Georgia imagined sitting there in shorts, the backs of her thighs chafed and chewed. She jotted down the license number.

At one of her high schools the only open electives had been home ec or auto shop. She spent a semester pounding out dents and sanding down Bondo and now smiled thinking of the havoc she could create with loose connections and crossed wires. Lumpless gravy and rising dough still baffled her.

No luck, all the doors were locked, and the hood latch was inaccessible.

A magnetic sign tipped from the passenger seat, one edge hooked under an extra brake pedal. Her cheek pressed to the windshield, she made out the words, *Caution, Student Driver* and *Scappoose School District*. Damn, tailed by a driver's ed car.

The junior high titillation of slumber-party prank calls beckoned her, and she dialed the number on the sign. She passed herself off as the mother of high-strung but oh-so-sheltered Greta Grimsby, explaining they'd just returned from their first mother/daughter driving lesson. Her voice added decibels as she explained that poor Greta felt so bad, she didn't mean to cut off that white car, and it was really, truly, an accident, but that rude man, the man Greta recognized as Mr. Kovac, had flipped them the bird. Greta was mortified, just mortified. What was the school going to do about such inappropriate adult behavior?

After Georgia lapsed into silence, the secretary said, "Yes, a car is checked out to Mr. Kovac. We'll look into it. Can I get your number?"

Georgia hung up, her urge to yank sparkplug wires quenched.

Above the burr of insects, she heard a skittering and crouched. She aimed her gun at the noise. A furry slipper of a squirrel scrabbled to a higher branch. She forced an overbite and nattered back, for a moment pretending she was hunting another dumb-ass like Jimmy, not a murderer.

211

A horn went off, blowing like a car alarm gone mad. Then shouting. A trapped Ted Brody stood beside his Lexus. She trotted back.

"Get your junk heap out of my dri—" Ted's mouth dropped open, and he paled. "Good God, have you gone off your nut?"

Georgia followed his sightline to the pistol still in her hand. She pressed the safety, leaned in the open window of her car, placed the Glock on the passenger seat, and backed away. Her empty hands held high, she said, "Sorry, sorry. No harm, no foul."

"No foul?" Anger flattened his voice. "You're just a cheap thug."

"Slow down. I want the documents Heath kept for you."

"You want? You want?" A new, flinty look in Ted's eyes made Georgia pay attention. "And if you don't get them, you'll what? Shoot me? You think this is one of Dawn's trashy novels?"

"Give me the documents and we're done."

"Don't threaten me. I have nothing to lose, and now, thanks to your incompetence, poor Marci is dead."

Memories from last night churned around Georgia.

A door slammed. Ted's car roared into life, and his window slid open. "I said, get that junker out of my way. You don't, I will." His Lexus inched forward and the front bumper tapped Georgia's fender. Her Corolla rocked back and he tapped again. While he inched around, his left tire almost tilted into a ditch.

He pulled even and gave her a smile, slow and glacial. "You've simplified my choices, my life."

By the time she jumped into the car and backed around, Ted had vanished onto Fairmount. And so had the hatchback.

*

After lunch, Georgia enlarged the photo snapped last night at Heath's, a letter addressed to Northwest Metals. Burke suggested an alternative dumpsite without environmental problems. Jonathan had been cc'd. His alliance with Burke still surprised her. Did Jonathan expect a big payday, or did he have a grudge against Ted? If Burke's proposal was accepted, Ted could kiss his dreams goodbye.

Even more puzzling was Heath's possession of the letter. Stockard had assumed that Ted financed Heath's property buying spree. Maybe not. If Burke bought Heath's complicity, he wouldn't take kindly to her betrayal. But Ted, on the brink of financial ruin and exposure, might resort to murder if he discovered her treachery. No matter how you cut it, the woman played a dangerous game. Or was it less complicated, Dawn eliminating her rivals with poor Gilbert as collateral damage? For all the woman's audacity, it was possible she really loved the dope.

Georgia massaged her temples. Heath's death and Gilbert's late night revelations kept dragging her back through the maze. Give it a break, think of something else. As a distraction she grabbed the cardboard box and dumped the contents on her bed. Gilbert had quoted Stockard's use of the word pathology. What pathology? Her mom was a drunk. No big surprise there. Georgia swept report cards, letters, a graduation certificate, everything but the scrapbook, onto the floor. Sitting with legs crossed, she dragged it into her lap.

Scallop-edged pictures in black and white filled the first pages. Most showed her mother as a young girl among older women in stern, dark dresses that hung to their ankles. Though they faced the camera, Georgia sensed strong profiles like the pictures of immigrant women queued up on Ellis Island. One of these might be her grandmother or an aunt, and it shocked her that she hadn't a clue who they were. She inspected each face. Her mother should have told her a story, described a celebration, named one name.

Next she concentrated on childhood shots. She counted six beach vacations when her mom boldly asked strangers to take their picture. The moment before the camera clicked, her mom would snap back her shoulders, smile wide, and say, "Tits and teeth."

Like a child learning to read, Georgia traced a fingertip left to right, left to right. She noted every detail, named names, interpreted the mood on each face. When she counted thirteen candles on a sheet cake with blue icing, she closed the book. Whatever she was looking for, it had happened after this. She gathered the scrapbook and loose photographs into a grocery bag. Let Stockard explain.

Tires squealed as Georgia swerved out of the parking lot. She rolled her shoulders and took deep breaths. Memories of being thirteen came to her in gentler waves, awe at her developing breasts and the pink tinge of blood in her bathwater. Somehow these changes had become tainted.

At the stoplight she snatched a photo from the bag. There she was in a skimpy yellow bikini. Her mother, back arched and hands folded to hide the roll of flesh above her bikini bottoms, shared the beach towel. Who'd taken this picture? From her mother's pose, Georgia knew it was a man. A frenzy she didn't understand hit her with the blue intensity of a blowtorch.

The traffic light must've switched to green, and the car behind her honked.

*

Georgia shoved aside a bag of groceries and slammed the scrapbook onto Stockard's counter. A loose photo drifted to the kitchen floor. "You, me, we're playing that old TV show, 'This Is Your Life.' But a twisted version—I'm the celebrity guest."

"I don't understand."

"Buzz, wrong answer. I'm the one who doesn't understand."

Georgia flipped pages until she found her thirteenth birthday cake then flicked that photo onto the floor. "See that? My hair's in a ponytail and no makeup, you can see my freckles." She turned the page and her finger stabbed at a picture of her in a low-cut blouse that revealed cleavage and the rim of a black bra. "Me going on fourteen, all whored up. I remember buying that bra, and my mom cooing, 'It's perfect, Georgie, all that lift.' Lift. Motherly concern for lift." Georgia bunched her breasts together and shoved them up. "She wanted this, boobs to the sky."

From Stockard's grocery bag Georgia grabbed flowers wrapped in green plastic, gerbera daisies, waxy-bright as if colored by crayons. "What the hell?"

"Friends called, I invited them to dinner."

"Then we better chuck these in water before they wilt." Georgia flooded water into a Mason jar. She yanked three times before the cellophane around the flowers ripped, and then she plopped the flowers into the jar. "Before I turned—nope, wrong word—before I debuted as a full-blown woman, Mom divvied up her attention. No man, then I'm center of the universe. But if there's a guy, I'm dumped on a friend for, it could be weeks. I hit thirteen thinking how astounding it was, now we're like best friends. Look at this, it's not me, it's how she wanted me. And I was so goddamned heartachingly itchy to please her." Georgia stepped back, studied the flowers, then nudged one to the left. "Perfect."

"I'll call my friends and cancel," Stockard said. "We'll have dinner, just the two of us. And these flowers, they're ridiculous, let's toss them."

"Nope, don't want to be a bother. Hey, I'll even help prepare dinner for your guests." Georgia emptied groceries from the bag, setting aside a packaged whole chicken. She dumped brownie mix into a bowl and rifled through drawers until she found a wooden spoon. After cracking an egg on the bowl, she plucked out bits of shell, and then slimed the yolk into the mix. "She pimped me. My own mother pimped me."

"But did she—"

"Did she what? Have me fuck her boyfriends? No. But things got intense. Weird. God, would she have crossed that line? You

215

should've told me."

"I wasn't sure."

"You should've told me."

"I was suspicious, never sure."

"Suspicious for how long? Out. I want it all out."

"For a long time."

"Since when?"

"The Hazlets. I placed you in the first available foster home. Your mother's boyfriend, Drew, he made an appointment, said he'd been engaged to your mother and quizzed me about getting custody."

"Sicker and sicker."

"I never would—"

"I know, but still, why, why didn't you tell me?"

"You adored your mother, and I was jealous. Yes, so jealous I didn't trust my own judgment. All those nights when she was falling-down drunk, I bet you kept her bedroom door open, checking in to make sure she hadn't choked on her own vomit."

"I never told anyone about— How did you know?

"I know you, I know you. This woman had a wonderful, smart-mouthed child, and God, so many times I wished you were mine. You adored her. I resented it and didn't trust my reasons for making you see the selfish drunk I saw."

Georgia set aside the mixing bowl and seized a cleaver from the drawer. After ripping away plastic, she squared the chicken on the cutting board. It looked embarrassed by its nakedness— pale, pimply flesh and the awkward jut of wings. Georgia chopped off a thigh then set the cleaver down.

Like a deck of cards arched taut then released, memories blitzed her. "I'm going to puke."

In the slice of a second she calculated her race to the bathroom—out the kitchen, across the rose-flowered carpet, down the hall, past the guest bedroom. She'd never make it. Her gut rose to her throat and she gripped the counter. Leaning into the sink she concentrated on the porcelain's tiny fissures like a map with thousands of crisscrossing tributaries. Her forehead burned with toxins and sweat filmed her face. When she straightened, Stockard handed her a dishtowel. Georgia drenched it under the faucet and slapped it to her forehead. The dishtowel fell. Stockard bent to pick it up, but with the side of her foot Georgia whisked the dishtowel and the fallen photos into the baseboard.

"I should've figured it out," Georgia said.

"You were fifteen and grieving."

Georgia braced herself against the counter. "A month or so before she died, my mom told me to kiss Drew goodnight. His lips caught me full on, not a long kiss but open-mouthed and slobbery. I felt his tongue. When I pulled away he said, "Ummmsmack," like it was all a joke. A week later he gave me a hug and his hand lingered. My mom stood two feet away, she had to see his fingers groping my boob. Maybe a week after that, I woke up in bed and found him easing the sheet off me. I screamed, and she ran into my bedroom. When I told her what happened, she said I must've been dreaming."

"God, that's awful."

"She wasn't the only sick one. After, after she killed herself— it's so disgusting." Splayed on the cutting board, the chicken's flesh looked vulnerable like the underside of arms or thighs. Georgia raised the cleaver, but on each downward hack, she shut her eyes.

"Stop, you'll chop off a finger." Stockard pried the cleaver from Georgia's hand.

"The same night she caught him in my bedroom, he broke it off. Not her, him. And God, how things changed. She was always drunk, even in the mornings. I've been saving the best for last." Georgia hadn't known she was crying and wiped away tears. "After, after she died, I blamed— If I hadn't refused Drew, he would've stayed with her, and, and she wouldn't have, she'd still be alive."

Stockard didn't try to stop her from leaving. Georgia walked out and imagined the snick of Stockard's knife notching through the chicken's joints.

*

A half-hour earlier Georgia had known, this man had known, everyone in the goddamn bar had known, they'd end up in bed.

She'd dismissed two earlier applicants. When the first guy asked to sit with her, she shrugged. Then he said, "It don't make no difference."

She didn't expect a meaningful relationship; God knows she'd given up on that crap, but intelligence? What tenet in the universe declared she could only sleep with witless males? "Sorry," she told him, "change of heart. Be a dear and bug off." The bitchery felt good, cleansing.

"Who do you think you are?" he asked. "I've seen you in here before, so don't act all pure like the driven snow."

With her finger she bobbed the ice cubes in her Scotch. "You know, I've always wondered, what's driven snow, and why is it so much goddamn purer than regular snow?"

Stranger one retreated. The second guy's mustache looked penciled in, and Georgia figured after a few drinks she'd lick her thumb and rub his upper lip clean like mommy smoothing down her little boy's cowlick. She checked the room and decided no need to hurry. One-night stands were as plentiful as stars in the sky, grains of sand on a beach, squeaks in her bedsprings.

The man chatting her up now, Shawn, hadn't made her laugh, and he wasn't better looking than the other two, but at last she'd hit the jackpot. He smelled of cigarettes. If she craved a smoke, she could bum one from him. Quick, pinch me now, it must be love.

"I hope you don't think, well, that I do this sort of thing often." Now for the campfire-Kumbaya moment. "It's been a rough couple days."

"Talking to strangers, sometimes it's easier."

Georgia smiled at his wisdom, his wrinkled shirt, his questioning eyes. They were blue and, because he was tanned, intense.

He checked his watch. "The bar's going to close, let's go someplace where we can really talk."

At least she wasn't playing games about intent—her jeans tight, shirt plunging. The hello-sailor clothes made her feel more honest.

"One more for the road," she said. Across the room, the waitress laughed with a group of college boys.

"I'll get our drinks at the bar," Shawn said. "Scotch rocks, right?"

Twitchy with anticipation, he reminded her of Turtle playing fetch. Hey, Shawn, calm down, you're a gnat's ass away from blowing this. I can still change my mind and pick curtain number two. As if he read her thoughts, his walk slowed to a twang with a hint of swagger.

They listened to the band, and she heard his foot tapping. When he finished his rum and coke, he said, "I want to spend the night with you. I'd suggest my place, but I have a roommate."

"Does that mean I won't see the bat cave?"

She knew the roommate excuse; he was either a slob or married. Instead of wearing a gold band that could be wriggled off in a dank restroom, married men should be tattooed around their finger. She checked his left hand for an untanned circle. None there, but if he made a phone call before they left, she'd ditch him.

"Talking to you, it helps." God, she was boring herself. "My apartment's not far." She touched the melting ice in her drink then drew a line across his wrist. Keep it up. Keep it up during the fondling, the phony cries of exaltation. Keep it up until you convince yourself that you don't need him.

He nodded and she nodded, sharing what he thought they

had in common. He gripped the table and leaned forward to give his smile intimacy. Something dark flashed in his eyes then scurried off before she could identify it.

27

Billy Kovac

The house crackled around Billy. Swaying, he waited to catch his balance then slipped off the bed and lurched to the door. The knob blistered his hand, and he kicked it open, awed by his sudden strength. His old hound dog dashed out of the smoke. Cinders swirled out of the hall, bit at his nose, and swallowed him up. A wall of heat drove him back and burning curtains lit the bedroom. He flapped his nightshirt at them, knowing this silly effort would not save him.

A black silhouette filled the entry, and a figure loomed over him.

Jonathan had warned Billy, *trust no one.* "Get away! Leave me alone!"

"Billy! Billy!" Embers sparked the carpet, and the man crawled closer, smothering flare-ups with his hands.

Braced by the drawer pulls on the nightstand, Billy steadied himself and clutched the table lamp, ready to pitch it at the stranger. A rough hand seized his wrist and the lamp shattered against the wall.

"Leave me alone." Billy crumpled to the floor.

Surprised by a cold wet towel flung over his head, he gave in and went limp. His nightshirt tightened across his chest and choked him. The man pitched Billy onto his shoulder and stumbled through the house to the porch.

The chilly night washed over him, and though his throat burned, he gulped down fresh air. Billy rolled onto his back in the damp grass and watched clouds sweep across the face of the moon. Fog hovered over the yard; this close to the river it wasn't unusual for tendrils to seep through the trees. No, not fog. Behind him the house sighed and snapped.

Had he blown out all the candles? Must've, he'd eaten two slices of birthday cake. But Gilbert and Theda hadn't been there. Why had they missed this birthday? He sorted through memories. The bayberry candles, not birthday candles. He couldn't remember lighting them, but he could already feel the heat of Margaret's blame.

"Where's Margaret?"

Chase licked his face, the tongue like sandpaper against his tender skin. He shoved the dog away and coughed and spit until he could sit up and lock his arms around his knees.

Out of the flickering dark, the man reappeared. His arms enfolded Margaret, and she leaned against him.

More asleep than awake, Georgia sensed the weight next to her. She'd dreamed about her mother: they were at a party, and she was on a bed nestled beside heaped coats. Another image drifted up, her mother sitting on their couch a few days before the suicide, wrapped in a comforter pocked with cigarette burns. Huddled beside her, Georgia would scrape a thumbnail across the burns and crisp them off like old scabs. Her mom no longer bothered to flick her cigarette ash, and while she talked and gestured in that wild way she had, Georgia watched the tube of ash lengthen.

"Men suck you dry." Her mother's jaw trembled, and the red tip of her cigarette stabbed at air.

Cigarette ash tumbled soft as a moth wing into Georgia's palm, and she dusted her hands over the ashtray. Around her mother's face where she'd held her cigarette too close, frazzled, burnt hair wired out. And she drank, the tinkling of ice as familiar and eerie as wind chimes on an autumn night.

The form next to Georgia snored, a harsh sound, then silence and a grunt.

What the hell's his name? Had she picked this guy because he morphed so easily into a blur, the last blot in a hazy line of one-night stands? Somehow she and her mother had come to the same place. A hand reached back and found her thigh. Shawn, his name was Shawn. She listened to his breathing, and when she identified a sleeping rhythm, she covered her breasts with the sheet and sat up.

Her clothes lay in a tangle a hundred miles away on the floor next to the bathroom. Shawn, so average, had made harsh biker love. At least he was quick. Men who bragged of their sexual prowess were the worst and could take hours. Georgia eased back the sheet, but exposing her body to morning light made last night too real.

She shook Shawn by the shoulder. "Come on, honey-pups, it's after six, you'll miss the bus, be late for work. The north forty needs plowing."

He smiled a tender recognition. "Georgia," and pulled her head into the damp muskiness of his chest hair.

Shit, she'd used her real name. She sugared her voice. "My name's Scarlett, honey, I was born on a plantation in Georgia, remember?" Take it slow. In the past there'd been scenes, she'd tease him out of the room. It was best.

"I've never met a Scarlett."

Christ, he bought it.

He leaned over his side of the bed, came up with a cigarette pack and matches, and unzipped the cellophane with a pull on the red tab. Making a big-ass deal out of lighting the cigarette, he tapped it then cupped his hand against a nonexistent wind. "You want one?"

"Don't tempt me."

"When'd you quit?" He picked a tobacco shred off the tip of his tongue.

"A couple months back."

In a sweet gesture she hadn't expected, he pursed his lips and blew smoke away from her face.

She jerked the cigarette out of his hand and inhaled long and deep before handing it back. "Ahh... Like I was saying, it's Wednesday, I mean on Wednesdays, Rhett comes by real early. He's got this temper and—" On her upper arm she noticed a bruise and tried to remember how it had happened. "See this?" She pointed to the purple blemish. "Rhett."

Shawn gripped her arm. His breath smelled like sour milk. She thought he was examining the bruise, but instead he stroked her shoulder, his thumb settling into the hollow between her collarbone and throat.

"Come on, you-all," she said. "Haul your sweet Yankee ass out of my bed."

Hesitant, like offering milk to a feral cat, he extended the cigarette to her. She snatched it and stabbed the burning tip out on her nightstand. The paper ripped, scattering tobacco. She smelled the scorched wood and raised a fist in the air. "As God is my witness, I will never smoke again."

"Shit, you okay? Where's the woman I met last night?"

"Oops, there she goes, over by the closet. Nope, sorry, you missed her, she's out the door."

He gaped at the door.

"You are tempting," she said, "but with Rhett, I never know what he'll do."

"You mean he's violent?" Shawn scanned the room as if checking for escape routes.

No knight in shining armor, this one. Out of bed and balancing like a stork, he inserted a foot into his pant leg then stuffed his briefs into his pocket. After the bedroom door shut she waited for the front door to slam. He'd rushed out and left his Bic lighter on the nightstand. She wrapped herself in a sheet and extracted her panties from the pile of clothes. Turtle waited, his nose pressed against the door.

"I know, I know. I've said it all a thousand times. Don't you start in."

He followed her to the kitchen, where she jammed her panties into the garbage pail under the sink. Coffee grounds clung to her fingers. Back in the bedroom she tore off bedding and stuffed it into the hamper. She showered in water so hot it blotched her skin and then lay down on the bare mattress. Fumbling, as if searching in the dark for a lost object, she touched her throat, her mouth, her chin. Sex, it meant nothing, sweaty bodies touching at essential points, like tangents in geometry. If sex equaled nothing, what her mother had groomed her for also meant nothing. The faceless fuck. Georgia curled on the mattress's blue and white ticking. She chewed her lip until the slivers of skin became painful and she tasted blood. Her hand pumped open and shut. Rage, like a sleeping animal, stirred.

*

Shell casings bounced around her feet; Georgia jammed another full clip into the butt of her gun and went at the bull's-eye. She'd put off coming to the firing range, but after last night, it felt right. Easing back, she concentrated on the trigger. No past, no future. Her final shot echoed through the room, and she reeled in the target. Thank God accuracy wasn't the issue: the spread looked like spatter from a shotgun, not a pistol. But for now, her anger had drained away. Penance by Glock.

Her phone went off, and caller ID illuminated Gilbert Kovac. He described the fire at Billy's.

"Is he all right?"

"He's exhausted and suffering from smoke inhalation. They're keeping him for observation."

"When can he answer questions?"

"He just fell asleep. I asked the doctor about visitors, and he said maybe later this afternoon."

"And you?"

"Me?"

"How are you doing? Do you need a ride?"

"I'm, fine. Thanks."

The moment she clicked off, her phone rang again. What had Gilbert forgotten? But it was Judith. So what now? Did Luke want more money? Well, the Quists had picked a piss-poor time to come begging.

"Lamb here."

"It's Judith, Judith Quist. Could you speak up, I can barely hear you. Where are you?"

"Stuck in traffic, road construction." She'd switched to full auto, open mouth and let the BS flow.

"I need to see you," Judith said. "I'm… I might be in danger."

"Be specific."

"It sounds ridiculous, I shouldn't have called."

"Nothing's too ridiculous. Trust your instincts, I can help."

"Meet me at the nursery."

"Be very careful. Stay out in the open, you're safest among people." Finding Heath's body had changed Georgia. Next she'd order Judith to take her vitamins and button her coat. She shifted the phone to her left hand, unclenched her right, and shook out tension. "Have you heard about Billy?"

"Has something happened?"

Georgia described the house fire and said he couldn't have visitors until tomorrow. She wanted to be the first person to question him. She felt herself sinking into exhaustion and hauled more urgency into her voice. "Anyone connected to Theda is in danger. I'll see you at the nursery."

"Thank you, I know I haven't—"

"Hey, one bitch to another, forget the apology."

*

The air conditioner dribbled warm air over Georgia's knees. She gave the vent a pat, hoping the right encouraging juju might heal the contraption; her TV always responded to a good thump while she chanted, "Shit oh dear, don't die on me now."

Through Linnton, over the bridge, and taking a right off Reeder Road, she debated with herself. By the time she parked at the nursery, she'd decided. Unless Judith was in immediate danger, she'd keep quiet about Jonathan's stalking. Knowledge was leverage, and Gilbert deserved her first loyalty.

Georgia wandered through the nursery smells, a rank mix of honeysuckle and compost, almost tangible in the heat. She heard a smoker's cough.

"Judith? That you?"

"Here, over here." The screen of foliage muffled Judith's voice. Georgia retraced her steps toward a shed behind the offices.

She followed a row of pegs supporting umbrellas, coveralls, hats, and raincoats. Dressed in shorts and armed with clippers, Judith stood at a worktable, trimming brown leaves and dried seed heads off flowers crowded into a terracotta pot. She smelled of cigarettes, and the urge for a drag walloped Georgia. Was it the price she paid for her one puff this morning? As if Judith read her mind, she lit up. Georgia maneuvered so smoke swirled around her. Judith laid the clippers aside and motioned Georgia to follow. They stopped at a wooden bench that faced the road.

"Now explain," Georgia said.

"I feel like I'm being watched here at work, while I drive home, even at my houseboat. Night before last I saw Jonathan, but well—I mean, it was just Jonathan."

"I need details."

A baby wailed beyond the hedge. Georgia waited for quiet and wiped sweat from her forehead.

"It's a small island," Judith said, "but I've spotted him too many times to dismiss it as coincidence. He never honks or waves. I've noticed him in my rearview mirror and driving past my houseboat. He's careful—no, stealthy—keeping car lengths behind me or driving by after dark. It sounds outrageous. I don't know what I mean, hell, we've been close since we were kids. He's like my big brother, but—" Judith examined her cigarette, then squared up to Georgia. "You're not surprised, are you?"

"The scales aren't dropping from my eyes."

"Why not?"

Georgia considered herself an inventive liar, but Judith had spotted the pretence. The woman had good instincts.

"When he talks about you," Georgia said, "reverence shines in his eyes, and this is going to sound ridiculous, but your name comes off his tongue like a purr."

"He always had a grade school crush on me." Judith shifted her weight to the other foot, nudging her body closer to Georgia's. Was this gesture the result of their girl-to-girl confidences?

Georgia held her ground. "Tell me about the other night."

"I heard noises, patter across the deck, something against my window. When I went outside, I knew someone was there. No, for a reason I can't explain, I knew Jonathan was there."

"Did you confront him?"

"What's the difference?"

"Does he know you know?"

"Doubt it."

"Good."

"Why good?"

"No need to force his hand. We'll push when we're ready."

"He's a friend. I don't want to lose that, never."

"Maybe you won't have to." What's one more lie? "For now, don't be alone with him, not for a second."

*

On the stretch between the nursery and Jonathan's house, Georgia's speedometer tipped eighty. Remorse percolated through her. Already she wondered if she could have prevented Heath's death. Now, since discovering Jonathan's stalking, she'd done nothing to curb his obsession. What if Judith turned up dead?

Anticipating the turnoff, she hit the brakes. Jonathan's secrets, her mother's secrets—all secrets festered in shadow. She tried to rein in her resentment toward Jonathan by picturing a blond child gathering up chicken heads. The two images didn't connect.

No car in his driveway. Good. She was in a kicking-down-doors kind of mood. But when she turned the knob, it opened. Georgia leaned in. "Honey, I'm home."

No answer.

The air inside was stale—no, something more, a sweet undercurrent of decay like rotting fruit. While waiting for his return, she'd conduct her own little tour. The kitchen's normalcy surprised her: sunny, yellow cupboards and a ceramic cookie jar shaped like a caboose. Down the hall she found a locked room. If you live alone, why lock up? Her door-kicking fantasies returned, but since the front door hadn't been locked—maybe? Maybe?

She circled the house, found the corresponding window and, swish, it opened slick as silk. She boosted herself over the sill and tumbled inside. A white sheet stretched over the bed without the comforting lump of a pillow. Georgia rolled away from the window and was stunned by the photos on the far wall: Judith in work clothes, Judith riding a tractor with her father, Judith in family portraits, in pages ripped from high school yearbooks, Judith floor to ceiling, in living color and black and white. Was there anything he wouldn't do to secure his place with Judith?

Across the room stood a giant dresser and on top a fish tank burbled, but no fish swam through the bubbles. Georgia opened the top drawer and found more Judith memorabilia—a lipstick-smudged paper napkin, black hair tied with red ribbon, canvas gardening gloves, and a shopping list in what must be Judith's handwriting. Each item was tucked into a black display box.

Buried under white t-shirts in the second drawer, she found an antique watchcase and popped it open. Inside were guitar fingerpicks—brass Dunlops for three fingers and a thumb, the other set of clear plastic—exactly like the ones she used. Did Jonathan play? No guitars here. Judith? Nobody had mentioned that. She slid the Dunlops onto her thumb and fingers, a glass-slipper-perfect fit. She scooped them up and dumped them in her pocket. These were going back home. She started reshuffling everything to their original order, then stopped. Screw it.

Was he collecting souvenirs of her for later fantasies? Okay, but why utterly destroy her guitar and leave it on the bed like a dead lover? She had no doubt; Jonathan had ripped her place apart. She tried shutting the drawer, but a pair of white cotton panties pinched in the corner. Stark white, they looked new, but the inking on the tag—100% cotton, see reverse side for care— had faded. She tugged on the elastic waistband and worked them loose, turned inside out. This had to be the treasure he'd snared from Judith's dumpster. Unwashed blood stained the gusset.

In the bottom drawer, tucked behind thermal underwear, was a black metal case. Georgia snapped back the clasps and flipped the lid. A Luger pistol. Was this his father's gun, the gun that had killed his dog?

A rustling came from outside. Seconds passed, but all she heard was the liquid babbling of the fish tank.

She lifted the Luger, ejected the magazine, and pulled back the toggle to open the breech—empty. A second search failed to produce a box of cartridges. The bedroom door unlocked from the inside with a turn latch. She lugged the box into the living room and placed it on the table next to the La-Z-Boy recliner.

After rummaging in the wastebasket beside Jonathan's worktable, she dumped crumbled wads of scrap paper under the curtains of the front window and heaped them into a fine mound worthy of a merit badge. No one would guess that she'd never been a Girl Scout. She flattened one ball of paper: lesson plans with INVERTEBRATE ANATOMY printed across the top. While twisting it lengthwise, her breathing became rapid and shallow. If her feet hadn't been set wide apart, she would've wobbled, giddy. Could revenge be this close, this delicious? Her palm against the wall, she steadied herself.

She pried Shawn's lighter out of her pocket The flint sparked and flame fluttered, orange and alive and vehement, writhing in the sunlight. By the time she reached her car this place would be engulfed, a collapsing ruin.

Through the door into the kitchen she did a slow sideways

dance shielding the burning future in her hand. She could finish this, it was her right, tit for tat. The paper became a torch, smoking, charred, consuming.

She dropped the paper into the sink, drowned it under the tap, and threw open the back door. Fresh air from the river scoured out the stink while she walked down the back porch steps to the top of the dike. The long wake behind a huge black tanker lapped the shore in a slow, persistent pulse. Rigid, she gazed across the water.

A bundle of hate, self-loathing, and irrational stupidity, she waited for her heartbeat to echo the beat of the waves. All the struggles of her last seventeen years would be wasted in this descent. If she lost control, what would happen to Gilbert? And Judith?

A car backfired and sputtered, huffing up the long driveway to the house. Welcome home, Johnny boy.

She slunk up the back steps to the porch, through the kitchen, and into the living room, where she angled the recliner toward the door. After flopping into it, she positioned the Luger on the table next to her.

*

"Hey, sweetie, it's about damned time. Remember your promise, if you're going to be late, call. Smell that?"

A confused nod. The door closed behind Jonathan.

"The meatloaf's ruined, my grandmother's recipe with onions diced the way you love them, burnt to hell, all burnt to hell."

He stepped back and reached for the doorknob. It felt right that something in her made him retreat.

"Take a little side trip stalking Judith, did you? Or are you saving that for later? Safer to wait until dark." She twisted in the chair and peeked through the front curtains. "Where's the driver's ed car? Or do you save that just to follow me?"

"What driver's ed car?"

"Jonathan, Jonathan, every word out of your mouth is a rotten, old whopper, I hear penicillin clears that right up. Save your lies for real crimes, like stuffing bees down Theda's chimney. Or, let me think here, I've got it, burning down your Uncle's house."

He threw the door open. "Out, out now! Here on the Island we shoot intruders."

Georgia pointed to the gun. "It's not loaded. Unless a butterfly net is a deadly weapon, I'm safe." She waited for him to respond. When he didn't, she filled the silence. "A nasty habit you have there, breaking into people's homes. Well, what's good for the goose—" She placed her hands behind her head and stretched her legs to show how reasonable she could be.

"You're nuts." Jonathan picked his way past her into the kitchen, and she followed. He stopped at the sink and snatched the scorched twist of paper. "What's this?"

The way he peered over his glasses annoyed her. "Oops, now you've caught me in a lie. No burnt meatloaf. I planned a little housewarming party but had a change of heart, so relax. Oh, by the way, I've seen your special collection, all Judith, all the time, wouldn't want to torch that."

He filled a glass with water, pressed it against his cheek, and glared. "You, get out now."

"You must be tired," she said. "Tell the truth and it's over, no more prowling. No more hurting people. Theda, Gilbert, Marci."

"You're crazy."

"A few words, the truth, and I won't mention your shrine to Judith. Tell me about the bees. From Billy's orchard, aren't they?" She cozied up her voice. "An old farm boy and a science teacher, you'd know how to handle them. Tell me, and your collection will be our secret."

His voice was thick, as if clotted by a cold. "Okay, the driver's ed car, I admit that. But everything else, just sick figments of your twisted mind. You don't have proof. Leave. Without proof, you can't do a thing."

Her focus snapped into place. Here it was, an almost confession. One solid push, he might give it up. "You can make it all stop, tell the truth and it's over."

His gold-brown eyes looked moist. The way he implored, holding both hands open, gave her an unexpected jab of pity. She felt an answer quivering on his lips.

"Go on," she said, "one word."

His mouth began to form a sound, but then the emotion in his eyes shut down as real as the closing of a door. "I'm calling the sheriff."

"Go to it."

Framed by pale lashes, his eyes fixed on her, and he said something else. But instead of his words, she listened to the current beneath his voice. Like her, he was teetering on a precipice. Sweat gleamed on his ashen, fine-grained skin, and the circles under his eyes looked like bruises. What would he do next?

She felt no limit.

Billy Kovac

A woman in white, not Margaret, leaned over Billy. She smelled of soap. Margaret must've been right, he'd finally broken his hip. He wiggled toes and lifted a leg, surprised by the lack of pain. His throat was raw, but he forced himself to swallow.

The nurse's face, shiny and puffy, made him think of a glazed doughnut. He struggled with memories: the sky red like fire, and him standing on a mountain his arms spread, Charlton Heston on Sinai. No, that wasn't right. He could see the lunch tray—a tea bag leaking rusty stains and vegetable soup—sparkling globules floating over carrots and barley. Solemn worries, like the pressure in his lungs and the restless beating of his heart, had replaced the daily ache of his joints.

"Where's Jonathan?" he asked.

"You have a new visitor," the nurse said. "I'll tell your friend you're awake."

The soapy odor receded. The visitor paused in the doorway, and Billy was stunned. Here was the man who had slung him over his shoulder. What the hell did he have on his hands? Gloves. Plump white gloves, just like Mickey Mouse. The man wore Mickey Mouse gloves. Billy decided to stay awake for that.

"I was leaving the barn and then, well, I saw smoke over your house." The man's words bumped out.

"You, you're one of the brothers."

This was not the pretty-boy brother. Billy checked the man's ankle: the bear trap was gone.

The man followed his gaze. "I stayed here last night, smoke inhalation, they removed my tracking bracelet."

The girl with one dimple came in. Billy remembered giving her candy, and he only gave Almond Roca to friends. He liked the way she ate it, sucking off the chocolate before crunching the hard part into tiny bites. The visitors looked at each other, startled, then something about their faces made Billy think of cats bumping shoulders to show affection.

The girl rested her hand on Billy's. "Can you talk about it?"

He could talk about anything. Pick a topic, he'd talk. "And she's dead?" Billy asked.

"You mean Marci Heath?"

He nodded. "How'd she die, or did I dream it?"

"Electrocuted. A hairdryer dropped in her bath."

"I have an alibi, Margaret can vouch for me."

Georgia waved for his attention. "Don't worry, no one suspects—"

His shoulders slumped. He realized he was acting like an old fool.

"You do have motive," she said, "so the police might show up and question you."

"I should put on my red tie, don't you think I should?"

"Absolutely, as soon as you leave here. Do you remember how the fire started?" she asked.

Fire. That explained it, the red sky, and the flickers every time he shut his eyes. Billy pasted the two images together. "A fire in my bedroom." The gauzy screen separating him from the past lifted. "I lit candles," he said, "before I went to bed. It was my birthday." He was thirsty. "No, I didn't light the candles." Talking hurt. The girl must've read his thoughts and handed him the glass of water instead of babying it up to his lips. Over the rim of the glass, he watched her write in a notepad. She might be a reporter.

"The candles," Billy said. "I hide matches in a sock. Margaret doesn't know, don't tell her."

"I won't." She made a cross over her heart. "If you're up to it, I need to ask more questions."

He was right. She was a reporter.

"Did you notice any chemical odors, like kerosene or alcohol?"

"Nope, and I have a good nose, never fails me."

"What color was the smoke?"

He said "Hmmm," as if considering possibilities.

"Think back, you're in the bedroom. Gasoline burns black, gunpowder yellow or brown."

"You know a hell of a lot about fires."

"When I was a paralegal I worked an arson case."

"It was the flames I watched, not the smoke."

"Can you describe their color?"

Color, color, yak, yak, yak. "The flames were flame-colored."

"Sorry, let me explain. Red flames mean flammable liquids."

"Red. When I burn brush, it's yellow, but this was red."

"Did your smoke alarm go off? Is that what woke you?"

He hadn't thought of that. "Could have. Or Chase woke me, my dog, Chase. The curtain caught fire. Red flames. I stood on the bed, and you—"

The man smiled.

"Margaret's a stickler," Billy said. "When we switch to daylight savings in the spring, she changes all the clocks and the smoke alarm batteries too." Those weren't Mickey Mouse gloves on the man's hands, they were bandages. The man was Daniel Quist.

Billy wanted to thank him, but the veil was coming down, blurry, like after rubbing his eyes. The white walls thinned to colors on a canvas, an ocean rimmed by red flickers, translucent glass.

"Sleep now," the woman with a sweet dimple said. Both visitors stood.

The man touched Billy's shoulder with his bandaged hand.

"Thank you," Billy said. The man had burnt his hands saving him. "I'm glad you're not running off to Disneyland."

The air conditioner blew hot air, and Georgia jammed the lever left. No change. One hand on the steering wheel, she gave in and opened the windows.

"Probably needs a Freon charge," Daniel said. "I can check."

"Can't give up the little dickens, not even for an hour."

She parked at the top of the Quist driveway. With no car distractions, their silence stretched long and clumsy. He twitched varying degrees of a smile. She wanted to supply a gesture that would make his expression settle in, but decided against touching his hand.

"Thanks for the lift," he said.

The way Daniel gripped the door lever pissed her off. What? Planning his escape? She mimicked his casual tone. "No big deal, I was going to Billy's house anyway."

"I better get, chores piling up."

He stepped from the car then leaned in through the open window. "Let me know the next time you're going my way." His voice was gruff with good humor, and she imagined him diving back through the open window. She was off again, collecting non-memories for her non-affair.

His gaze switched to something above her head. "And take care."

Goddamn blue eyes.

Georgia goosed the gas pedal, and her car coughed before grumbling back to life. She wasted a wave on the back of Daniel's plaid shirt then drove past the cornfield mumbling, "Yup, yup, shucks, shucks."

When she saw Billy's house, her schoolgirl daydreams withered. Sunflowers still cast shadows across the front porch, but the fire had jumbled the back of Billy's house into a charred husk.

Billy said the flames were red. Could she trust his memory? And she should've asked if any windows had been open. The mind that arranged Theda's death might avoid anything detectable like gasoline, but in summer open windows would be overlooked and any draft would feed the flames.

She circled the house. Three windows were open—Billy's bedroom, the kitchen, and the bathroom. She stepped over yellow tape that read *Fire Line Do Not Cross* and climbed the porch. The flames had not demolished the front room, but Billy's green velvet chair, slouched in the corner, was a sodden mess.

Down the hall a splinter of light gleamed under the bedroom door. Georgia swung it open. Though light flooded the room, it was still bleak. Ash shrouded everything: floor, dresser, and the skeletal remains of Billy's bed. The gray haze distanced Georgia as if she stared through a grimy window into an abandoned factory.

When she focused the camera, objects appeared sharper, more real. Click. Next to the window a scorch, like an inverted triangle, climbed from the floor up the wall. The alligator pattern suggested that the fire had started here. Click. A groan warned her—weak floorboards. She stepped back. Joists near the wall must be damaged. She focused the long lens on a scaly imprint etched evenly across the wall. Click. The pattern would be irregular if someone had flung gasoline, but taking a natural course the flame had flared up. Click. Nothing sprinkled across the floor. Hidden in the bottom drawer, just where Billy said they'd be, she found matches.

Georgia stepped back, and broken glass snapped under her heel. Fire should've blown the window outward. She leaned out the window and scanned the ground. No boot prints. Note to self—ask the arson investigator if a fireman had smashed any windows.

In the hall the reek of smoke and ash lost force. She reached to unfasten the plastic cover of the smoke alarm. Even standing on tiptoe, her fingertips barely brushed it, and she lugged a stool in from the kitchen. Pressing the button, nothing sounded. Had Margaret forgotten to install a new battery? Or had someone replaced a viable battery with a dead one?

*

Georgia eased off the gas and coasted past the Quist house. Her eye followed the curve of the driveway where Daniel had disappeared. Damned moony crap. She hit the gas.

What the hell? She braked.

No longer vertical, the wall of the barn bulged out. A yellow metal boom with a scoop had punched through the red siding. She slammed the car into second, U-turned, and angled through the front gate. When she hit the brakes gravel ricocheted off the barn. Shouting voices came at her as she ran through the open door.

Daniel paced, waving his arms. "Good God, Judith, how many times have I told you, stop and think? Always in such a damned hurry."

"Danny, Danny, Danny, don't—" Hands stretched out, Judith sank onto a hay bale. She wiped at tears, and streaks of grease smeared down her cheeks.

Georgia stepped between them. "Christ, what happened?"

Daniel pointed at the backhoe, a mechanical beast, its head rammed through the wall. Where boards had splintered, sunlight framed the hole. Daniel's mouth moved but no words came. Georgia followed tread marks from the backhoe to a pair of metal ramps, empty, supporting nothing.

"I wanted to help, that's all, what with Danny's burned hands, and I knew the backhoe needed to be lubed, I forgot to chock the wheels and—" Words caught in Judith's throat. "It must have popped out of gear."

Somewhere Georgia heard Hank Williams quietly honky-tonking the blues. Daniel hit the off button on the CD player. He slapped his bandaged palm on the workbench and winced as he rushed back at Judith. "Why the fuck? You know better."

He advanced, and she shrank away.

Georgia grabbed his wrist. "You. Back off. She's in shock. She doesn't need your grief." Georgia pushed him away, then crouched next to Judith, and her arm circled heaving shoulders.

"Hey, sweetie, you're okay, everything can be repaired. I'm going out to the car and grab a camera. Pictures will make things easier for the insurance man. And you, Daniel, make up with your sister."

Georgia dawdled back to the car, let emotions settle. Family. Unexpected loneliness flooded her. She missed Stockard. Seventeen years ago Stockard had not distracted her with toys; instead, she taught Georgia to estimate time using her fingers. Each finger parallel to the ground represented fifteen minutes. Georgia held her hands at arm's length and tried it again. Counting eight fingers between the top of the hill and the sun, she reckoned she had two hours until sundown.

The car door open, she let hot air escape, and sat askew on the seat jotting notes. What had happened to her easygoing farm boy? This Daniel, irrational and quick to anger, could have run down Luke or, she had to be honest, even Theda. She tossed the pad on the seat and held up her hand. Seven fingers. With the sun at her back she stopped at the barn door. Her shadow fell across the backhoe.

Judith looked up, her right hand blocking the glare. "I sent Danny off to the Cracker Barrel to buy me a pack of smokes. This will be our little secret." She withdrew a wrinkled cigarette package from her pocket, straightened a bent cigarette, inhaled once, and handed it over.

Georgia sucked in nicotine. Her cheeks hollowed at the effort, and she watched the cigarette tip glow red. "How'd you know about me and cigarettes?"

"I'd blow smoke in different directions and watch you scamper around to catch a sniff. Your expression—"

"Unadulterated lust?"

"Yeah, that's the one."

In a farewell fondle, Georgia twirled the brown filter between her thumb and forefinger, then handed it back.

Judith's shoulders relaxed, "Actually I wanted Daniel gone... We need to talk."

"You talk, I'll take pictures." Georgia started at the front bucket of the backhoe and methodically snapped her way across the barn toward the hole in the wall. "Talk. You're not talking."

"I lied about the accident."

"What?" Georgia straightened.

"You saw what he's like, I didn't want him tearing off after Jonathan."

"Jonathan? You're losing me."

"It sounds crazy. The backhoe was on the ramp, and I was under it with the lube gun, this way." Judith indicated a line at a right angle to the metal ramps, head toward the wall. "I didn't hear anything because of the music and then it, the backhoe, started rolling. I twisted out, it just missed me. I saw the backside of a man disappearing, and I'd almost swear it was him, Jonathan, his size, light brown hair."

"How sure are you?"

"It happened fast and the wheels blocked my view, but yeah."

Georgia flipped out her phone. "We need the sheriff."

Judith snatched the phone. "These walls..." She shivered. "C'mon, let's talk outside."

Georgia followed her out the door, and they sat on a patch of grass with the mangled wall at their backs.

"Remember," Judith said, "I told you that Jonathan threw pebbles at my window? Well, I left something out, not to mislead you, but it just sounded, the only way I can put it, is sick. I still can't believe what I did."

Judith offered another drag. Georgia shook her head.

Strain showed around Judith's eyes. "Standing under the porch light in my T-shirt and robe, I sensed Jonathan—like when you stop at a light and the guy in the next car checks you out. Even if you don't face him, you feel his eyes burrowing. I believed that if I acquiesced, no, that's not the right word, if I acknowledged his presence, I'd be free of him. Saying it out loud sounds naïve, or just plain stupid."

Judith stabbed out her cigarette. Sparks glinted in the dry grass, and she spit on her fingers to snuff out the embers.

"I walked back inside," Judith said, "but I could still feel him watching, and I grew angry. You want a show, I'll give you a show. I went from room to room, opening blinds, turning on lights, then I centered myself in front of the largest window and dropped the robe. Standing in my old T-shirt and panties I did a pirouette, a slow circle for his inspection. Saying it out loud in daylight, it sounds nuts."

"You were angry."

"I really thought that if he believed he'd won me, maybe he'd leave me alone."

"We need a restraining order."

"Give me time to think, my God, it's Jonathan, the gawky boy who never took off his glasses, even when we went swimming. He did this funny breaststroke, and his head poked out like a turtle. Jonathan taught me how to climb trees, even dared me to fly off with him."

Georgia hadn't planned to reveal more, but Judith needed a shock. "You're not the only one who left out a few details. I followed him following you, watched him dig through your garbage. This afternoon I confronted him and he denied nothing."

Judith stretched her legs into shade, plucked a blade of grass, and tore it down the center seam. "Jonathan taught me how to make a whistle using a blade of grass. I've forgotten, do you know how?"

"Forget that. You've seen his butterflies. Now imagine yourself pinned to that wall."

Judith laughed, crisp bursts that stopped and started.

She must still be in shock. Georgia considered shaking her. "You've been friends forever. I'll make you a bet."

"What?"

"You've never seen his bedroom, have you?"

"God, you're right. I've been in his house hundreds of times, cooked meals there, taken pees, but that door's shut, always."

"It's not shut, it's locked. The room's a shrine. Ladies and gents, my tribute to Judith Quist." Georgia explained the photomontage, the boxes of souvenirs, the cotton panties. "Live and let live, what crap. We can go to the courthouse now."

The blood left Judith's face. "Give me a day to sort this out." She handed back Georgia's phone.

To the north, dust rose above the cornfield. Instead of coming back to the barn with cigarettes, Daniel had returned to the fields. He must be waiting for her to leave. The sun, a lemony chrome, was without much force.

*

In the rearview mirror Georgia could still see the Sauvie Island Bridge. The phone rang. Caller ID read Judith Quist. Before she pulled off the highway, she knew Judith had decided to meet Jonathan.

"He called me," Judith said. "It's been what, ten minutes since you left, and he called. I almost asked if he was checking to make sure the backhoe crushed me. But he didn't sound surprised to hear my voice. He sounded tender—can you believe it, tender? I must be wrong, if he'd just tried to kill me, he wouldn't chat like that, not Jonathan. He doesn't lie, not to me."

"Has truthful Jonathan mentioned Roy Burke?"

"The real estate guy? What's Jonathan got to do with him?"

"The two are in cahoots." Georgia heard fumbling. "You still there?"

"Hold on, I need to light up."

Georgia clung to wisps of a new idea—*Jonathan worshiped Judith, therefore*—but the thought dissolved. Judith must've propped the phone between shoulder and cheek. A hoarse intake of breath ended when she exhaled into the mouthpiece.

"He wants to talk," Judith said, "tonight."

"Holy shit."

"You deserve to know, that's why I called."

"First, let's go to the sheriff. If anything goes wrong—"

"And what, watch the cops shoot him? I won't have him hurt. And don't think about calling the sheriff on your own."

"Then I'm coming with you. Even if you say no, I'll follow, so you might as well agree. He has a gun, did you know that?"

"That old Luger? Sure. My father might've been a bully, but he was a pacifist. No guns in our sanctified house. Jonathan would sneak it out and we'd plink tin cans. I was curious, you know, forbidden fruit."

"He's dangerous, why take a chance?"

"Hey, being used as bait, that's not my style, but if he hurts one more person—I can't let that happen."

"Judith?" Georgia started the car, cut into traffic, and headed back towards the bridge. "Judith, you there?"

"I'll call him," Judith said. "Set up the meeting, then tonight I'll get him to confess."

"How?"

"I don't know, but I will."

*

A pair of jet skis surged past Judith's houseboat. The deck seesawed and Georgia's stomach lurched. At the front door, sinewy vines snaked out of ceramic pots. She kicked the vines aside and knocked.

No answer.

Georgia gripped the doorknob, and her memory careened back to finding Heath: the air heavy with steam and lavender, then Heath's body, buoyant in the bath water. Georgia shouldered the door open.

Grease still smeared Judith's face. She sat cross-legged in the center of the room, looking like an urchin out of Dickens. She beckoned Georgia inside then murmured into the phone. "I know you'd never hurt me, of course we'll meet." She rolled her eyes at Georgia. "That PI showed up, she gave Daniel a ride home from the hospital. Anyway, she blathered on about your locked bedroom, how I was in danger, said I need a restraining order."

Judith had to know she was listening, but out of polite mumbo-jumbo, Georgia turned to the wall and studied a watercolor of a sloop sailing through a squall.

Judith laughed. "You're right, she's one tiresome bitch." Judith turned from Georgia. Her little hmms and uh-huhs tangled with his comments like a pair of teenagers nuzzling in the dark. "Private... Yes, yes... The nursery, an hour, by the shed in back... Same here..." Her voice flared. "I don't need protection, just do what I ask. I'll handle the rest." Another laugh. She hung up then turned to face Georgia. "It's set. Give me a minute, I have to change and hook everything up."

"Hook? Hook what?"

"No sense getting him to confess if I can't prove it. My phone has a voice recorder, even a plug-in mouthpiece I can use like a remote mike. At the nursery we all have them for making notes in the field. I can record every word." Judith peeled off her shirt as she rushed down the hall.

Should she call the sheriff? Yeah, and tell him what? Blow the bugles, Jonathan Kovac might have tried—almost one-hundred percent certainly did try—to squash Judith Quist under a backhoe.

The living room opened to the kitchen, and Georgia hunted up a glass in the cupboard next to the sink. She glugged down water then stared through a tiny window filmed with cooking grease.

The moon, nearly full, hung above the Columbia River. A fleeting shadow swept across the deck, and Georgia raced out the back door. Nothing there except a bowl of cat food on a rubber mat. Did Judith feed all the strays? Rex Hickle's back deck, complete with curlicue iron benches, even a rug, offered no hiding place. Ducks paddled by. Georgia tossed kibble to a trio of mallards. More ducks skimmed onto the water and squabbled for food.

An earlier idea lingered, *Jonathan all mushy, worshiping Judith*. Again the thought faded, but this time she snatched it and hung on—*and then he tried to kill her?*

Georgia found Judith in the kitchen prying the lid off a bottle of aspirin. Some of her fingernails were sculpted, others ragged with chipped red polish.

"Why has Jonathan changed?" Georgia asked.

"What the hell are you talking about?"

"He didn't wake up and say, 'Ah, this morning I'll rig a backhoe and smash the love of my life.' Why the change from adoration to murder?"

"Maybe he's unstable because, well, because he's unstable."

"Even schizophrenics act on logic, skewed, but still logic, voices in their head, television jingles handed down by God."

Judith massaged her temples.

"Before you two meet," Georgia said, "I need to know why he changed."

Judith shook aspirin into her palm, reached for the counter, missed, and dropped the bottle. Pills pinged across the floor. They both dropped to their knees, scrabbling for tablets.

Judith stopped. "Ted."

Georgia sat back hard on the linoleum. "Ted?"

"I'll get a broom."

"No," Georgia said. "Explain."

"Jonathan knows that Ted's my lover, and that we planned to run off together." Judith's eyes softened, and her mouth went slack.

Shit, Georgia knew that look.

"Ted's a bad habit," Judith said, "like smoking. When I was little, I threw tantrums over the tiniest scratch, even believed a Band-Aid had magic powers. Ted's like that. I can't explain any better."

"How long have—"

"Six years, but I'm ending it. Too big a price."

"You just told Jonathan you didn't need protection, you'd handle it yourself. Did you mean protection from Ted?"

"Jonathan wants to give me his old gun."

"Ted cheated with you, right? And Theda found out?"

"Miss Do-Good, full of lofty intentions, she convinced him I wasn't right, blah, blah, blah. Back then she played the bratty older sister, and she's still doing it."

Now Ted, even Dawn, had motives to kill Judith. "The glitter?"

Judith laughed. "You know about that?"

"But I thought Marci Heath—"

"Marci." Judith spat out the name. "Vapid little twit. No imagination that one. While making love, Ted used to plan new garden beds." Judith left the room.

Georgia funneled a few aspirin tablets into the bottle. Fuck it. She tossed the bottle at the refrigerator, let Judith sweep up the mess, and tromped back to the living room. A portrait filled the wall behind the dining table. No mistaking Judith's arched eyebrows and widow's peak. Georgia squinted at the signature. A self-portrait. Judith had mentioned a stint in art school. Puzzle pieces shifted. At the art studio the sculpture was Ted's, but the charcoal nude and the caricature of Heath were Judith's.

Georgia started to turn, but something drew her back. At the edge of the portrait, almost lost in shadow, were the fingertips of a reaching hand. Did this represent Jonathan stalking? Or Ted coming to her?

Possibilities flew at Georgia like an eruption of birds. Theda had tried to protect Judith from Ted, probably told him she's too gullible, too young. Although Georgia had hammered at Ted, he refused to reveal his lover's name: a point of honor he said, a promise to Theda. Who would Theda protect from Ted? Heath? No. But she might protect the little girl who'd grown up next door.

Georgia took another leap. The driver's ed car, she'd seen it twice, once after leaving the Brodys', and then at Ted's mansion. Jonathan hadn't followed her; he was spying on Judith's lover.

Judith entered the room, face scrubbed and hair combed. For some reason this reassured Georgia.

"I ran the wire under my bra strap, it keeps peeking out." Judith unbuttoned her shirt and fiddled until Georgia stepped over and untangled it. "There." Judith wiggled the wire. "That's better."

"After we park, switch it on then forget it, you'll act more natural. If Jonathan blinks wrong, you scream. I still want to call this off, I'd feel better if—"

"I'll drive," Judith said.

"First, I need to grab my gun."

"No one's shooting Jonathan."

"And I said I'm getting my gun."

"One last thing." Under Judith's steady gaze, Georgia waited. "I'm doing this for the part of me that's glad Theda's dead."

"I know."

*

Lights from the parking lot shone over the nursery, but a vault of darkness covered the potting shed. Georgia zigzagged around tangled hoses, empty pots, and stacked bags of mulch, searching for the best place to hide.

She heard a voice: a woman's voice.

Was Judith talking to her or Jonathan? Georgia ducked behind an oak tree, its silhouette so black it might've been painted. Wind gusting off the Columbia River had stolen the day's warmth.

Now two voices—male and female. Georgia rose a few inches and saw Judith's flowing skirt. Before she saw Jonathan she heard him laugh, high and intense. She'd never heard him laugh before.

Judith's voice carried better than Jonathan's. "That PI said you're working with Roy Burke to stop Northwest Metals. That's not like you."

"No, it's more like Ted, always dickering then crowing about his shrewd deals."

"Forget Ted."

"Isn't that why we're here?"

"Your butterflies, and teaching. You've never cared about money."

"But you have."

"You mean the other night when I said I'd run off for money? Good God, you know me better than that, just talk. Poor, mistaken Johnny."

Georgia heard him hiss something about "pity." She crept closer and tripped over the octopus-roots of another oak, cracking her knee against the August-baked ground. She fingered a tear in her jeans and moisture that must be blood.

"Did you hear that?" Jonathan's voice.

"Raccoons," Judith said. "Remember, I talk to the animals."

His laugh rippled out deeper and more severe.

Did Judith's presence bring out this assertiveness? Or did he sound different tonight because Georgia knew he'd tried to kill Judith? She crept closer and settled behind stacked bags that smelled of bark dust. Inching back, she squatted and transformed herself into an abstract shape.

"You can't take me seriously," Judith said. "I was spewing nonsense, when I win the lottery la-de-dah kind of nonsense. God, I want this to be over."

Georgia heard exhaustion in Judith's voice. The woman was good.

"It's crazy," Judith said. "In the barn I thought I saw, for an instant, I thought you tried to kill me, that's how crazy I'm feeling. But now I think you're right, it must've been Ted. I'm breaking it off with him. Look what happened to Heath." She stepped toward Jonathan and held out her hand. Georgia expected them to hug. Instead Judith said, "The night Theda died, I know you were there. Admit it."

Georgia strained for his answer. A car drove by, windows rolled down, music blaring at summer volume.

"I didn't hear you," Judith said. "What'd you say?"

Good girl. The music faded, but all Georgia heard was the periodic swish of passing cars.

"Answer me," Judith said. "Did you go to Theda's house that night?"

"Yes," he said. "I was there."

Georgia restrained herself from whooping out loud.

"And you pushed that dog into Gilbert's shop, tore up Lamb's apartment?"

"Yes, yes."

Judith was too cocky; wind it up, move under the lights, hit the road. Georgia reached across her chest and rested her palm on the butt of the gun.

"No matter what," Judith said, "I always thought we'd trust each other, but nothing stays the same, does it? We've crossed an imaginary line. I want to go back to the way things were."

"Me too." Jonathan stepped toward Judith then stopped in front of a tree. His form lost shape, became black on black.

"You can trust me." It looked like Judith was talking to the tree. "All I want is to feel safe again. You're the only one I never

251

lied to. Today was—"

"I know."

Judith spun out comforting phrases. Georgia caught the melody, if not the meaning, and sensing the end, inched closer.

Judith held out her hand. Jonathan separated himself from the tree and reached out.

"You brought it," Judith said. "I haven't seen it since we were kids."

My God, she must mean the Luger. Georgia drew her gun.

Judith stepped back. "Jonathan you're wrong, you've got to trust me. Why would I record us? It doesn't make sense."

Jonathan and Judith merged. A blast and flare.

Energy burst into Georgia's throat, but no scream escaped. She leapt towards them, gun extended and pointed at the one standing figure.

Judith swayed over Jonathan's body. "Oh God, oh God, oh God. He saw the wire."

Georgia knelt, fumbled for her penlight, and flashed it onto Jonathan's face. A worm of blood trickled from his nose. Farther down she found the hole in his chest and pressed. "Call nine-one-one."

"He saw the wire, ripped it away, then pointed his Luger at me and I pushed it away and, and—"

"Call an ambulance! Now! I'm losing him." Georgia felt a violent beat, not the soft rise and fall of breathing, his heart pumping blood through the wound.

Judith made the call.

*

Georgia heard the lament of a siren then others joined in. She told the paramedics Jonathan had been alive a minute ago. She'd watched him shudder like someone cold. It seemed imperative they know this. The taller man shook his head. Georgia looked up at the sky to stop her tears, and the stars blurred.

252

The first deputy sheriff, stout with red hair, introduced himself as Driscoll. Random pieces—bees, dogs, Gilbert being shoved—tumbled out of Georgia. She stopped, breathed deeply, and started again. The forensics team arrived, and a blond woman snapped pictures.

A man in a suit motioned for Driscoll, and he excused himself. He returned and asked Georgia to repeat everything in chronological order. She described Theda's death, the threats against Gilbert, Judith's belief that Jonathan would confess to her. Driscoll frowned. He was right, this was her fault. She hadn't stopped Judith from meeting Jonathan.

A blanket wrapped around her shoulders, Judith sat on a bench across the parking lot. Another deputy with a notebook squatted beside her asking questions. He stood and called out, "Driscoll, come here. There's a recording."

Although Georgia had told him that Judith recorded everything, Driscoll registered surprise. She followed him. The recording began with Judith chatting, airy and funny. The voice seemed unrelated to the woman rocking on the bench. Jonathan's laughter reeled out at them. His voice grew impatient as he confessed going to Theda's house, luring Turtle into Gilbert's shop, ransacking Georgia's apartment, then his tone softened. After her remark about not having seen the gun since they were kids, he might have said, "I love you." The recording ended.

Paramedics boosted Jonathan onto the stretcher and zipped the body bag closed.

Judith rode with Driscoll to the Justice Center in Portland. Georgia followed, driving Judith's car. Hours passed before Georgia signed a statement. The desk sergeant told her that Judith Quist hadn't left yet, and Georgia waited in a chair near the door. Next to her a middle-aged woman in a business suit sobbed into a piece of paper. Ink smudged her nose. There had to be Kleenex in this damn place. Georgia dug into her pocket, came up with a fast-food napkin, and handed it to the woman.

Whiskey fumes knocked her back.

Judith emerged through a metal door and Georgia took her arm.

"Poor Billy," Judith said. "This will knock him flat. When is he getting out of the hospital?"

"Tomorrow. My car's still at your place."

At four in the morning the city was desolate. Scraps of paper and torn bunting, debris from an end-of-summer parade, bunched up in the gutters.

"I'll tell Billy about Jonathan," Georgia said.

"It has to be me. Everything I care about turns to crap. I need a warning bell around my neck like lepers used to wear."

"I should have stopped you."

Judith's laughter echoed in the empty streets. "I'm not trying to comfort you, it's a skill I never acquired, but you couldn't have stopped me."

"I'm sure Billy will stay with Gilbert, at least until he's better," Georgia said. "For now, we need sleep. I'll come by your houseboat at eleven, and together we can pick Billy up."

From the deck of the houseboat, Judith waved goodbye. Georgia listened to waves slap along the beach. Jonathan was gone. Everyone was safe. She phoned Gilbert and let him know about his cousin's death. On the drive back to town Jonathan's voice came to her, distant and muffled, the way she'd heard it on the recording. "Yes, I was there…" And finally, "I love you." This time Georgia heard the phrase.

31

Gilbert Kovac

Gilbert Kovac jerked awake. Last night Georgia's account of Jonathan's death had left him frazzled, and he'd almost slept through the alarm. Theda's instructions had been exact: "I must become one with the sun."

At the first stoplight, he brushed his fingers across the box on the passenger seat. He'd opened it and, yes, Theda was ashes. Mixed in, he saw shards of bone and bits of fused metal from the zipper of her orange spangled dress. He'd sealed the box in glossy white paper, neat and precise, each fold familiar. Now that he knew who had killed Theda, the stab of grief beneath his breastbone had relaxed into a relentless ache he could almost manage. After this, he'd stop at a grocery and stock up on Billy's favorites: pitted olives, mango sherbet, and sweet pickles. That gave him time to change the bedding in the guest room before Georgia and Judith delivered Billy. He switched lanes, and tires screeched behind him. He'd promised Theda he'd be ready, and now if he was late he'd have to repeat the ceremony tomorrow.

Gilbert wheeled to a stop at Sellwood Park and retrieved a folding camp shovel from the trunk. The leather soles of his loafers slipped along dew-slick grass until he stood on a bluff above the Willamette River. This would be the last time he and Theda strolled to her favorite willow. He transferred the white box to the crook of his arm.

Oaks Amusement Park was silent below him, the Ferris wheel motionless in predawn gray. Downriver the tops of Portland's glass and steel spires glinted in first light. A map detailed the history of the Oaks Bottom Wildlife Refuge, and a dirt trail angled down the slope before fading into a tangle of alder and ivy. Filled with tree snags and purple loosestrife, a lake stretched north between the bluff and an elevated railroad bed. Mallard ducks flapped out of morning shadow toward the sun. Theda loved this place and had hounded city council to save it.

He clipped the camp shovel to his belt. At the first switchback, he glanced down and caught a quiver in the branches. Mats of wild morning glories swept up the hillside, and white fluted blossoms erupted through the foliage. He hit flat ground, the river's floodplain, where the trail forked. Theda preferred the path to the right, the one leading away from Oaks Park. Quieter, more meditative, she'd say. He stepped aside as a pair of dachshunds strained at their leashes and towed a white-haired woman down the trail. The dogs jerked by. Gilbert shrank back but forced a smile.

Half hidden in a thicket, a broken-down couch faced two easy chairs and a coffee table, discards from a suburban living room dropped into a swamp. Signs of homeless people increased each time he and Theda visited the Bottom. Theda would rant then stop and say, "When you're hungry, the environment is a luxury."

Across the river the clamor of commuter traffic swelled. The path curved away from the lake, and muted by tall maples, those sounds evaporated. Light from the rising sun met the top of the West Hills. Theda had been clear about the timing: when sunlight strikes the willow, she would be free.

The path opened onto a meadow dotted with Oregon grape, shrubby ash bushes, sprawling dogwoods. They often came here with a picnic lunch. This place revitalized her, she said. He stopped at the willow. Its branches stretched over the water, and he placed the white box next to the trunk. In the tree's shadow he knelt and snapped the shovel open.

He heard her voice. "This will be my spot. Cast a handful to the wind, a handful to the water, and then bury me in the roots of this willow."

Gilbert stabbed his shovel into the ground. Bent to digging, he repeated the secret name they had shared as children. "Moulee."

Tears glazed his cheeks. He'd know when it felt right to leave.

Behind him a branch snapped. After that, sounds came to him clear and separate, and he attributed each noise to a scuttling raccoon or leaves quaking in the wind. Still his hands trembled, and he felt certain that someone watched. He licked his index finger, as he'd watched Theda do hundreds of times, and held it up. The air remained unmoving.

32

Georgia Lamb

Georgia knocked on Judith's door again, then shouted her name, rattled the doorknob, and checked down the length of the deck. Multnomah Channel reflected sky and clouds back at her.

"She's not home."

When Georgia turned, her knee bumped a tall flowerpot. It rocked on its base but remained upright.

Rex Hickle leaned on his deck railing. "You peddling more brochures?"

"I was supposed to meet her."

"Don't know about that, I said 'hi', and she mumbled something about picking up her uncle. That was an hour ago." He checked his watch. "To be precise, an hour and seven minutes ago." He said more, but his words were lost to the mechanical hiccup of a motorboat starting.

Georgia nudged the pot again. It wobbled. Packed with potting soil, a planter that large should be immobile. She kneed the other pot. Stable, solid, vertical. Last night she'd almost tripped when her feet tangled with the vines; now the vines were gone. So this morning, racked with grief over Jonathan, Judith surrenders to an attack of domesticity and swaps out the vines for stubby yellow marigolds? Why?

Georgia tipped the wobbly pot on its side, clamped it between her thighs, then sorted through her bag until she found a plastic Bic pen. Using it as a probe, she punched through a drainage hole. Thunk. The pen hit something hard, not dirt.

She clutched the marigolds and yanked them free. Crusted with mud, the roots wriggled like worms as she flipped them aside. Dirt speckled her face and stung her eyes while she burrowed and scooped and tunneled

"Stop, you're making a mess, you've gone crazy!" Hickle ran from his houseboat to the dock and down Judith's gangway. He grabbed Georgia's shoulder. "You can't rip out marigolds, there are laws."

She twisted loose, but he snagged the neck of her T-shirt and pulled until she choked, sputtering spit and dirt. Georgia's fist hammered his bare big toe.

He squawked and hopped on one foot. "That's assault and this, this muck, it's everywhere. I'm reporting you."

She clawed away the last inch of dirt, wrenched a sealed plastic box free, and wiped it across her Levis. Inside the box she found the manila folder with two coffee cup stains, the same folder she'd seen in Heath's hands. She flipped through pages until Burke's letterhead stopped her. It was the original of the copy she'd photographed at Heath's.

"I told you she's gone." Hickle squatted. "I'm informing your organization about your inappropriate conduct." He retreated then turned back to face her. "And I'm doing it now."

She thumbed through more papers until she came to Billy's signature: William F. Kovac, in a palsied pale-blue script. It was a letter of intent to sell, simple and non-binding, between Ted and Billy. Pure boilerplate. As a paralegal, she'd seen a few, but the excessive details puzzled her. Usually these letters were general with specifics to be negotiated later, but Ted wrote this up as if it were a done deal, finalized. None of this made sense; Billy had decided not to sell. But dated six months earlier with Heath as a witness, Ted had given himself wiggle room in case Billy had a change of heart. Behind her she heard quick steps. An extension cord over his shoulder, Hickle gripped his vacuum and swung onto the deck.

Georgia scrolled through previous calls on her phone and hit redial for Good Samaritan Hospital. At the eighth ring someone answered.

"Has a patient, Billy Kovac, been discharged?"

"Let me take a quick check," the woman said, "How do you spell Kovac?"

"K-O-V-A-C."

"Nothing's written down, should be something here, I'll put you on hold."

"No. This is urgent, please—"

Last night Jonathan had confessed to killing Theda. No, that wasn't exactly true. Georgia shut her eyes and the memory drifted up. Judith's voice, loud and distinct, came at her, and then she heard Jonathan. Yes, he admitted going to Theda's house, but said nothing, not one word, about killing her. Just when Georgia expected him to describe the climb the ladder to the roof, Judith had cut him off, claiming he'd detected her wire. Like he had so many other nights, Jonathan shadowed her, but Judith, not Jonathan, climbed the ladder to drop bees down the chimney. He had only watched. At the precise moment before he incriminated her, Judith had ripped the wire loose. The timing had been perfect, and Georgia imagined her thrill at playing such a tight game.

The growl of Hickle's vacuum stifled the hospital Muzak.

Georgia jerked the plug from the socket. "Leave or I toss it."

"I don't understand why—"

"To be more precise, I will hurl your vacuum into the Columbia River." Georgia's fingers ached from gripping the receiver. She switched the phone to her left hand and bargained with the universe: *Anything, anything, but keep Billy safe.*

"Sorry this took so long." Finally a voice. "Mr. Kovac checked out at ten-fifty. You just missed him."

Georgia hung up.

Now what? Judith had Billy, but what was her plan? She couldn't just kill him and dump his body into a ditch. Not creative enough and the police would never dismiss his death as an accident. Although terrified that Judith had everything worked out, Georgia was sure she still had time and dialed the cell phone she'd given Billy.

He answered on the sixth ring. "Hello?"

Thank God. "Billy, say 'Hi, Margaret.'"

"Hi, Margaret."

"This is Georgia, but answer like you're talking to Margaret. Now say 'Uh-huh.'"

"Uh-huh."

"Is someone driving you?"

"Uh-huh."

"Listen to what I say and act casual."

"Uh-huh."

"Two things I want you to do, Billy, don't trust anyone but me and stall, stall, stall. Okay?"

"Uh-huh."

"Now using all your strength, focus. Can you do that?"

"Course I can."

"Give me a hint, where are you going?" Georgia clenched her fist and inhaled, ready to repeat the question.

"You still there?" Billy asked.

"I'm here. Now give me a clue, where are you headed?"

"We need to pick up my good dentures."

Had Billy slipped into one of his foggy places? No, he'd bragged that he had all his own teeth. Code: they were headed to his house.

The phone went dead.

33

So today he was going to die.

Billy strained to remember what Georgia had said on the phone. All he came up with was, "Hi, Margaret," and "stall, stall, stall." Didn't take a genius to spot the panic in her shaky voice. And Judith, who'd always struck him as icy, kept pawing at him. He recognized her effort. On the farm before he put an animal down, his gestures stank of deceit and apology.

Billy's hand trembled, but beneath his fumbling he discovered a durable calm. All his life, calving and butchering were parts of a cycle. Or was the calm from those pills? Judith had insisted they fill his prescription. She'd read the label out loud, "Four pills every hour," then handed him four tablets and a water bottle. He'd hesitated, remembering that the doctor had said, "One pill every four hours." But he swallowed them anyway. Judith had paid for the medication, and he didn't want to seem ungrateful.

At least his death would be memorable, might make the front page: William Finley Kovac—murder victim. Next Thursday, when his poker buddies dealt seven-card stud, nothing wild, instead of debating the prospects of this year's high school football team or wondering if spring rain would rot the hay, they'd speculate about his death. Last summer after Harley Ferdy fell off his horse, funerals and death had sneaked into their bull sessions. Most favored drifting off while asleep.

Not Billy. He'd be digging in his garden. Each spring after the ground warmed, he worked his fingers past crusty dirt into dark, crumbly loam. Forget cherry blossoms or fancy-pants perfumes, soil smelled like sunshine and shade. Beat that. After tilling, he'd thumb in seeds for his first crops of the year, radishes and sugar snap peas.

Judith drove past the barn where years ago her father held his revivals. A backhoe had punched its way through the wall. What the hell! Were they building a damn church? Visions of Bible thumpers swarming over his property gnawed at him until they coasted into his driveway.

Sorrow quivered through him. Where was the back of his house? Between charred rafters he saw great gaping holes. "I won't go in there."

"We'll just be a minute." Judith said something more, and he strained to listen, but all he heard was blood whooshing through his ears.

Once more he started to protest, but Judith touched him and his throat closed up. She left her hand draped across his knee. The longer he stared down, the more he despised her fingers. She tried to make them look limp and kind but couldn't stop the twitching.

Another pill must've kicked in because he didn't mind her hand so much. Pushing it away seemed a cumbersome chore, and he decided to climb into the back seat for a short catnap. He nudged the passenger door open and heard the throb of a tractor out in the cornfield. Daniel had carried him from the fire, but the chance of Daniel saving him twice was slim.

Judith gripped his arms. Because she was short—the top of her head barely reached his chin—her strength startled him. She propelled him, staggering, onto the gravel. He bet a cat felt like this when someone lifts it by the scruff. Billy tried to shake her off, but her grip tightened.

Debris clogged the driveway, and he threaded his way around a rug with the fringe singed off, dining chairs toppled onto each other, and Margaret's antique mirror that looked like a perfect, oval pond. Shuffling two more steps, he worked himself into a stop then studied the yellow warning tape.

He had her. "It says don't cross."

She ripped the tape and let the yellow streamers flutter off.

He considered resting on the blackened mattress, but it was wet and pulpy. The grass looked more inviting. While he angled toward a shady patch, he gave into his limp, letting his strength accumulate for the moment when he'd need it.

He reached a swatch of shadowy grass. "Nope. Not going farther."

An uneasy energy buzzed off Judith. While Billy waited for her response, he scratched between neck creases where his skin felt damp.

He heard the car door slam.

Maybe she'd decided to drive off and leave him here. But he looked up and there she was, marching back to him, pill bottle in one hand, cane in the other. He'd already swallowed too many pills, but his determination was oozing away. He didn't realize Judith was talking at him until she stopped, the way you first notice a fan after it goes silent. *Stay awake*, he told himself. He had to warn Jonathan about this woman.

Billy buckled onto the grass and rolled away from Judith. She stepped over him, but soothed by the lazy whirr of grasshoppers, he barely noticed.

34

Georgia Lamb

Georgia tried tweezing out words but caught only Judith's sentences snaking through Billy's fits and starts. She ached to scream, "Billy, I'm here," but Judith was strong and might have a weapon. Georgia must rely on surprise. One end of a scorched table leg crumbled into ash when she wrenched it free. She missed the holster snug against her ribs, but this morning she'd put away the baseball bat, the pepper spray, the Glock; a ritual to erase the nightmare of Jonathan's death. Case closed.

Floorboards crackled under her weight, and avoiding the blackest patches, she followed a crazy path, like stepping on stones to cross a stream. Down the hall and past the bathroom, the shrill contrast between dark and light intensified as if chamber by chamber she was entering Judith's mind. Outside Billy's bedroom, soggy blankets tossed about on the floor muffled her footsteps toward the door.

"What's happening?" Confusion distorted Billy's voice.

Dread prickled the back of Georgia's neck. Anyone who crossed Judith died—Theda, then Heath, and last night Jonathan.

"Don't you recognize me?" Judith asked. "I'm the preacher's wife, Ardith. You always liked me. Remember the time you caught me sneaking out of a prayer meeting? You told me, 'Thou shalt not laugh.' Said that was my husband's first commandment."

Georgia understood the tactic. Push him into the past, make him easier to control.

She exploded into the room.

In one motion Judith slammed Billy to his knees. Georgia heard the whack of his kneecap against wood, then a gurgle.

Judith pressed the cane across his throat. Flames had licked a black swath up walls consuming rafters, and sunlight sluiced through a great opening in the ceiling. Georgia felt the shadow of a cloud move across her cheek.

"Drop it," Judith said.

Georgia opened her hand, and the stump of the table leg clattered to the floor. "Why? Why all this?"

Judith's gaze seemed to stop before it met Georgia's eyes. "They, you, nobody would leave us alone."

"You and Ted?"

Bathed in filtered sunlight, Judith's face became faultless, lit with exultation as if murder was a creative act. Georgia had seen the same expression while she described the bee equipment—the veils and the smoker. She enjoyed squirming close to murder, the same way she'd enjoyed teasing Georgia with her cigarette smoke. Play it brash, Judith liked the rush.

"Did you enjoy killing Jonathan?" Georgia asked.

"He cared more for this old man than he cared for me." Judith's voice veered into singsong and her self-righteousness billowed. "Once he guessed about the fire, I couldn't trust him, but, no, I did not enjoy shooting him."

"An honest emotion, that's a first."

"Jonathan acted on his own. I had no choice."

"Not true." How far could she push? Georgia took another step.

A smile twitched across Judith's face. "Too bad. I was beginning to like you."

Keep her curious, keep her talking. Georgia pictured a little girl biting her own arm to avenge a broken music box. She inched forward.

"Step back. You're too fidgety."

Not willing to give up the ground she'd gained, Georgia stayed rooted. Judith tightened the cane. Spit bubbled at the corner of Billy's mouth.

"I said step back or I smash his windpipe." Her skin stretched taut across her cheekbones, yet her eyes were loose, this new face hard and at the same time wild. "Have you ever felt your throat?"

Georgia ignored her.

"Do it. Do it now."

Georgia lifted her hand to her neck.

"Fragile like bird bones, breakable, don't you think?"

"Did Ted help you kill Theda?" Georgia asked.

Judith shivered. It passed so quickly Georgia wasn't sure if it came from her lips, her shoulders, or the cane, but the woman had made a decision. "Ted has no idea all I've done for him."

"Does Ted know you killed Theda?"

"I first met Ted here, in this house. He was talking to Billy, standing right where you are now." For a second her eyes darted across the room as if pinpointing the exact spot was important.

Georgia sprang.

Judith teetered then threw her arms out for balance. Georgia grabbed Judith's calf, but the caution light in her brain flashed a second late. Judith kicked, and Georgia's head snapped back. One by one her fingers relaxed. *Hold on*. Her grip slid down, and she clenched Judith's ankle long enough for Billy to crawl away.

The cane chopped at Georgia's temple. A sulfurous stink shot through her nostrils, blossomed in her head. She floated into a rubbery nausea and rolled away. Again the cane slashed, but Georgia used her foot to block it. Judith was stronger; Georgia had to be smarter. With both hands she latched onto Judith's arm and twisted until the cane clattered across the floor.

Georgia staggered to her feet and exaggerated her confusion, ready to sidestep the next attack, but Judith hung back. She wanted to prolong the fight. Squared off, they circled one another. The room was quiet except for hard breathing and the scrape of shoes across the floor.

"Stop it. Both of you." Billy's eyes, exaggerated by his glasses, looked bewildered.

Georgia hurtled forward and seized Judith's shoulder. They tripped over Billy. He clutched the cane and pulled himself to his knees, jabbing and prodding, waving it like a sword. Judith stumbled backward against Billy, and he caromed off the wall headlong into the doorjamb. Blood splashed from his nose.

His foot shot out and tangled with their legs. Judith swayed. Georgia's arms tightened around her waist, maneuvering closer and closer to the black floorboards along the wall. Georgia rocked back, dove, and they plummeted toward the window. Wood splintered with a brittle pop, pop, as floorboards gave way. Georgia on top, they sprawled across the joists. For a moment they were suspended, intertwined. She banged Judith's head against an exposed two-by-twelve, and they plunged through the floor into the crawlspace.

"Christ." Stunned by dazzling pain Georgia twisted onto her stomach. Face in the dirt, Judith whimpered. Blood trickled through black hair. Georgia straddled Judith, pinning her shoulders, wrenching her arms behind her.

"Billy, your phone, dial nine-one-one." Georgia repeated her instructions before he took the phone from his pocket.

His golden-brown eyes watered. "Where's Jonathan?"

*

Three days had passed.

Wispy bands of cirrus clouds creased the morning sky. During the heat wave, hollyhocks along the south side of Stockard's house had wilted, but the papery core of each dead blossom still showed its original color—yellow, white, purple. Last night the temperature had dipped, and trees lining the spine of the West Hills looked faded.

Under the stooped head of a sunflower, Stockard brushed dirt crumbs from her coveralls. The plastic red cherries stapled to her straw hat jiggled as she crossed the lawn and settled into an Adirondack chair. "How are you doing?"

"Better," Georgia said. "I still picture Jonathan lying on the ground, even feel his blood spurting through my fingers. Somewhere I read that the survivors of Hiroshima had the image of the blast etched onto their eyes."

Georgia sat on grass still fresh with morning dew. She plucked a blade and remembered Judith asking if she knew how to make a grass whistle. Georgia's mother had showed her how, but all she remembered was the grass blade tickling her lips.

"Judith coaxed stray cats into the open," she said, "and used that same skill to lure damaged people."

"You mean Jonathan?"

Georgia nodded. "Do you think Judith mourns him?"

"I doubt she experiences emotion like other people. Wild chances and thrills substitute for genuine feelings."

"God, the woman choreographed everything. Even got me to help her fuss with the wire for the remote microphone. After Jonathan admitted being at Theda's, she cut him off before he could say anything incriminating about her. She pretended that he spotted the wire, and I never doubted that he ripped it off."

"We know Judith killed Theda," Stockard said. "But my friend in the DA's office doubts they can prosecute. He said they're concentrating on the other murders, Jonathan and Marci. And the attempt on Billy."

An image of Judith came to Georgia, smaller and clearer, as if viewing her through the wrong end of a telescope. "I was baffled until I realized two people were arranging the accidents. Jonathan became Judith's silent partner. She wanted to kill her enemies; he wanted to frighten us into ending the investigation. That's why the degree of violence kept changing. One day Jonathan leaves Halloween masks on Gilbert's porch; the next day Judith pushes Gilbert onto the train tracks. But when Judith set fire to Billy's house, she'd gone too far. Besides, Jonathan knew too much."

"Those papers I gave you, did they help?"

"It turned out that money was only part of the motive. Judith wanted to satisfy Ted's greed, but she craved revenge more. When Theda discovered him cheating, she convinced him that his relationship with Judith wouldn't work. Judith's hatred of Theda grew over the years."

"I don't understand that. Theda was the least spiteful person I know."

"Years ago Ted chased after Judith. Theda broke it up, but the two of them hooked up again. Without the big bucks from Northwest Metals, Judith worried that Ted might not leave Dawn. Then Theda's campaign to save the Island frustrated her plans."

"But Heath, why kill her?"

"Jealousy for one," Georgia said. "Seduced by Ted, Heath became his accomplice in real estate fraud. His signature wasn't on any contracts, but he scooped up all the cash. I think Heath decided not to risk prison. She threatened to expose him and called me. Judith couldn't let that happen."

"With you as a witness, Judith's recording, and Marci Heath's papers, the DA thinks they have a good case. Did Ted know about the killings?"

"I don't think so. Even Ted has limits, but that won't matter to the federal prosecutor or Dawn's lawyers."

"Theda called him her lovable loser," Stockard said.

A bee, late-summer plump, landed inches from Georgia's hand, twitching a purple stalk of salvia. "This mess has loads of losers. Ted and Judith are on the way to jail. Now that Billy controls Jonathan's property, Burke's dream of a golf resort is bust. And the landfill expansion won't happen."

"How's Billy?"

"Healing and showing off his broken nose, but Gilbert's a good nurse. And Billy, how can I put this, makes Gilbert less rigid. Yesterday I stopped by; Gilbert had a surprise for me. He called you, didn't he?"

"Called me?"

"To find out what kind of guitar I had. He replaced my Hummingbird."

"Guilty."

"He's a sweetie pants—never thought I'd call him that. He'd hate it. And now he hunts up the perfect gift while dealing with Billy's muddled grief. Billy forgets, and everything must be explained again." It felt like she'd been talking on and on, but she couldn't stop until it had all been told. "Everyone said Jonathan should've been Billy's son and now Billy has that grief, a father losing his son."

Stockard pushed the straw hat back from her forehead. "If you lose a husband, you're a widow. If you lose parents, you're an orphan. But if you lose a child, the cruelest loss of all, there's no word. There should be a word."

Boisterous laughter bubbled over the hedge from the neighbor's yard, and a whiff of tobacco smoke blew by and faded. The image of her mother came, but softer, without longing or resentment.

Stockard braced the arms of the chair and heaved herself up. "I'll finish with the garden then fix our tea."

Someday Georgia might tell Stockard about her attraction to Daniel, but not yet. Judith's arrest must have devastated the Quist family. She hoped that Daniel would forgive himself for giving up small confidences that night in the barn and remember how fiercely he'd defended his sister that afternoon when he thought she was in danger.

Stockard flexed her fingers; even while gardening she wore turquoise rings. Her hands were large and strong and, what Georgia needed to sense most, familiar. The rhythm was comforting to watch. Again and again Stockard's hand dipped into her coverall pocket then swept above the bare soil scattering seed. A winter cover crop.

About the Authors

Ann Brandvig and Rick Becker have worked as magician's assistant, carpenter, newspaper gofer, and choreographer.

Rick never set out to be a writer. He intended to become an astrophysicist but discovered an intense dislike for calculus and a crazy passion for poetry. That led to prizes from the Academy of American Poets. One snowbound winter deep in the wilds of NE Washington, his nearest neighbor gave him a shopping bag full of paperbacks. By spring thaw murder mysteries had him hooked.

For Ann it was never an either-or proposition. She always wanted to be a novelist and Gene Kelly's dance partner. After teaching in Portland, Oregon's performing arts school, she hung up her tap and jazz shoes but never lost her love for Miss Marple and Philip Marlowe. She and Rick fused their passion for mystery and wrote the *Killing Jar*.

Discover more about PI Georgia Lamb at

http://www.greycellspress.co.uk/about/

http://georgialambpi.wordpress.com/

https://www.facebook.com/georgialambPI